The ferry captain cried, "Raise oars!"

The drummer stopped, lifting the small cudgels he used to beat out the pace, and the rowers raised their oars. Almost immediately, the ferry slowed, then drifted to a stop in the thick brown silt. The passengers fell silent and stared out into the darkness. The rowers sat utterly still. The sudden atmosphere of tension on the boat was palpable.

"*Listen!*" said the dwarven captain.

Then they all heard it, unmistakable, a sound cutting through the darkness, slowly growing louder. It was a swishing sound, punctuated at intervals by a low, deep, muted thud.

Something was moving through the silt, something very large . . .

. . . the sound of footsteps.

The ferry captain screamed out, "Giant off the starboard side! Full ahead, double the beat!"

DARK SUN® Books

CHRONICLES OF ATHAS

The Brazen Gambit
Lynn Abbey

The Darkness Before The Dawn
Ryan Hughes

The Broken Blade
Simon Hawke

Cinnabar Shadows
Lynn Abbey

TRIBE OF ONE

Simon Hawke

The Outcast • *The Seeker* • *The Nomad*

PRISM PENTAD

Troy Denning

The Verdant Passage • *The Crimson Legion*
The Amber Enchantress • *The Obsidian Oracle*
The Cerulean Storm

DARK SUN WORLD

The Broken Blade

SIMON HAWKE

TSR

THE BROKEN BLADE

Random House and its affiliate companies have worldwide distribution rights in the book trade for English language products of TSR, Inc.

Distributed to the book and hobby trade in the United Kingdom by TSR Ltd.

Distributed to the toy and hobby trade by regional distributors.

Cover art by Brom.

First Printing: May 1995
Printed in the United States of America
Library of Congress Catalog Card Number: 94-68139

9 8 7 6 5 4 3 2 1

ISBN: 0-7869-0137-3

TSR, Inc.
201 Sheridan Springs Road
Lake Geneva, WI 53147
U.S.A.

TSR Ltd.
120 Church End, Cherry Hinton
Cambridge CB1 3LB
United Kingdom

For Mike Stackpole,
respected colleague and boon companion

Acknowledgments

With special acknowledgments to Robert M. Powers, Sandra West, Bruce and Peggy Wiley, Marge and James Koski, Liz Danforth, Emily Tuzson, Daniel Arthur, Vana Wesala, Jennifer Roberson, Allen Woodman, Brian Thomsen, Rob King, Russell Galen, and all my students in the Sonora Writers Workshop, who keep me on my toes.

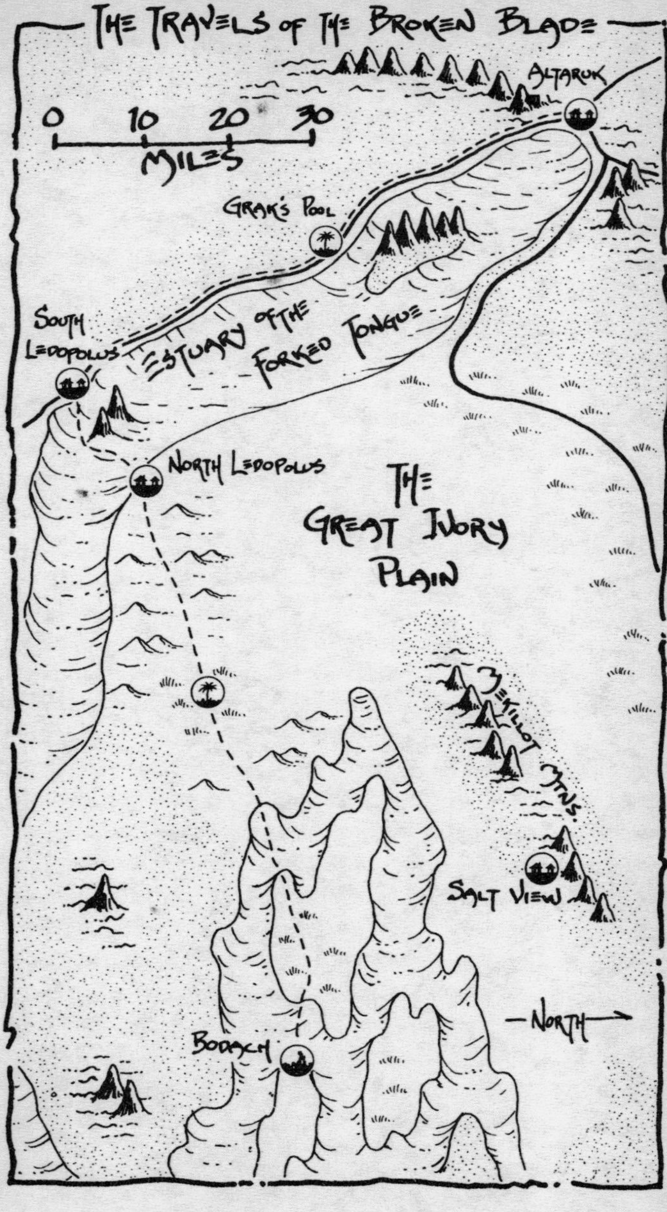
The Travels of the Broken Blade
0 10 20 30
Miles
Altaruk
Grak's Pool
South Ledopolus
Estuary of the Forked Tongue
North Ledopolus
The Great Ivory Plain
Killot Mtns.
Salt View
North
Bodach

PROLOGUE

A dust-covered, blood-spattered young mercenary passed through the elaborately carved wood gates and into a wide courtyard, a space paved with dark red bricks and lushly landscaped with desert plants. The graceful fronds of a pagafa tree shaded a large fountain, surrounded by stone benches intricately decorated with glazed blue and yellow tiles. In garden beds densely planted with purple-flowering broom bush, red and yellow desert paintbrush, and white-furred old man cactus, large, variegated desert agaves grew over six feet high and twice as wide, their curving spiked leaves striped in blue and yellow. Beside a blue-needled agafari, a weeping desert acacia swayed gently in the breeze, its yellow puffball blooms attracting dozens of hummingbirds, which flitted among the branches like tiny darts.

It was a lovely, peaceful, bucolic scene, the gentle trickle of the fountain adding to the restful atmosphere. It was a stark contrast to the scene the young mercenary lieutenant had just left.

Matullus paused by the fountain. Taking a deep breath, he unwound his blue and yellow turban and dipped one end of it into the water, soaking it thoroughly. It would not do to confront Lord Ankhor all covered in blood. The news he had to give him was bad enough. He wiped away the dust and blood on his face, chest, and arms. The blood was not his own. The man whose blood it was, the captain of the house guard, had died suddenly and terribly. He had been standing right next to Matullus when it had happened.

They had responded to an alarm in the merchant plaza. That, in itself, was no unusual occurrence. The crowded central plaza of Altaruk, with its many merchant stalls, was frequently the scene of arguments and altercations, but this one had quickly become a full-scale riot. The disturbance that had set it off turned out to be merely a diversion for the attack that followed, and it had all happened so quickly that Matullus wasn't even sure who had attacked whom.

The house guard had come marching in quickstep down the aisle between the rows of tented stalls, where they found a crowd gathered around a couple of combatants, who circled each other with obsidian knives. As Matullus pushed through the mob to separate the two men, it happened.

There was a blinding flash of blue light just beyond the crowd, and someone screamed. Matullus heard the unmistakable low whump of thaumaturgic energy bolts striking human bodies, and suddenly everyone was screaming and bolting from the scene. The guard formation fragmented as the crowd shoved past, and Matullus drew his sword, trying to find the source of the attack.

He glimpsed several white-robed figures moving quickly behind a row of merchant stalls, and a chill ran through him. The Veiled Alliance!

"Guard!" the captain shouted. "Assemble on me! This way! On the double!"

"Captain," said Matullus, "those men are—"

"*Move,* Lieutenant!" the captain shouted without pausing to hear him out. "*Now!* Go!"

They pushed their way through the milling, panic-stricken throng, past the prone and moaning figures of people who had been knocked down and trampled by the mob.

The next thing Matullus knew, he was lying facedown in the dirt. He had tripped over a body, or what was left of a body: the corpse was charred beyond recognition. Where the chest had been there was now a gaping, blackened hole, its edges cauterized by intense heat. Matullus recoiled in horror, and that was when it happened.

His captain was bending over him, holding out his hand, and saying, "Get up, man, come on, get—" when he disappeared in a searing flash of bright blue light. A soft, dull sound followed, like a hammer striking meat, and the captain came apart in an explosion of blood, entrails and viscera.

For a few moments, Matullus could not see. The blinding flash of thaumaturgic energy had washed everything out, and bright, pinpoint lights danced before his eyes. He yet felt the heat of it, and of the spattered blood.

The captain's eviscerated, blackened corpse lay just a few feet away, thrown back by the power of the energy bolt, and there was not much left of him. One arm and shoulder were missing, most of his chest was gone, and his hair and flesh had been instantly incinerated. Matullus gagged at the sight and heaved his guts out, there in the street.

By the time he rose unsteadily to his feet, it was all over. The entire merchant plaza had emptied, save for a few determined vendors who desperately tried to save goods from burning tents.

Bodies lay everywhere, some alive and moaning, some unmoving, trampled by the fleeing crowd, and some, like the captain's, incinerated by the devastating magical assault. Matullus stood there amid the flames and rising smoke while the guard squadron gathered around him.

"Sir, what happened?" one of the mercenaries asked, wide-eyed. They had drawn swords and knives and were glancing nervously about.

"Where's the captain?" someone asked.

Matullus pointed with his obsidian sword. "There . . . what's left of him."

He was gratified when two other mercenaries became sick at the sight. At least he was not the only one.

The fire brigade was already arriving, and there was nothing left to do but watch for looters. Matullus detailed the remainder of the squad to do so, then returned to the barracks, where he immediately sent reinforcements, under the command of a guard corporal. He, unfortunately, had a much less pleasant duty to perform. Lord Ankhor would have to be informed at once.

With a sigh, having cleaned himself up as best he could, Matullus wound the turban back around his head and tucked the long, wet end underneath his cloak.

He took a deep breath and squared his shoulders to the building before him—the mansion of the House of Ankhor, one of the largest, most powerful merchant houses of Athas. The adobe walls of the sprawling, four-story building dominated the surrounding area, rising above the one- and two-story buildings of the town around it. Even the exterior of the house spoke of opulence and luxury. The tan stuccoed walls were artfully textured by expert craftsmen, and the windows and archways were bordered with blue and yellow glazed ceramic tile. The gracefully stepped and rounded topcaps of the walls naturally led the eye toward the center of the mansion, where an arched parapet bore the house crest of Ankhor. It was a swallowtail flag divided horizontally in two bars of blue and yellow, and it flapped against a background of yellow tile.

Though the House of Ankhor maintained offices and residences in all the major cities of Athas, this was its headquarters in Altaruk, where the Ankhor family lived and from which they ran their merchant empire.

Matullus crossed the courtyard and went through a portal, down a walkway leading through an atrium and through the doors of the mansion. The steward greeted him as he came in.

"Guard Lieutenant Matullus to see Lord Ankhor on a matter of great urgency," he said.

"Very well, sir, follow me," the steward said. He led him across the high-ceilinged front hall of the mansion and up a flight of tile-covered stairs to the second floor. The floors of the hall were covered with expensive Drajian rugs woven in elaborate patterns of red and blue and gold. Wrought iron braziers from Urik provided the illumination, and wooden chairs and benches from Gulg, elaborately carved and set with obsidian and precious stones, lined the hall. Every detail testified to the vast trading empire of the House of Ankhor and the immense wealth of the Ankhor family.

The steward had Matullus wait outside the offices while he entered to announce him. A moment later, the carved agafari door opened, and the steward said, "Lord Ankhor will see you now."

Matullus nervously moistened his lips and drew himself up. He took a deep breath and entered the airy room beyond. It centered on a rectangular brick fireplace big enough to roast three full-grown men. The walls were whitewashed in a dull cream shade, and the ceiling high above had thick, round wooden beams running across it—old growth agafari trees harvested in the Mekillot Mountains. There were several arched niches built into the walls, and these held statuary, expensive pottery, and other luxury goods imported by the house. Several tall iron braziers were placed around the room, and censers on either side of the fireplace filled the air with the piquant scent of mountain moonflowers.

On the far side of the room, in front of three narrow, arched windows, stood a wide desk crafted from hundreds of blocks of agafari and pagafa wood inset with obsidian. The worth of that desk alone could have fed an average family for years. In front of the desk stood two wooden chairs of exquisite craftsmanship, with soft cushions artfully embroidered in blue and yellow.

One of those chairs was occupied by an elderly man with long gray hair, a lined, narrow face, high forehead, hooked nose, and deeply sunken eyes. He wore a thin chaplet bearing the hammered-silver house crest and white robes trimmed with blue and yellow in geometric designs; Lyanus, the minister of accounts for the House of Ankhor.

The man standing at the windows behind the desk was considerably younger. He was handsome, in his early thirties, tall and slender, with shoulder-length black hair and dark brown eyes. Unlike Lyanus, whose pallor gave evidence of a life spent mostly indoors over ledgers, Lord Ankhor was deeply tanned, and his fine features had the look of a sensualist.

Since his father, Lord Ankhor the Elder, the

patriarch of the house, had become infirm in his advanced years, Lord Ankhor the Younger had taken control of the family empire, and his shrewd business acumen had led the house to great profit in recent years. He was magnanimous in rewarding success among his employees, and equally intolerant of failure.

Matullus felt a knot form in his stomach as he crossed the room to stand at attention before the massive desk. He gave the mercenary salute, thumping his left breast with his right fist, and bowed his head respectfully. "My lord," he said.

"Ah, Matullus," said Lord Ankhor, turning to face him. "I see smoke rising from the merchant plaza. I take it you bring news of what's transpired?"

Lord Ankhor's tone was casual and pleasant, but that meant nothing. Matullus had heard Lord Ankhor sentence men to fifty lashes in exactly the same tone of voice. "My lord, we were attacked."

Ankhor raised his eyebrows. "The House Guard of Ankhor, attacked? In the merchant plaza?"

"We had learned of a disturbance, my lord, and when we arrived, we found two men fighting in the plaza with knives. However, the fight was merely a diversion. As we moved in to break it up, we were attacked by magic."

Ankhor frowned. "By magic, you say?"

"Yes, my lord. I saw it myself. It was the Veiled Alliance."

"You *saw* them? Attack the *house guard?* I don't believe it. Where is Captain Varos?"

"Dead, my lord. Killed in the attack."

"Incredible," said Ankhor. "Tell me *exactly* what happened, without leaving out the slightest detail."

Matullus described exactly what had occurred, from the moment they received the alarm to the moment of the captain's death, leaving out the part about his throwing up. Ankhor listened carefully, as did Lyanus, saying nothing until he was through. Then Lord Ankhor spoke.

"You say you saw the flash of light from just beyond the crowd, and then you heard someone scream—before anything else happened?"

"Yes, my lord. That was the moment the attack began. The crowd panicked and dispersed our formation, but I caught a glimpse of men in the white robes of the Alliance just as Captain Varos gave the order to assemble and move forward—"

"Did you tell Captain Varos you saw men in robes of the Alliance?"

"I tried to, my lord, but there was no time. Captain Varos gave the order to advance, and then I fell over a body, as I told you, and in the next instant, Captain Varos was killed. It all happened so fast. . . . It was a well-planned ambush, my lord. There can be no mistake."

"It was an ambush, all right, but you were almost certainly not the targets," Ankhor said.

"My lord?"

"The Veiled Alliance has nothing to gain in attacking my house guard. We are not political. Their enemies are defilers, not merchants. Clearly, they stalked defilers, not you. They must have spotted their quarry and launched their attack before you blundered into it."

"But, my lord, the captain was killed."

"An accident, no doubt," said Ankhor. "He was merely in the wrong place at the wrong time. You do not even know who killed him. From your description, it is clear that spells were exchanged. The Alliance has always been careful not to injure innocent bystanders. Defilers have no such scruples. Varos could have been killed by one of the Alliance or one of the defilers they were after. Either way, it was almost certainly a mistake. You were just caught in the middle. Varos was a brave man and a good fighter, but much too headstrong. Well, I had planned to replace him, anyway. This merely simplifies the task."

"My lord, I will do my utmost to do you credit," said Matullus, bowing respectfully.

"*You?*" said Ankhor. "What makes you think I am offering you the job?"

Matullus looked up and blinked with surprise. "But . . . my lord, as Captain Varos's second-in-command, I . . . I naturally assumed—"

"Only fools assume things, Matullus," Lord Ankhor replied. "A wise man *knows,* and if he does not know, he takes the trouble to find out. You would do well to remember that. You are young yet and do not have enough experience. No, this constant skirmishing between the defilers and the Alliance has become too troublesome. Something must be done, and the job calls for a top-ranked professional.

"I had already sent for Captain Varos's replacement, and he is to arrive shortly. But until Kieran assumes his duties, you will act as temporary commander of the house guard. Try not to get any more of them killed, if you can manage it."

"Kieran, my lord?" said Matullus with surprise. "Kieran of Draj?"

"You know of him, then?"

"I know his reputation, my lord," Matullus said. "What mercenary does not? But I heard he had retired."

"I was able to induce him out of retirement to lead my house guard," Ankhor said, "so you had best prepare the men. If everything I've heard of him is true, you can expect Kieran to crack the whip from the very moment he arrives. He sounds like just the man we need at a time like this. Now, go clean yourself up. You stink of blood."

"Yes, my lord," said Matullus, bowing and backing away several steps before turning to leave.

Once outside, he heaved a sigh of relief. It could have been much worse. It stung his pride to be so summarily dismissed from consideration as the new captain of the house guard, but at the same time, he had been passed over for nothing less than the very best.

Kieran of Draj was a living legend among mercenaries, a veteran campaigner who had covered himself in glory and achieved the dream of every mercenary, to retire a wealthy man. And he had done it before he had reached his fortieth birthday. Matullus wondered how much Ankhor had offered him to tempt him out of retirement. It must have been a princely sum. To be second-in-command to a man like Kieran of Draj would surely make his reputation. And a reputation was worth money in this business. Matullus smiled. Lord Ankhor had not blamed him for the death of Captain Varos, and it could well be the luckiest thing that had ever happened to him.

* * * * *

"I had not known you'd hired a replacement for Captain Varos," Lyanus said after Matullus left. "How long ago did you reach that decision?"

"Oh, some time ago," said Ankhor, dismissing the question with a wave of his hand.

"You normally consult me on such matters."

"Your knowledge of trade is second to none, Lyanus," Ankhor replied, "but hiring mercenaries is a bit outside your field of expertise. Why, do you disagree with my decision?"

"No, my lord, I know nothing of this Kieran of Draj. I was merely curious. . . . But, as you say, the matter is outside my expertise. Still . . . I might have been effective in conducting the negotiations. I am sure I could have saved the house some money in concluding arrangements with this man."

Ankhor smiled. "Oh, I doubt that, Lyanus. And that was no slight to your bargaining abilities. Kieran stated his conditions clearly, and they were absolutely non-negotiable."

"May I inquire what they were, my lord?"

"One hundred thousand gold pieces for one year of service, with half payable up front and the rest in equal monthly installments."

Lyanus's jaw dropped. "*One hundred thousand in gold!*" he said with disbelief. "But . . . but that's outrageous!"

"Yes, it certainly is," said Ankhor. "And at the end of the first year, the contract is subject to renegotiation."

"And you mean to tell me you *agreed* to these incredible demands?"

"I imagine Kieran was no less amazed than you when I accepted his terms," said Ankhor with amusement. "He expected me to refuse, of course. That was why he named so ridiculous a sum. He had no wish to come out of retirement, especially not to command the guard of a merchant house. This is a man who had distinguished himself in war. However, once he stated his terms and I agreed to them, he had no choice but to accept. Otherwise I could have accused him of dealing in bad faith, and that would have besmirched his reputation. A man like Kieran lives and dies by his reputation."

"But, my lord . . . *why?*" Lyanus said, aghast. "You could easily have hired an entire battalion of mercenaries for such a sum!"

"It is a significant expense, I agree, but we can easily afford it," Ankhor said. "Besides, if I had hired a battalion of mercenaries, it would not have created the impression I intended."

"But . . . I do not understand, my lord," Lyanus said with a puzzled expression.

"The Merchant Code requires us to be nonpolitical," said Ankhor, "but we are, of course, very much concerned with politics. One cannot transact business profitably otherwise. I wanted everyone to know that the House of Ankhor will spare no expense in hiring the very best to lead our guard in this turbulent time—a man whose reputation is established and beyond question. We share with the House of Jhamri the responsibilities of policing Altaruk; both houses are headquartered here, and I wanted everyone to know just how seriously we take that responsibility."

"Lord Jhamri, in particular," said Lyanus, catching on.

"Precisely," Ankhor replied with a smile. "My father spent his entire life competing with the House of Jhamri, and it wore him out. They were always bigger, always wealthier, and they always regarded us as upstart newcomers. At social functions, they treated my father as a second-class citizen, as a peasant unfit to rub shoulders with them. Oh, they were unfailingly polite, but their condescending tolerance was a slap across the face. I have never forgiven them that, and I never shall."

"But you recently signed a partnership with the House of Jhamri," said Lyanus.

"Because trying to compete with them in the marketplace is pointless," Ankhor said. "We could never match their resources. Whereas if we join them in partnership, we can take advantage of them. Jhamri thinks he has beaten us. He believes I am more pragmatic than my father, that in allying with his house, I have made a wise decision that ensures our survival and extends his own holdings, since the agreement places him in the preeminent position.

"Well, he is half right, at any rate. I *am* more pragmatic than my father. I realize that competing with the Jhamris is not the way to beat them. The way to beat them is to join them . . . and undermine them politically."

"And Kieran is part of your plan?" Lyanus asked.

"Exactly," Ankhor said. "I had my agents negotiate with Kieran on behalf of the House of Jhamri, in my new capacity as junior trading partner. His salary will come out of my pocket, of course, but he will wear the red of Jhamri, not the buff and blue of Ankhor."

Lyanus frowned. "I fear you've lost me, my lord. You mean, you have, in essence, given this Kieran as a present to Lord Jhamri's house? Where is the profit in this? And how can he lead our house guard if he wears the Jhamri colors?"

Ankhor smiled. "You have an excellent mind for detail, good Lyanus, but a poor one for intrigue. Lord Jhamri will see my employment of Kieran on his behalf as a gesture to ingratiate myself with him. It is just the sort of thing a man in my position would be expected to do.

"After years of competition, he has finally brought the House of Ankhor to its knees, and in my new position as his subsidiary trading partner, it would seem perfectly logical for me to curry favor with him as evidence of my good faith. After all, my father was his enemy, and as his supposedly weaker, more pragmatic son, whose primary interest is in enjoying a self-indulgent lifestyle, I will play up to his expectations by trying to prove myself his friend. He will, of course, have no idea how much I am paying Kieran, and it would be impolitic of him to ask. And a condition of my contract with Kieran is that he not reveal the amount of his salary.

"However," Lord Ankhor continued, "at the proper time, I shall allow that information to leak out. Meanwhile, Kieran will command my house guard because Lord Jhamri will insist on it, especially now that I have tragically lost Captain Varos. The fool could not have gotten killed at a better time. Lord Jhamri already has a captain for his house guard, and it would not be practical to demote him in Kieran's favor, especially when he has done nothing to deserve it.

"No, he will magnanimously offer Kieran to me, to command my own guard, but I will insist that Kieran wear the Jhamri red and act as the nominal co-commander with Jhamri's own captain. A merely titular appointment, with no real authority behind it. The two units will continue to remain separate. At the same time, Jhamri will have the satisfaction of having all of Altaruk see the commander of the Ankhor House Guard wearing his colors, a clear sign to everyone of who is in control. He will think he has outmaneuvered me, and I will be seem to have placed myself at a considerable disadvantage for the sake of public safety."

"Very shrewd, my lord," Lyanus said. "If, indeed, it comes out as you predict."

"Rest assured, it will," said Ankhor. "These recent outbreaks of violence in Altaruk have steadily been growing worse, and everyone is greatly concerned. The Alliance has always maintained a strong presence here, because the defilers have never had much influence.

"However, defiler numbers have been growing, and the Alliance is stepping up efforts to eliminate them. Each faction tries to spy out the other, and Altaruk has become a hotbed of intrigue. If things keep up at this rate, we shall soon be caught squarely in a full-scale mage war. And that would be very bad for business."

"And you have a plan to prevent this conflict?" asked Lyanus.

"Oh, I always have a plan, Lyanus. Kieran is only the first part of that plan. The public part, for there is also another, very private part. The first part is the fire I light under the House of Jhamri, and the second is the ice."

"The ice, my lord?" Lyanus asked, puzzled.

"Yes, an ice that will freeze the very soul, Lyanus," Ankhor said with a smile so warm and pleasant that it sent a chill through the old minister of accounts.

Lyanus had learned to watch his young master's eyes when he smiled. This time, they were terrifying—dead and flat, devoid of emotion. In that moment, Lyanus wondered if Ankhor had a soul. "I . . . I do not understand, my lord."

"All in good time, Lyanus," Lord Ankhor replied as he turned back to the window to watch the merchant plaza burn. "All in good time."

ONE

It was almost dawn on the Great Ivory Plain, and the twin moons cast a ghostly light on the seemingly endless expanse of sparkling, hard-packed crystal. As the night wind shifted, blowing from the east, Sorak seemed to hear the tormented cries of the lost souls wandering the streets of Bodach, whose crumbling spires rose in the distance, barely visible in the bright, silvery moonlight.

Perhaps it was his imagination. Surely not even an elfling could hear across fifty miles of desert. And yet, tricks of the wind could sometimes carry sound far out in the trackless wastes of Athas, especially here where nothing grew, here on the shimmering crystal plain. As the desert breeze blew across the silt basins to the east, rustling through the palm fronds of the oasis, Sorak was almost certain he could hear the faint sounds of a tortured wailing, a chorus of ululating voices that chilled him to the bone. It was a sound he had hoped never to hear again.

Soon, the sun would rise and the living dead of Bodach would slink back to their hiding places in the ruins. The wind would cease to bear their fearsome wails across the desert, and the city of undead would fall silent as the sands swirled through its deserted streets and plazas. A deceptive stillness would once again descend upon the Great Ivory Plain as the dark sun baked its crystal surface with temperatures high enough to boil blood.

During the day, Bodach seemed merely an abandoned city on a narrow spit of land jutting into the great silt sea—the isolated, crumbling ruins of a once great civilization that had flourished upon Athas in an age when the world was green and the sea filled with water, not with brown and swirling silt. But at night, horror stalked Bodach, and those who fell victim to the city's undead rose again to join their ranks, doomed by an age-old curse to spend eternity protecting the lost treasure of the ancients.

What Sorak had found in the city of undead was of greater value than any material treasure. He had found a gateway into Sanctuary, the refuge of the Sage, and it was there that he had learned the answers to the questions that had plagued him all his life. It was there that he had found himself, and in the process, came close to losing everything, even his life.

As he stood upon the low and rocky ridge that sheltered the oasis at the edge of the great salt plain, Sorak glanced back toward Ryana, sleeping in her bedroll by their campfire. Together, they had survived the city of undead, and their journey to find the Sage had taken them from their home in the forests of the Ringing Mountains all the way across the harsh and foreboding desert Tablelands. Along the way, they had fought marauders and mercenaries, half-giants and defilers, corrupt aristocrats and paid assassins, and a host of undead warriors. They had even defied the wrath of the Shadow King, Nibenay, himself. They had come a long way from the beginning of their quest and had both sacrificed a great deal to follow the Path of the Preserver. Their lives had changed immeasurably since they had set out on their journey, and as Sorak stood there, the cool night breeze ruffling his long, dark hair, he thought back to how it all had begun.

* * * * *

From childhood, he had been a tribe of one—a half-breed with a dozen personalities, some male, some female, each with distinctive attributes. A wandering pyreen had found him half dead, alone out in the desert. When the shapechanger realized that his ordeal had fragmented his young mind, she had brought him to the villichi convent, nestled high in an isolated valley of the Ringing Mountains.

The villichi were a sisterhood of warrior priestesses who had vowed to follow the Way of the Druid and the Path of the Preserver. They were women born with fully developed psionic powers, mutants ostracized from their communities. They were taller than most women, broad shouldered and long limbed, and most were marked with albino features—snow-white hair, eyes ranging from palest green or gray to pink, and pale, almost translucent skin that burned easily in the hot Athasian sun. Each year, robed villichi priestesses went out on pilgrimages to search for others of their kind, but never in all the history of Athas had there been a male villichi. In all the years the convent had existed, no male had set foot in its walls.

Though he was male, Sorak was accepted by the high mistress of the convent, both out of her reverence for the pyreen and because she had detected his inborn psionic powers. He was not only an elfling, born of a forbidden union between halfling and elf, he was also a tribe of one, a condition so rare that it was known only among villichi. He was an outcast, as were most villichi, and if he was not villichi himself, then he was as close to being one as any male had ever been. The high mistress took him in and named him Sorak, an elvish word for a nomad who travels alone.

Sorak grew up among the villichi sisterhood. One of them, Ryana, a villichi girl his own age, became his closest friend. They grew up together, played together, trained together in the exotic warrior arts of the villichi, and studied the Way of the Druid. But as they grew older, youthful friendship and affection gave way to love and sexual attraction. And Sorak found himself tormented, torn between his own desires and those of his other personalities.

The female personalities residing in him could accept Ryana as sister or friend, but not as lover, so Sorak left the convent to seek out his destiny and discover the truth of his origins. But Ryana would not be parted from him. When she found out that he had left, she broke her villichi vows, fled the convent in the middle of the night, and followed him out into the desert.

Together, they sought the Sage, the reclusive and mysterious preserver wizard who had embarked upon the long and arduous course of metamorphosis into an avangion, the only creature capable of standing against the power of the dragon kings. Only the magic of the Sage was great enough to help Sorak discover his past, and only preserver magic, which did not destroy the dwindling natural resources of Athas, could cure him of his rare condition. To accept the help of a defiler would have violated everything he had been raised to believe, and would have doomed him to forsake forever the Path of the Preserver. However, in searching for the Sage, Sorak had attracted the attention of the dragon kings and their defiler minions, who regarded the preserver wizard as the sole threat to their power.

In Bodach, Sorak and Ryana faced not only an army of undead, but the murderous champion of the Shadow King, a ruthless killer named Valsavis. They prevailed, but only at great cost. Guided by Kara, a pyreen known as the Silent One, they had found the gateway into Sanctuary in Bodach. It was a magical doorway into another time and place, in an age when Athas was still green. That was the secret of the Sage, and it was why none of the dragon kings had ever been able to find him. They sought him in the present, but he had used his magic to find a refuge in the distant past.

In Sanctuary, Sorak found the answers he had so long sought. He had already deduced that the Sage was the same person once known as the Wanderer, who had chronicled his peregrinations across Athas in a book known as *The Wanderer's Journal*. What he had not known was that the preserver wizard was his grandfather.

The Sage cast a spell on Sorak, which enabled him to see into his past. He discovered who his parents were, and what his truename was, and what had become of his people. Through the magic of the Sage, Sorak saw how the Moon Runner tribe of elves had been destroyed by a necromancer called the Faceless One, a defiler wizard hired by Sorak's halfling grandfather.

However, finding out those answers both set Sorak free and severed him from the only security he had ever really known. The voices of his multiple personas would never speak to him again. The wise, maternal Guardian; the stoic Ranger; the calculating Eyron; the brash and irrepressible Kivara; the beastlike Screech; the gentle, childlike Lyric; and the others . . . all were gone now. They had joined with the Sage, living on inside him as he entered the next stage of his transformation. The act that empowered the Sage's evolution also healed Sorak's fragmented personality, and now Sorak was left feeling more alone than he had ever felt before.

"All living creatures are alone, Sorak," Ryana told him afterward in an attempt to ease his pain. "That is why they mate and bond in friendship."

"Yes, I know," he replied. "But it is one thing to know it, and still another to experience truly being alone for the first time. I have never known the feeling. For as long as I can remember, I have had the others with me. Now, I feel their absence, the emptiness in my soul. It feels as if a part of me is missing."

Nor was his multiplicity the only thing he lost.

When he had left the convent, High Mistress Varanna had given him a gift, a wondrous sword named Galdra—the enchanted blade of elven kings. It had been entrusted to her safekeeping by a pyreen elder, who had received it from the hand of Alaron himself, last of the ancient line of elven kings. Sorak had not known the nature of the blade's enchantment when he had received it, but he learned that it would cut through anything, and that other blades would shatter upon contact with its elven steel. He knew, too, that if Galdra fell into the hands of a defiler, its magic blade would shatter—and that was precisely what happened when he fought Valsavis, champion of the Shadow King.

When Valsavis seized the sword, a blinding explosion of white light shattered the enchanted blade. Now, all that remained was the hilt and about a foot of broken blade. Of the legend once engraved on it in ancient runes—"Strong in spirit, true in temper, forged in faith"—only the elvish symbols for "Strong in spirit" now remained. A defiler's hand had touched it, and the enchantment was broken.

* * * * *

As he stood alone upon the rocky ridge in the first orange-tinted light of dawn, Sorak drew the broken blade from his belt and held it up before him, staring at it as it gleamed with a faint blue eldritch light, the remaining trace energies of the enchantment. Why keep it? It was useless as a sword, and Sorak bore Valsavis's iron sword now, anyway. But Ryana had insisted that the legend of Galdra still stood for something and could be of use to them. Sorak grimaced wryly as he thought of it.

It was said in the songs of elven bards that whoever bore the sword Galdra was fated to become the Crown of Elves, the ruler who would once again unite the scattered tribes under one king. In his travels, Sorak had encountered elves who had believed that he would be that king, but he wanted no part of any elven crown.

Though his mother had named him Alaron after

the long-dead elven king, Sorak felt the name did not belong to him. For as long as he could remember, he had been Sorak, the Nomad, and now that he had finally learned his truename, it did not seem to fit him. He was no elven king, no elven kingmaker.

So why keep the broken blade? Ryana thought it important, as did Kara. "Keep it as a symbol of what you have achieved, and what we struggle for," the pyreen told him before they parted.

But was it really a symbol of achievement, Sorak wondered, or a symbol of a life left behind? He was no longer a tribe of one, an elfling with a dozen different personalities. Now, he was merely Sorak the elfling, the Nomad, around whom unwanted legends had already sprung up. Such notoriety brought only trouble, and he had enough trouble as it was.

For the first time in his life, he felt alone and vulnerable. Yet, for all that he had lost, he had gained the one thing he had never thought that he could have. Ryana.

He turned his back upon the great salt plain and gazed down the slope into the small oasis where Ryana slept, curled up in her bedroll near the smoking embers of their campfire. He thought back to the day she had declared her love for him. It seemed almost a lifetime ago. . . .

* * * * *

As usual, after weapons training in the morning, the villichi students went down to the stream to bathe. In a desert world, a running stream was the rarest of luxuries, yet Sorak and his villichi companions took it for granted. The Ringing Mountains around them were covered with thick, old-growth forests, and he spent long days hiking through the lush woods, or running with Tigra by his side, a tigone that had been his constant companion since his childhood.

Instead of joining the others at the lagoon, Sorak and his best friend Ryana wandered off to a special spot a bit farther downstream. As they sat together on a large rock outcropping in the middle of the stream, feeling the coolness of the water rush over them, Ryana told him how she felt. "Sorak . . . there is something I have been meaning to ask you—"

"I know what you are going to ask. I have known for some time." He had seen it coming and had dreaded the moment when she would finally give voice to her feelings. She had known he was a tribe of one, but because his other personalities all spoke with his male voice, she had not suspected that some of them were female, and he had been afraid to tell her. When she learned the truth at last, it took her completely by surprise.

Shocked and dismayed by his disclosure, Ryana fled to the temple tower, where she began a period of solitary meditation.

That was when Sorak appeared before High Mistress Varanna and told her he was going to leave the convent. He felt his continued presence would only bring heartache to Ryana, whom he cared for very deeply, but could never have. The vows taken by villichi priestesses did not permit them to have mates, and even if they had, his female personas would never have allowed it.

Though he had lived with the villichi sisterhood, he was never one of them, and as an adult male living among them, he knew he would only be a source of discord. He thought that by leaving, he would free Ryana from the burden of loving him.

Instead, she forsook her vows and followed.

* * * * *

Now, freed of his multiple personas, Sorak was able to accept her as a lover at long last, and that made all the difference. The harsh light of morning softened in his eyes as he looked down upon Ryana, sleeping below. In Sanctuary, they had made love for the first time, and they vowed that they would always be together, no matter what the future brought.

He pulled the broken blade from his belt. It might still have made a useful knife, even though the tip resisted all his efforts to sharpen it into a tapering point. Useless, though it yet sparked faintly with a crackling discharge of blue energy, like a guttering candle.

So much for the legend of the Crown of Elves, he thought. A broken blade, a broken people, scattered throughout Athas in small desert-dwelling tribes or living in the cities, where they performed the most menial of labor or eked out lives as gamers and merchants in the squalid, overcrowded elven quarters. A legend, perhaps, would give them some small hope for their future. Those who still believed in it, at any rate. But if they met with the reality, then they would see only a nomadic wanderer with a broken sword, not a fabled blade borne by an elven king. Why shatter their illusions, as the touch of a defiler had shattered the steel of the blade?

Why shatter more lives? Sorak's ancestors had done enough of that already. . . .

* * * * *

The Sage, his maternal grandfather, was the only family Sorak knew. He did not know if his paternal grandfather, the halfling chieftain Ragna, still lived, but hoped he was dead. If Ragna lived and Sorak found it out, the halfling would live no longer.

Sorak would never understand what sort of father could condemn his own son to death by fire for mating with a female of another race. Ragna had meant for him to die as well, and but for a chance casting of a spell, Sorak had survived.

Ragna's commission to the Faceless One was to cast a spell to slay every last elf in the Moon Runner tribe. Sorak had been spared only because he was not a full-blooded elf. He was a half-breed, born of two races that were natural enemies. The spell cast by the Faceless One had failed to strike him down, as it had struck down all the others, and though he was a sworn enemy of all defilers, Sorak despised the Faceless One above all others. He knew nothing of the wizard but his name, yet somehow, somewhere, he would find him. And then his father and his mother and her tribe would be avenged. Death to the sorcerer, and to the grandfather who commissioned him.

It was a cold and ruthless resolution. An unsettling thought.

And there were so many thoughts streaming through his head these days. He could not get used to the curious feeling of being all alone in there.

He was having trouble sleeping. When he was a tribe of one, Sorak could rest by letting one of his other personalities come to the fore and take over. He would fade back and "go under," as if sinking down into warm darkness, sometimes aware of what was happening outside and sometimes not, while his body remained awake and in the control of one of his other personalities.

Now that he was just alone, he had to learn to fall asleep the way that everyone else did. Sooner or later, he grew tired, and then sleep would come. However, being part elf and part halfling meant his body possessed immense physical reserves. Since leaving Sanctuary, he had found he could go for days without sleep. He would lie down to rest, as he had done the previous night, but while Ryana quickly fell asleep, he remained awake, his mind relentlessly active as if it sought to fill the void left by his other personalities.

It was a new life, a new way of being, and he was

not yet accustomed to it.

Often, at night after Ryana fell asleep, he would start talking to himself, a habit many people had, but Sorak would half expect to hear an answer. He would start to speak to one of his personalities aloud, as he had often done before, and when no answer came, he would remember again there would be no answer, and then the crushing loneliness would descend on him like an immense weight on his chest.

* * * * *

Sorak felt the warmth of the dark sun as it slowly rose on the horizon. Soon, Ryana would awaken, and they would fill their waterskins from the oasis pool and set off once again, en route to North Ledopolus, one of two dwarven villages located on opposite banks of the Estuary of the Forked Tongue, roughly thirty miles southwest. From there, they planned to cross the estuary to South Ledopolus, through which the caravan trade route ran from Altaruk to Balic.

Neither he nor Ryana had ever been to that part of the world, and all they knew of it was what Sorak's grandfather had written in his journal, a copy of which Sorak carried with him. However, it had been written many years ago, and they had no way of knowing if the information it contained was still accurate.

According to the journal, the dwarves of South Ledopolus were trying to build a causeway to

Ledo Island, a long-dead volcano that rose in the center of the estuary. At the same time, the dwarves of North Ledopolus were trying to do likewise, thereby hoping to meet in the middle and connect the two villages with a bridge that would open a shorter caravan route from Gulg and Nibenay to Balic and the other cities south of the Tyr region. The bridge would benefit both villages and increase the traffic coming through them.

But the giants who lived on Ledo posed an obstacle. They had no desire to see their island become a connecting point between two dwarven villages, with the increase in traffic, and so they kept tearing down the causeway that the dwarves were building. Constant battles raged between the giants and the dwarves, and Sorak had no idea if there would be a bridge across the estuary when they reached it or not.

The dwarves had ferries that plied the estuary, above and below Ledo Island, but the giants often attacked these, as well. The dwarves therefore navigated with great care, taking ferries across the deepest parts of the estuary to avoid the giants. But the silt shifted on the bottom, and it was difficult to gauge the estuary's depth, so any ferry crossing was a gamble.

Even so, Sorak knew they had to take that course. The only other alternative was to head north across the Great Ivory Plain and take the trade route along its northern boundary. They had crossed the plain once already, and Sorak was not anxious to repeat the long, arduous journey.

Once they had crossed the estuary and reached the caravan trade route that ran past South Ledopolus, Sorak had no idea which way they would go. He had expected to receive some sign from the Sage, but as yet, there had been no message from his grandfather. He knew only one thing—wherever they were bound, they would be going toward trouble, not away from it.

Throughout Athas, in the larger city-states, the dragon kings held sway. In the smaller towns and villages, their defiler minions were always active, seeking to extend and consolidate their power. The preservers were outnumbered by defilers everywhere, so much so that preserver adepts and their supporters had been forced underground.

They functioned as small, semi-independent groups collectively known as the Veiled Alliance. To be exposed as a member of the Alliance meant certain death, so members functioned in great secrecy, working against the power of the defilers in whatever ways they could.

The structure of the Alliance assured anonymity. It was divided into secret cells, with each cell being aware of only two other cells on the same level, and only one above it. In this way, if any one cell were exposed, it could quickly be cut off, and the members of the cells in contact with it absorbed into other groups. This system kept defilers from penetrating the structure of the entire organization.

Fortunately for them, the defilers were not united. The dragon kings were in fierce competition with each other. Even so, they commanded far more power than the preservers. And that power was slowly, relentlessly destroying Athas.

Yes, the dark sun rose upon a dying world. With each passing year, more and more of the planet's resources were used up by the defilers in their greedy quest for power. Some said it was the science of a bygone age that had changed the climate and reduced most of the world to blasted desert, but Sorak knew it was defiler magic.

He walked back down the rocky slope and approached the small pool of the oasis. For a moment, he simply stood there, staring down into the dark blue water.

Behind him, Ryana stirred softly. "Good morning," she said, as she sat up behind him and stretched. "Have you been awake long?"

"I have not slept."

"Again?"

He sighed, heavily. "My thoughts are too much with me."

"What were you thinking about?"

"Legends," he replied. "And about the difference between fable and reality. Sometimes reality leaves much to be desired." And with that, he tossed the broken blade into the pool.

Ryana leapt to her feet and ran to his side. "No! What have you done?"

He grabbed her by the arm before she could dive in after it.

"Let it go, Ryana," he said.

She stared at him, uncomprehending. "*Why?*"

"Because I am not a king," he said. "And legend or no legend, the blade is broken."

"But it still could have been a symbol!"

"Of what? Of the elven prophecy? Defilers could just as easily claim that with Galdra broken, the prophecy has proven false. I may not have much faith in it myself, but neither do I wish to see defilers twist it to their own ends. If there is to be another elven king someday, then let it be my grandfather. The avangion will have the strength and wisdom to rule well. I find it challenging enough to rule myself."

"But think what you have thrown away!" Ryana said with chagrin.

"I have," said Sorak, staring into the pool where Galdra had sunk out of sight. "I have discarded the reality, and in doing so, I have preserved the legend. I do not regret my choice. Come, let us fill our waterskins. We still have a long way to go."

TWO

They were out there tonight, waiting. Waiting with their sweaty hands and leering faces, with their tongues moistening their lips and their eyes gleaming with anticipation. Cricket could hear them, shouting and laughing boisterously, pounding on the tables and calling for more drinks. The caravan from Balic had arrived in South Ledopolus that afternoon, and tonight the place was full, packed with traders, travelers and mercenaries. The humans were the worst. Ordinarily, only a few humans frequented the house, but when a caravan was in town, they came in droves, with money clinking in their purses and hands reaching, feeling, pinching. . . .

"All right, my lovelies, we've got a full house tonight," said Turin, pulling aside the beaded curtain as he came into the dressing room. The squeaky-voiced dwarf paid no heed to the various states of undress of those within. "They'll want their money's worth, and I know you'll give it them, won't you?"

"Because when the customers get their money's worth, they're happy, and when the customers are happy, Turin's happy," Rikka chanted, imitating his high voice. Turin gave them the same speech every time a caravan came through town. Just once, thought Cricket, it would be nice to hear a different sermon.

"Don't worry, Turin," Rikka said, sashaying to him with a bump and grind, her large breasts bouncing as she moved. She stopped in front of Turin, who came up to about her waist. She reached down and tousled the dwarf's thick red hair. "We'll part them from their money, then you'll part us from ours, as usual."

Turin took the casual impertinence in stride. "Just remember, my dears, the more you make—"

"The more you keep," the other girls said in unison as they continued getting dressed in their dancing costumes and applying their makeup.

"That's absolutely right," said Turin, rubbing his pudgy little hands together in anticipation. "And it's a fine, rich caravan this time, from the House of Jhamri. They're fresh from delivering goods to Balic, and they've got plenty of money in their purses. It's our duty to ease their burden a bit on the return trip. So let's have a good show tonight, and be sure to circulate among the patrons when it's not your turn on stage. We want them drunk, diverted, and delighted."

"Wasted, wanton, and wiped out," said Rikka with a grin, kissing Turin on the top of his head.

"Exactly," said the dwarf. He patted her rear end affectionately, and his hand lingered a bit too long.

Turin was like an old woman shopping at a fruit stall, thought Cricket. He had to feel everything. He had his favorites among the girls, and the ones who indulged him the most were allowed the most leeway. Nevertheless, Cricket had not followed their example, and whenever Turin reached for her, she adroitly moved away.

Turin had not pressured her, at least not on his own behalf, but on several occasions, he had drawn her aside and made a point of telling her she ought to be more friendly to the patrons. Being "friendly" meant sitting at tables, or better, on laps, allowing certain intimacies as patrons bought her drinks—which were no more than colored water—and asking if they would like a private show upstairs. For a fee, patrons of the Desert Damsel could rent a room, paying by the half hour, and receive a private dance. Any other transactions that occurred there, behind closed doors, were extra. That was how the other girls made most of their money.

Cricket was the exception. She had never gone upstairs with any of the customers, and she would sit at their tables only so long as they kept their hands to themselves. The moment any of them tried to touch her, she would politely excuse herself and leave.

"A word with you, Cricket, if I may?" said Turin to the half-elf, coming to her side as the other girls filed out of the small dressing room.

"If it is the same word, then it is the same reply," said Cricket, checking her makeup in the mirror. Even sitting, she was the same height as he.

Turin shook his head. "Cricket, Cricket, Cricket," he said, petulantly. "Why must you be so difficult?"

"I am not difficult at all," she replied, carefully applying a bit more rouge to her cheeks. "I always come to work on time, and I never short the house on its share of the tips, as some of the other girls do. I am never rude to any of the customers, nor do I sit on their laps to pick their pockets. I was hired to dance, and that is what I do. If anything more was expected of me as a condition of my employment, you should have made it plain in the beginning."

The pudgy dwarf sighed with resignation. "You take unfair advantage of me," he said in a whining tone. "You are the most striking-looking girl I've got, and the best dancer, too. You know I could not afford to lose you. . . . By the way, which of the girls short me on the tips?"

Cricket smiled. "That would be telling tales."

Turin grimaced. "Well, I expect most of them do," he said with a shrug. "Why should you be any different?"

"Because I do not break my agreements," she

replied, turning to face him. "If I compromised on my agreement with you, it would be only a short step to compromising on my agreements with myself, and I do not wish to lose my focus."

"Your focus?" he repeated with a smile. "That is a dwarven concept. What would a half-elf girl know about focus?"

"I know what dwarves have taught me," she replied. "It is a very useful concept, and I am a quick study."

"And what is your focus?" Turin asked with a condescending little smile.

"You of all people should know better than to ask a thing like that," said Cricket, raising her eyebrows.

Turin nodded. "Indeed," he said. "One's focus is a private thing. I see that you have learned at least that much. Forgive me for my rudeness."

"No offense was meant, and none taken."

Turin smiled. "Spoken like a dwarf," he said. "Whoever taught you, taught you well."

"I live in a dwarven village," she replied. "I try to learn the customs, as a courtesy."

"You are an unusual young woman," Turin said. "You are not like the others."

"Yes," she agreed, "that is a large part of my appeal."

"And some of the other girls resent you for it."

"They all resent me for it," she said. "But I did not come here to make friends, only to make money."

"And only on your own terms," said Turin.

"The other girls are already busy out there, circulating, yet you always remain backstage until it is your turn to dance. You could make a great deal more if you were more forthcoming with customers, you know."

"On the contrary, I would make a great deal less," said Cricket.

Turin stared at her thoughtfully for a moment, then pursed his lips and nodded. "You may be right, at that," he said. "Well, that bard should be finishing up his song by now, so I'll need to go and start the show." He grinned. "There's nothing like a bard to get things rolling. By the time he's finished, they'll be dying for some real entertainment. It's a hungry crowd. Let's really drive them wild tonight."

"That I can do," said Cricket.

Turin went back out into the main room, then Cricket heard the clamor of the crowd as the bard finished his recitation and Turin took the stage to announce the first dancer.

A moment later, the beaded curtain parted, and Edric the bard came in, looking weary and exasperated. He was dressed as usual in a loose-fitting gray tunic belted at the waist, use-worn breeches of brown leather, and soft, high-topped moccasin boots. So far as Cricket knew, they were the only clothes he owned. With a heavy sigh, he put down his harp and eased his long, lean, elven frame into a chair, running a hand through shoulder-length silver hair.

"Tough crowd tonight?" asked Cricket sympathetically.

Edric grimaced. "Indifferent to the point of pain," he said, his voice heavy with frustration. "It was like trying to sing into a sandstorm. I don't know why I bothered taking this job. It's you girls they come to see, not me. They talked and shouted throughout the entire performance. Still, at least they didn't throw things. That's something to be thankful for, I suppose."

"I'm sorry, Edric," Cricket said. "You deserve a more appreciative audience."

"Well, I fear I won't find one here," said Edric wryly.

"Why not sing for me, then? There is still time before I have to go on stage." She tossed him a coin. "Sing for me, Edric."

He caught the coin adroitly. "There is no need for this, Cricket," he said. "I would be glad to sing for you for nothing."

"And I am glad to pay," she said. "I can afford it, and an artist should be rewarded for his efforts."

Edric smiled and picked up his harp. "Very well, then. Is there a special song you would like to hear?"

"Sing for me 'The Song of Alaron,' " she said. "Not the whole ballad—there isn't enough time. Sing the sad part, about the fall and the prophecy."

"Ah," said Edric, nodding. "An excellent choice. I have not sung that one in quite a while."

"You still recall it?"

"How could I not? I am an elf," he said with a smile as his long fingers delicately plucked the harp. Cricket sat back in her chair and closed her eyes, and Edric began to sing, reciting the words with a measured cadence in a deep, mellifluent voice.

> "And so it came to pass that the noble Alaron, last of the long and honored line of elven kings, was cursed by the evil Rajaat, who feared the power of the elves and sought to sow disunity among them. With his defiler magic, Rajaat cast a spell upon the noble Alaron, so that he could sire no sons, and so the royal line would die out with him. And the evil that he wrought upon our people is with us to this day. May his name live long in infamy."

"May his name live long in infamy," Cricket repeated softly, as was the custom when the song was performed around the elven campfires in the desert. Edric smiled and continued.

> "Rajaat then sowed discord among the tribes, using bribery, deceit, and magic, and in time, he succeeded in driving the tribes apart into many warring factions. Only the noble Alaron resisted him, but he was unable to bring the tribes together once again.
>
> "And so the kingdom fell."

"And so the kingdom fell," said Cricket, nodding with her eyes still closed. And Edric went on.

"Then the noble Alaron was forced to flee, pursued by Rajaat's evil minions. They caught up to him and the remnants of his tribe at a place called the Lake of Golden Dreams, and it was there the dream died for our people. A mighty battle followed, and all the tribe was slain. Mortally wounded, the noble Alaron alone escaped into the forests of the Ringing Mountains.

"There, he fell down in despair and waited for death to come claim him. He had done his utmost, and he had failed, but he had not bowed down to the foe. May his courage be remembered."

"May his courage be remembered," Cricket echoed with feeling. Edric nodded, plucking out the notes of the refrain, and then went on.

"And it came to pass that as he lay dying, a wandering pyreen came upon him and stopped to bring him peace and ease his final moments. With his last breath, the noble Alaron gave her his sword, the mighty Galdra, enchanted blade of elven kings. With his last breath, he asked one final boon of her.

" 'Take this, my sword, the symbol of my once-proud people,' he said to her. 'Keep it safe, so that it should never fall into the hands of the defilers, for the blade would shatter if they tried to use it. I was cursed never to have a son,' he said, 'and a proud tradition dies with me. The elves are now a beaten people. Take Galdra and keep it safe. My life is but the blink of an eye to a pyreen such as you. Perhaps, someday, you will succeed where I have failed, and find an elf worthy of this blade. If not, hide it from the defilers. I can at least deny them this.'

"And with those words, he died. And so the kingdom of the elves died with him."

"And so the kingdom of the elves died with him," Cricket repeated, her voice tinged with sadness. Edric's fingers plucked out a dirge of soft chords as he continued.

"And our people became decadent, and the tribes scattered far and wide, most to live as nomads in the desert, raiding and stealing from both humans and each other, forsaking their honor. Others went to live in the cities of humans, where they engaged in commerce with them and mixed their blood with theirs and forgot the glory of their once-proud race.

"And yet, a tiny spark of hope remained, nurtured in the hearts of our people. That faintly glowing spark was the legend of the Crown of Elves, passed on through the generations. To most, it was merely a myth, a story told by elven bards around campfires to while away lonely desert nights and bring a few moments of solace in the squalid elven quarters of the cities, where our people lived in poverty and degradation. But to all, it was a glimmer of hope. And thus we recall the legend."

"And thus we recall the legend," Cricket said softly. They were both caught up in spirit of the song, and the noise from the main room seemed to recede into the distance as Edric played and sang.

"There shall come a day, the legend says, when a chieftain's seventh son shall fall and rise again, and from his rise, a new life shall begin. From this new life will spring a new hope for our people, and it shall be the Crown of Elves, by which a great, good ruler will be crowned, one who will bring back the elven forest homeland. The Crown shall reunite the people, and a new dawn shall bring the greening of the world.

"So it is said, so it shall be."

"So it is said, so it shall be," Cricket echoed, her eyes shining. Edric plucked out the final chords, took a deep breath, and exhaled heavily, then put down his harp. For a moment, they simply sat in silence.

"Thank you," Cricket said finally, her voice barely a whisper.

"No, thank *you,*" said Edric. "It has been too long since I have sung that song. And it is good to have another share it."

"Even a half-elf?" Cricket said, somewhat rueful.

Edric reached out and placed his hand on her knee. She allowed the contact, for she knew it meant merely friendship. "The same elven blood flows through both our veins, my dear."

"Only yours is pure, while mine is mixed."

"Perhaps, but yours is no less red than mine," said Edric with a smile, giving her knee a reassuring pat before removing his hand. "And in a place like this, what do bloodlines matter?"

"In a place like this, perhaps they don't," Cricket replied with a shrug of resignation. "But there are places where they do matter very much."

"Was it your father who was human, or your mother?" Edric asked.

"My father."

"Ah, so your mother was tribal, then."

"Yes, how did you know?"

"It took no great powers of deduction," Edric said. "In cities, elves are less clannish, and those of mixed blood are not uncommon, whereas in desert-dwelling tribes, such things are not easily accepted."

"No," she said, softly, "they are not."

"And do your parents still live?"

"My mother died five years ago, old before her time from laboring as a scullery maid in a tavern owned by humans. I never knew my father."

Edric nodded. "Regrettably, such things are not uncommon these days, either."

"Were you ever tribal?"

"Once, many years ago, but that was in another lifetime," he replied.

"Why did you leave?"

He shrugged. "I fell in love."

"Ah." She smiled. "With an elf girl from the city? A half-elf woman, perhaps?"

"Worse than that, I fear," he said, smiling. "With a human man."

"Oh," said Cricket, with surprise. And then she chuckled.

Edric raised his eyebrows. "That amuses you?"

"No, forgive me," she said. "You misunderstand. That was not the reason I laughed."

"Then, pray, enlighten me."

"It's only that Rikka will be crushed," said Cricket. "She has had her eye on you, in case you hadn't noticed."

"Rikka is the tall one, with the dark hair and the large . . . ?" Edric pantomimed the features.

"That's Rikka," Cricket said with a grin. "She thought you were avoiding her because she is Turin's favorite."

"Ah. Well . . . that was not the only reason."

Cricket giggled. "So what happened with your human man?"

"He was not similarly disposed, I fear," said Edric. "Last I heard, he married a tavernkeeper's daughter. It was a tragic case of unrequited love. I was very young and foolish in those days, and given to grand and hopeless passions. Such are the things that make a bard. What of you? Has there never been a grand passion in your life? I can't believe there have not been ample opportunities."

"Not the sort of opportunities I sought," she

said. "I am still waiting."

Edric looked surprised. "Do you mean to say you've never . . . ?"

Cricket shook her head. "No. Never."

"Well, I would not have guessed," he said. "From the sultry way you dance, I would have thought you were well versed in the arts of love."

"That is what most men would assume," Cricket replied wryly. "But it takes no great skill for a girl to be seductive, especially if she is pretty. One merely learns from watching the way men react."

"Hmmm. Do the others know?" asked Edric.

"That I am a virgin?" Cricket shook her head. "I think they would be even more surprised than you. They think I'm merely stuck up. At first, they thought perhaps I might prefer women, but they soon discovered I was not so disposed, to borrow your rather diplomatic phrase."

"Why do you stay here? You could make a great deal more by dancing in a city, or even in a larger town. Why here, in a small dwarven village on a distant caravan route?"

"It was where fortune took me," she replied. "But it is not where I intend to stay."

"Oh? You have plans, then?"

"I have been saving my money ever since I started here," said Cricket. "Or as much as I could save, after I had paid for food and clothes and lodging. Prices are inflated here, and when you're known as one of Turin's dancers, the price always goes up. Still, I almost have enough put aside to purchase first-class passage in a caravan. After tonight, with any luck, I should have more than I need."

"And then?"

"And then I will be quit of this pestilential hole," she said, with an intensity that surprised the bard. "I have already made inquiries. In two days time, the caravan departs for Altaruk, and I'll go with it." As if suddenly realizing she might have said too much, she glanced at Edric sharply and added, "I trust I can depend on your discretion. Turin would try to keep me here if he knew my plans."

"You may depend upon my silence," Edric said.

"I am willing to pay for it," said Cricket cautiously.

Edric looked offended. "My dear girl," he said, in an affronted tone, "do you truly think that I would sell you out?"

"There are those who would, if they were in your place," she replied.

"Then they have no honor," Edric said. "As it happens, I have already booked passage with the caravan, myself. Not first class, I fear, since I shall be singing for my supper, but I was going to say that I was looking forward to your company upon the journey. Now, I think perhaps you might scorn it."

Cricket sighed and looked down with a rueful grimace. "Never," she replied. "Forgive me, Edric. I did not mean to insult you. It is just that I do not trust easily. I am not used to having friends."

"There is an old elven proverb," Edric said with a smile. "It is better to have a score of friends than a score of coppers. Then you can ask each friend for a loan of *two* coppers, and you be well ahead."

Cricket chuckled. "I like you, Edric. You make me laugh. And I do not laugh very often these days."

"Well, we shall have to see to it that you are more frequently amused," he replied. "Frown lines would look bad on such a pretty face as yours."

The beaded curtain was flung aside and Turin stuck his head in. "Get ready, Cricket. You are up next," he said, then disappeared.

Edric frowned. "You don't suppose he heard?"

Cricket shook her head. "I do not think so. But it makes no difference. When the caravan leaves South Ledopolus two days from now, I am leaving with it, and nothing anyone can say or do will stop me."

"That's the spirit," Edric said, as Cricket got up and adjusted her clinging black gown. "Now go out there and dance up a storm."

"Yes," she said. "That I can do."

THREE

The village of North Ledopolus was even more unassuming than Sorak had expected. It was little more than a scattering of small, flat-roofed, one-story adobe buildings clustered along a few narrow, dirt streets. The village was situated on a bend in the Estuary of the Forked Tongue, separated from its sister village, South Ledopolus, by about ten miles of ugly brown silt. In the middle of the estuary rose the craggy, volcanic peaks of Ledo Island, dominating the view for miles around.

North Ledopolus was smaller than its sister village, which had grown because of its position on a caravan route. The northern village was smaller in another way, too: it had been built by dwarves and for dwarves. South Ledopolus, on the other hand, had many structures built to human scale to accommodate caravan crews.

Sorak could see little reason for a village to be situated on the north shore of the estuary. There were no trade routes running past, no natural resources there. North Ledopolus stood completely isolated, bounded by the estuary on one side and the Great Ivory Plain on the other.

Its only reason for existence was the causeway the dwarves sought to build across the estuary. If they could complete the project and successfully defend it from the giants who lived on Ledo Island, it would open a new trade route, connecting Balic to Gulg and Nibenay. There was also the possibility of a second trade route, northeast to the gambling city of Salt View.

Though far removed from major trade routes, Salt View was a popular destination for adventurers and pleasure seekers. Situated in the southern slopes of the Mekillot Mountains, it was a freewheeling gambling mecca where virtually any sort of entertainment could be found—for a price. Those who sought its expensive, libertine diversions paid handsome fees to join small, well-protected caravans from Gulg or Nibenay to Salt View. Such a trip was not without its hazards, however. Aside from the dangers of the harsh and inhospitable terrain, there was the added risk of an attack by marauders, who lived in the foothills of the Mekillots and preyed on travelers and raided the caravan routes to the west.

A trade route from North Ledopolus could skirt the southern edge of the crystal plain and run across the desert to the oasis where they had camped the previous night. From there, it could continue around the great silt basins to the east, following their shores before turning north, toward the Mekillots, crossing the salt plain at its narrowest point. It would make for a much easier and safer journey to Salt View then approaching it from Nibenay or Gulg.

If the bridge across the estuary could be completed, Sorak was sure the governing council of Salt View would share the expense of establishing the new trade routes, and North Ledopolus would quickly grow from a small village to a large and thriving caravan town. Knowing this, the dwarves had labored ceaselessly for years to bridge the estuary, carrying the burden of the elaborate construction and doing battle with the giants.

The merchant houses of Altaruk could easily have supported the dwarven venture with additional construction crews and mercenaries. For that matter, Sorak thought, any of the great houses could have raised an expeditionary force to drive the giants out of Ledo Island. However, for undertaking such a costly enterprise, they would doubtless expect a proprietary share in the causeway, and that would reduce the potential profits to the dwarves.

It seemed to Sorak that the dwarves were going about it the hard way. If they had cut one of the merchant houses in for a proprietary share of the causeway, the estuary would have been bridged by now, and any losses the dwarves might have sustained from a merchant house taking a percentage of the tolls would have been offset by the increased revenues.

But dwarves were uncommonly stubborn, and once they had determined their focus, nothing would deflect them from it. They wanted full ownership of the causeway and would settle for nothing less. As a result, *nothing* was exactly what they had, even after years of struggling to complete the project.

Well, not quite nothing, perhaps. They had clearly made some progress. The construction that extended into the estuary from South Ledopolus reached almost halfway out to Ledo Island. From North Ledopolus, another section of the causeway stretched across the silt, extending about two miles from the shore.

The giants could not wade out from the island to attack the bridge at just any point. In some places, the silt would rise over their heads and drown them, so they could destroy only whatever sections they could reach. This meant the dwarves made progress with one section while the giants attacked another. Then the silt would shift along the estuary bottom and the situation would be reversed.

Where the sections of the bridge began, near either shore, the dwarves had widened the causeway considerably, not only to allow for the eventual passage of large caravan vehicles, but also to accommodate defensive fortifications, including catapult emplacements and towers for archers.

Those recently constructed sections of the causeway that extended farther out across the estuary were narrower and not yet fortified. Consequently, they were more vulnerable to attack.

For the dwarves, the trick was to take advantage of the estuary's shifting depth, extending new construction as quickly as possible when the giants could not reach it and gambling that there would be time enough to widen and fortify those sections before the giants could wade out to destroy them. Little by little, the dwarves made headway, but progress was excruciatingly slow, and one successful attack by the giants could undo months of work.

Apparently, that was exactly what had happened recently, for a large section of the bridge extending out from North Ledopolus was newly wrecked, and dwarven work crews labored to repair the damage.

With each new catapult emplacement and each new defensive tower built along the causeway, the giants' assault retreated. But before those works could be extended, more pilings had to be driven down into the silt and reinforced, and new sections of the span constructed. More effort was expended in widening and fortifying the causeway than extending it. The dwarves had learned the hard way that it was pointless to extend the causeway beyond the protective reach of the catapults and towers. As a result, the bridge was slowly taking on the appearance of an elongated fortress, complete with battlements and crenelated towers constructed from thick adobe brick. Eventually, both sections would reach the island in the middle, and then the giants would find themselves under siege. The dwarves were already grimly preparing for that final battle.

As Sorak's grandfather had written in his journal, each year, as a result of steadily increasing revenues, the dwarves' mercenary force grew a little larger. However, the dwarves paid a price for building and maintaining their private little army, and it wasn't just a matter of monetary expense. Mercenaries were a rough and unruly lot, and discipline had never been one of their virtues. Mixed in with a standing army under the command of seasoned officers, they could be controlled. But with a force composed entirely of mercenaries, who chose their own officers, discipline was a serious problem. While North Ledopolus was a quiet, sleepy dwarven village, South Ledopolus had become a rowdy, rough-and-tumble desert town where mercenaries did pretty much as they pleased.

The dark sun was sinking on the horizon as Sorak and Ryana booked passage on the last ferry of the day, paying with one of the silver coins they had brought back with them from Bodach. They could easily have loaded up their packs with gold and precious jewels from Bodach's vast treasure hoard, but such wealth would attract too much attention. Ceramics made up by far the largest percentage of the world's coinage, followed by silver and then gold. An aristocrat with purseful of gold coins would raise no eyebrows, but it would be decidedly unusual for two plainly dressed pilgrims to be paying in such currency, so they had taken only silver. They packed away no more than they could comfortably carry, but enough to see them through for a quite a while. And more than enough to tempt any would-be robbers, so they were discreet in how they carried it, keeping only a few coins in their purses and the rest hidden in their packs.

The ferry they boarded was constructed of blue pagafa wood, held aloft by the exertions of a floater—a psionicist specially trained to keep boats afloat on the shifting silt. It was a long, flat, open-decked boat about thirty feet from end to end and about twelve feet in the beam, with low gunwales and ten oarlocks to each side, with low bench seats for the dwarven rowers. There was a heavy mast set forward toward the bow, with a gaff-rigged sail stitched from dark green lizard hide. But despite the rising night wind coming in off the Great Ivory Plain and filling the patchwork, triangular sail, the oarsmen still needed to row. Even with the wind, the ferry made slow progress across the thick brown silt.

There was no place for them to sit, except on the deck. As they dropped down cross-legged among the other passengers, a mixture of dwarves and mercenaries heading across to South Ledopolus, Sorak tried to imagine what it must have been like in the ancient times, when the estuary was filled with water, when boats had plied it with the speed of the wind.

Ryana glanced at him curiously. She was well accustomed to his silences, but until recently, those silences had often indicated he was listening to his inner voices. Now, she was no longer sure quite what they meant. She knew it must be very difficult for him to learn how to accept the change. "What were you thinking of just now?" she asked.

"I was wondering what it must have been like in the old days, when boats sailed upon water," he replied. "I think I would have liked to be a sailor."

Ryana smiled. "It would have been a fitting occupation for a nomad."

"We shall have to try it someday," he replied.

She frowned. "But . . . how could we?"

Sorak smiled, something he did not do very often these days. "We may be going back again, one day."

She said, "Ah," and nodded in sudden comprehension. He meant Sanctuary, of course. In the ancient time where the Sage had magically established his retreat, the world was still green and water filled the seas. It flowed swift and cold in the estuaries and the rivers, and the wind that blew over it was richly laden with its scent and moisture. In the time of Sanctuary, Athas had not yet become the dying world of the dark sun.

For a moment, they sat in companionable silence as the muscular dwarven rowers bent to their oars, laboring to pull the ferry through the silt. Sorak's thoughts went back to the brief time they had spent in Sanctuary. It seemed more like a dream now than reality, but it *had* been real, and that brief taste of a lost reality had fed his hope that perhaps, one day, it could be found again, and the fate that had befallen the world at the hands of the defilers could be reversed.

He wanted to discuss it with Ryana, but could not speak of it without risk to the Sage. Only among the Veiled Alliance, who fought the same secret war against the dragon kings, could they ever speak of it, for the Alliance, too, awaited the avangion. But no one, not even the Sage, knew how long the metamorphosis would take.

With each painfully completed stage of the complex transformation, an immense amount of energy was expended, and no further progress could be made until recuperation was complete. Then, once more, the whole process would begin again. In a way, thought Sorak, it was like dying and being reborn, over and over and over.

He wondered what his grandfather would look like when the transformation was complete. Exactly what sort of creature *was* an avangion? Its name appeared only in a few half-forgotten myths, and in none of them was the avangion described, for no one had ever seen one. In all the long history of Athas, there was no record of a living avangion. Still, the world's history was shrouded in myth and legend. Much was unknown about the ancient days, and it was almost impossible to separate fact from folklore.

Most likely, the avangion was a creature that existed only *in potential*. The spells to create an avangion were what existed in fact, but they had never been successfully employed before. Until now. It took a mage of a very advanced level even to attempt those spells, and great skill in magic was not all that was required. To undertake the long and arduous process of the metamorphosis required a degree of dedication, discipline, and self-sacrifice few people would possess.

In many ways, the process was similar to that followed by the sorcerer kings in their transformation into dragons. Each step in the long and complex metamorphosis required the casting of many intricate spells, even the simplest of which took weeks or months to prepare. The casting of each of those many spells had to be performed in an exacting, flawless manner, linking them together to initiate each separate stage of the transformation. It drained the adept almost to the point of death, and when the final spell in each stage was cast and the activating invocation spoken, there came the incandescent pain of the incremental transformation as the powerful magic went to work, restructuring the body, tearing it apart and reconfiguring it in ways that would leave the adept writhing on the floor and screaming in agony for days on end. And the pain never went away completely. Once the metamorphosis was under way, there could be no turning back, and the adept had to resign himself to living with the pain until the transformation was complete—a process that took many years.

Sorak remembered how the Sage had looked when they finally came face to face. His grandfather had seemed able, and in good humor, but was in great pain. Sorak could not imagine what it must be like, living through each day in constant pain, knowing that at best, there would be periods during the recuperative stages when it lessened in intensity, but never went away completely. He did not know if he would have the strength for that. He had thought his quest to find the Sage had taxed him, but now he knew that it was nothing compared to what his grandfather had to live with every day.

Sorak had not seen any family resemblance. His grandfather's appearance had changed greatly as a result of the transformation. His tall, lean elven frame had become even thinner beneath the loose, floor-length robes he wore. His hands had grown frail and delicate, the wrists astonishingly thin, the fingers long and almost skeletal, like talons . . . birdlike. Yes, that was it. His grandfather's nose was aquiline, and the facial bone structure was sharp and prominent, the skin stretched taut, the brow ridge more pronounced, the eyes sunken and hooded, like those of a desert hawk. He walked in a shuffling manner, slightly stooped over due to his shoulder blades, which had protruded as if they were growing . . . sprouting into wings.

Sorak looked out at the evening sky as the dark sun disappeared over the horizon and imagined an avangion in flight, a huge, hawklike creature, part bird, part man. Or, in this case, part elf. And he thought, what better fulfillment to the elven prophecy? The Crown of Elves, indeed. Sorak had not been a king, but a kingmaker. How could the tribes fail to unite behind such a potent symbol?

The ferry captain's cry of "Raise oars!" interrupted his reverie. The drummer stopped, raising the small cudgels he used to beat out the pace, and the rowers raised their oars. Almost immediately, the ferry slowed, then drifted to a stop in the thick brown silt. The passengers, who had been conversing among themselves, fell silent and stared out into the darkness. The rowers sat utterly still. The sudden atmosphere of tension on the boat was palpable.

"What is it?" asked Ryana, and was immediately shushed by the other passengers.

"*Silence!*" said the dwarven captain. "*Listen!*"

And then Sorak heard it, unmistakable, a sound cutting through the darkness, slowly growing louder. It was a swishing sound, punctuated at intervals by a curious sucking noise followed by a low, deep, muted thud.

Something was moving through the silt, something very large . . .

. . . the sound of footsteps.

The ferry captain screamed out, "Giant off the starboard side! Full ahead, double the beat!"

The drummer instantly pounded out the new pace with his cudgels, two beats to the second, and the rowers bent to their oars with urgency, their muscles straining as they pulled the ferry through the silt. They dipped their oars to the first beat, then the heavily corded muscles on their arms and backs stood out in sharp relief as they pulled with the second.

The passengers, a mixture of dwarves and mercenaries, were all standing now, staring off to the right, straining to catch a glimpse of the approaching threat. Some of the mercenaries had their hands on the pommels of their swords, while those who carried crossbows immediately snatched them up and fitted bolts.

The giant was off to the right, somewhere in the darkness. The first of the twin moons, Ral, had risen already, but it was only in its first quarter, a crescent that cast almost no light. Now, as they waited apprehensively, Guthay rose, adding a slight amount of illumination. The only sounds were the steady beats of the drum and the swishing, thudding, sucking noises of the giant's footsteps as he waded through the silt. They were steadily growing louder.

Ryana unslung her crossbow from her shoulder and fitted a bolt. She pulled back the string and waited, tensely, staring out into the darkness off the starboard side.

"Let me have that," said Sorak.

Wordlessly, she handed him the crossbow, knowing his elfling night vision was far superior to her human sight.

"Triple time!" the captain cried, and the drummer increased the beat, gritting his teeth with tense anticipation as the rowers fought to make headway against the resistance of the silt. Sweat stood out on their faces and poured down their bare, muscular backs.

The mercenaries were all staring silently and intently out into the darkness off the starboard side, holding their bows ready, while the dwarves nocked arrows to the strings of their short, double recurve pagafa bows.

The sounds of the giant's approach were much louder now, practically drowning out the drumbeats as huge feet struck the soft bottom of the estuary with deep, muffled thuds, then pulled free from the silt with unsettling sucking noises and swished through the thick, resisting powder.

Sorak saw him first.

The giant's shadowy form appeared off the starboard side, about thirty yards away. Sorak could not yet make out his features, but the creature was huge, with a wide chest that looked like a thick slab of rock moving through the darkness. The silt reached to the giant's waist, so it was difficult to tell his height, but appeared to be between twenty and thirty feet tall, weighing six to eight tons. The giant's massive arms were like tree trunks raised over his head, and Sorak could see that he was carrying a huge boulder. It was all too clear what he intended to do with that boulder. If it struck the ferry, they would all be smashed to pieces.

There was no time to lose. Sorak did not know how far the giant could throw the stone, but he looked perfectly capable of reaching them from where he was. And with each huge step, he came closer. Sorak raised the crossbow, aiming for the giant's face, estimating where his eyes might be. At the same instant, the creature's powerful arms bent to throw the boulder. Sorak released the arrow, and it whistled through the darkness, striking home just as the giant threw the boulder.

A deafening bellow of pain filled the night and, an instant later, the huge rock struck the silt off the starboard side, missing the ferry by mere feet. The displacement of the silt raised the ferry sharply, almost tipping it over on its side, but it quickly settled once again, and the dwarves resumed their frantic rowing as the passengers all started letting bolts and arrows fly, aiming them toward the giant's screams. For once, Sorak was grateful it was silt that they were rowing through, not water, for if it had been water, the splash from the boulder would surely have swamped them.

He fitted another bolt and shot again. He was rewarded by another scream of enraged pain as the shaft struck home, and he now saw the giant claw at his face. The other warriors let arrows fly as fast as they could shoot, firing over the heads of the rowers, who strained at their oars with all their might. The drummer relentlessly pounded out the beat, eyes wide with fright, breaths coming in gasps. The silt undulated as the giant beat at it with fury and frustration, and then, without warning, another boulder struck the surface of the silt just off the port bow.

"Another one!" someone shouted, pointing toward a huge silhouette looming in the darkness.

There was no question how far the giants could hurl their boulders. The one who had just thrown was some twenty-five yards off the starboard bow, and he had overshot them. As Sorak's elfling gaze penetrated the darkness, he could see at least three others coming up behind him.

"*Row,* damn your eyes! *Row!*" the captain shouted hoarsely.

He couldn't raise the beat any more; the oarsmen were already rowing as fast as they could. They were now roughly parallel with Ledo Island, halfway out across the estuary, and the giants were wading out to cut them off. The captain stood at the tiller, bending over it and steering to the left. The bow of the boat slowly swung around, describing a wide arc as the captain tried to put more distance between them and the giants.

With no way to tell how deep the silt was, the boat's path was anything but sure. The silt rose up around the giants' chests as they approached, so the bottom fell off sharply at this point. The question was, would it continue to deepen or level off?

There were three giants up ahead, closing on the starboard bow. The fourth giant, the first they had encountered, had now been left behind, but despite his wounds, he had not given up pursuit. With any luck, thought Sorak, he'd been blinded. Enraged, the creature slogged steadily through the silt, bellowing in pain and fury as he tried to catch up to the ferry.

The captain's change of course was taking them obliquely away from the giants because he was still making for the opposite shore. But the giants were just ahead of them and closing. Their footsteps made a chorus of loud swishing, thudding, and sucking noises as they struggled through the silt.

Sorak looked out into the distance, ahead of the boat, and he could see torches flaring up along the partially completed section of the causeway extending out from South Ledopolus. The flames from some of those torches rose in a spiralling course, carried by mercenaries that climbed up onto the defensive towers to man the catapults. But were they in range?

The bow of the boat rose sharply as another boulder struck the silt just ahead of them. Every archer aboard was shooting bolts and arrows as fast as possible. The other passengers held tensely to swords, praying they wouldn't have to use them. If they did, it would already be too late.

Sorak shot another bolt and was rewarded by an enraged scream of pain that shook the night. It was so loud, his ears rang. The giants were getting closer, and it looked as if the ferry might not make it.

The mercenaries on the defensive works of the causeway knew their trade. They brought the catapults into play quickly. Sorak saw trails of fire arcing through the night, illuminating the frightening tableaux of men scrambling over war machines. It took only a few shots to find the range, and then the flaming projectiles were coming down upon the giants.

Four beasts remained, counting the one still lumbering behind them through the silt, and all were now clearly visible. They were huge, ugly brutes, with dark red skin and matted hair reaching to their shoulders. Their powerful upper arms were thicker than Sorak's torso, and their hands were large enough to crush the boat to splinters. Their facial features were misshapen; brow ridges protruded sharply over their eyes, and their noses resembled snouts. Several of them had grotesque canine teeth that grew outward, curving into tusks.

The creatures were close enough now that Sorak could smell their stench, and it made him gag. Another boulder struck the silt just off the starboard bow, landing close enough to scrape the hull as it fell. The boat heeled over sharply, and part of the gunwale broke away with a loud, cracking sound of splintering agafari wood.

They were over a deeper part of the estuary now, for the silt was coming up almost to the giants' collarbones. Still they pursued, refusing to give up with their quarry so close at hand.

Several of them batted at the falling missiles as if at annoying insects, but one of the projectiles struck home, hitting a giant directly on the head. He cried out with pain and staggered, almost going under, and his oily, thickly matted hair caught fire. The giant's panic-stricken screams rent the night as he batted wildly at his hair, trying to put out the flames. It apparently did not occur to the dim-witted creature to duck his head under the silt, which would have put the flames out in an instant. He simply stood there, screaming and swatting at himself with his huge hands.

The ferry captain was screaming, too. He was shouting himself hoarse as he urged on the rowers, who needed no urging, with death so close at hand. A giant loomed up just off the starboard bow, almost close enough to seize the prow of the boat. Sorak raised the crossbow and took careful aim. The bolt whizzed through the air and struck the giant right between the eyes, penetrating his skull and killing him instantly. He immediately sank beneath the surface, and the swell of the silt raised the prow of the boat high as he went down with a hideous sound. The other passengers cheered as the giant fell, but the rowers were oblivious to everything except the frantic drumbeat as they pulled for their lives.

One of the mercenaries was struck squarely in the chest by a spear the size of a small tree trunk. It pierced his upper body completely and carried him over the side, dead before he struck the silt.

The flaming missiles continued to fall, lighting up the night sky. The giant whose hair had caught fire had managed to put out the flames at last, but he had given up pursuit and was staggering back toward Ledo Island, holding his head in his hands and moaning with pain. The giant they had first encountered had also given up pursuit and was wading unsteadily back toward the island, crying out his defiance as he stumbled toward the shore. One giant was dead, but that still left one more, and that last one was a bit more canny than his comrades. As the missiles from the catapults fell all around him, he ducked beneath the silt and disappeared from view.

"*Row, curse you, row!*" the captain screamed at the top of his lungs. The passengers waited tensely, their eyes scanning the surface of the estuary.

For a moment, the only sounds were the steady, rapid beating of the drum, the creaking of the oarlocks as the rowers pulled with all their might, and the hissing of the flaming missiles falling into the silt.

Then the giant broke the surface, right beside the boat, and Sorak found himself staring into a monstrous, silt-encrusted face with red-rimmed eyes that burned with hatred. One powerful blow, and the ferry would be smashed to kindling.

Sorak did not hesitate. He jumped between two of the oarsmen and leapt onto the gunwale, launching himself off the side and directly onto the giant's head. In one motion, he unsheathed his sword and grabbed a fistful of the giant's hair in his other hand, twisting it around his wrist.

"*Sorak!*" Ryana screamed.

Sorak leaned over and swung his sword, slashing into the giant's neck and severing the large jugular vein. The giant roared as blood fountained from his neck, gushing powerfully out for a dozen yards. The giant clapped one hand to his neck to stop the massive flow of blood and, with his other hand, tried to sweep Sorak from his head, but Sorak anticipated the move and swung down from the giant's head, holding onto his hair.

He dangled at the nape of the creature's neck, bracing his feet against the giant's spine, and with a powerful blow, chopped into the vertebra where the spinal column met the skull. The giant grunted and died, falling forward and barely missing the boat, which pulled past him.

As the giant sank beneath the silt, Sorak found himself struggling to stay up. It was like trying to swim through quicksand.

"Sorak! Catch the rope!" Ryana shouted.

A line arced out from the ship and struck the surface of the silt about a foot from Sorak. He grabbed it at, still holding onto his sword with one hand, and twisted it around his wrist.

"I have it!" he shouted.

"Hold on, stranger!" he heard the captain cry. The rope went taut, and Sorak felt himself pulled through the silt. He swallowed hard. Another second and the boat would have been out of reach. Several of the passengers, including the captain, pulled hard on the rope, drawing him in. Moments later, they were leaning down and lifting him over the side. He collapsed, coughing, onto the deck and felt several hands on him, raising him to his feet. His body was encrusted with silt and caked with giant's blood. His hair was thick with it, matted down and plastered to his face and skull.

The passengers gathered around him, patting him on the back and congratulating him. The oarsmen cheered, though without pausing in their rowing. They would not be completely out of danger until they were well past Ledo Island.

Ryana put her arms around him and crushed her lips to his, heedless of the crusty silt covering him from head to toe. "If you ever do anything like that again, I'll kill you," she said.

He grinned. "I'd sooner face a dozen giants than

a scornful Ryana."

The passengers around them, both dwarves and mercenaries, laughed. With the danger past, they were all giddy with relief.

The captain stood before him. "That was the most foolhardy thing I've ever seen," the powerfully built dwarf said, "and the bravest. You saved all our lives. What is your name, stranger?"

"Sorak. And thank you for throwing me the rope."

The captain nodded. "I feared you were lost. We could not have turned around in time, and in truth, I must confess I would not have risked it."

Sorak nodded. "I understand."

The captain frowned. "Sorak. Are you by any chance the one they call the Nomad?"

"That is the elvish meaning of my name," said Sorak.

"Then I have heard of you," the captain said. "And I would be pleased if you and your companion would dine with me tonight."

"The pleasure would be ours," said Sorak. "But I shall have to find a place to bathe first, and make myself presentable."

"Then allow me to extend to you the hospitality of my humble home," the dwarf replied. "Then I'll treat you to the finest night of entertainment my village has to offer. Now please, sit down and rest. Give him room, the rest of you!"

Sorak gratefully sank to the deck and stretched out.

"Here, rest your head in my lap," Ryana said,

sitting down beside him.

"No," said Sorak, shaking his head. "I am filthy, and I stink with giant's blood."

"Here, take this," one of the mercenaries said, offering him a waterskin. "You can at least rinse off your hair and face."

"My thanks," said Sorak. He leaned over the side while the mercenary poured the water over his head and Ryana helped him scrub the filth off. A few moments later, he was relatively clean from the neck up.

"Are you injured?" the mercenary asked, looking him over.

"No, just a little tired," Sorak said.

"You were lucky," said the mercenary. "Either that or very skilled." He smiled. "Which was it?"

"A bit of both, I think," Sorak replied with a slight smile.

The mercenary grinned. He had perfect teeth, unusual for a man in his midthirties. The usual remedy for a toothache was to pull out the offending tooth and, if the patient could afford it—which most could not—replace it with an artificial one made of obsidian or silver. Most people took poor care of their teeth and suffered the consequences. This man was an exception. His teeth and well-muscled physique showed he took good care of himself, and kept well groomed. His skin was clear and tanned, his shoulder-length blond hair clean and glossy, his face clean shaven. Few mercenaries bothered to take such scrupulous care of their appearance. He was a handsome man, and he knew it and took pride in his good looks.

Out of habit, Sorak glanced toward the man's weapons. Two long, stiletto daggers were tucked into his belt, and he wore a heavy sword in an elegantly crafted and embossed leather scabbard. The crossguards were simple, straight, functional, and made of iron, as were the daggers. The hilts of all three weapons were wrapped with silver wire. Weapons made of iron were uncommon and expensive. This mercenary had not stinted on his equipment.

Neither had he stinted on his wardrobe. His feet were shod in well-made drakeskin boots cuffed at the knee, expensive not only because drakes were dangerous reptiles, but also because their hard black-and-red pebbled hide was extremely tough and difficult to work. A true craftsman had made those boots. The black-and-gray striped kirreskin breeches and the matching forearm bands were equally expensive, as was the mercenary's sleeveless, laced-up tunic, made from the brown speckled hide of a cloud ray and studded with black onyx.

Everything the man wore was made from highly dangerous game. The only way he could afford such apparel on a mercenary's salary was if he had provided the skins himself, and that spoke volumes about his prowess as a hunter.

"A bit ostentatious, perhaps," said the mercenary, noting Sorak's scrutiny, "but I find that flamboyance makes a strong impression. A poorly dressed mercenary is a poorly paid one. I am called Kieran."

"Sorak." They shook hands.

"I know. I heard you tell the captain. Apparently, your reputation precedes you. He seemed impressed when you gave him your name."

Sorak shrugged uncomfortably. "Whatever reputation I may have is much exaggerated."

Kieran smiled. "Oh, I doubt that, judging from the way you handled that giant." He glanced toward Ryana.

"Oh, forgive me," Sorak said. "This is Ryana."

"It is an honor, priestess," Kieran said, inclining his head respectfully. "The reputation of the villichi sisterhood is known far and wide."

"You are most gracious," said Ryana.

"Are you seeking employment in South Ledopolus?" Kieran asked Sorak.

"I have not yet decided," Sorak replied.

"Ah, well in that case, perhaps I may tempt you with an offer. I am on my way to Altaruk, where I have accepted a post as the new captain of the guard for the merchant house of Jhamri. I could use a man of your abilities, and the merchant houses pay top wages, as you doubtless know."

"Thank you, I shall consider it," said Sorak.

"Take your time," said Kieran. "The caravan of Jhamri is even now in South Ledopolus, but it is not scheduled to depart for another day or two, and you can leave word for me with the captain."

"Thank you, I shall," said Sorak.

Kieran nodded. "I will let you rest," he said, then moved off to give them some privacy.

"Why did you agree to consider his offer?" asked Ryana. "We do not even know if we are going to Altaruk."

"I did not wish to seem impolite, after his courtesy," Sorak replied. "Besides, the merchant houses pay very well."

"But we are not in need of money," said Ryana, glancing at their packs sitting on the deck beside her.

"Yes, but it would not be wise to advertise that fact," said Sorak.

She nodded. "I see your point. Good thinking." She looked up toward the bow. "It seems we have a welcoming committee."

The boat was pulling up to the dock at South Ledopolus, where an anxious crowd was waiting with torches, having seen the battle from the shore.

"Well, it seems your arrival in South Ledopolus is destined to cause quite a stir," the ferry captain said, gazing at the crowd as they approached the dock. "By tomorrow morning, the whole village will have heard of your battle with the giant. It's likely you won't have to pay for any of your drinks during your stay."

Sorak sighed wearily. "I was looking forward to a bath. The last thing I want now is to be peppered with questions."

The captain grinned. "A lot of men in your position would relish the prospect of an audience eager to hear a tale of battle. But never fear, I will have one of my crew escort you to my house while I distract the crowd. Please make yourselves at home, and I will join you after I am finished here."

"You are very kind," said Sorak.

"Nonsense. You saved my boat. I am happy for the chance to show my appreciation. Make ready the bowlines!"

The lines were thrown out to waiting hands on the dock as the rowers stowed their oars and the boat drifted gently up against the moorings.

"This way," said the captain's mate, coming up beside them. "We will disembark from the stern while the others file down the gangplank. That way, we can lose ourselves quickly in the crowd and make our way into the village. I will take you to the captain's house."

"Thank you," Sorak said, lifting his pack.

"No need," the dwarf replied. "It is we who are in debt to you. Come, let's go."

As the crowd on the dock surged around the gangplank, anxious to hear firsthand reports of the battle, the mate jumped off the stern and landed lightly on the dock. Ryana followed, then Sorak, and they quickly made their way around the outer fringes of the crowd and down a narrow side street of the village.

It occurred to Sorak that he and Ryana were forever either sneaking out of a town or sneaking into one. This time, however, a welcome awaited them and there was no one on their trail. It made for a refreshing change. It would be nice if things remained that way for a while.

Perhaps that was too much to hope for.

FOUR

The ferry captain's home was much larger than they had expected. It was a two-thousand-square-foot adobe house built around an atrium, with a walled courtyard entrance. It had been constructed to human rather than dwarven scale, as were most buildings in the central part of the village. The floors were flagstoned with attractive, pale pink slate, and throughout the house, the doors were made of beautifully figured, hand-carved pagafa wood. Inside, everything was neatly arranged. Most dwarves liked order, and the ferry captain was no exception. His home was elegant, yet simple, with well-made, functional wood furniture and few decorations save for some house plants and some exquisite black-fired dwarven pottery. He was unmarried but had two servants, an elderly dwarven couple who kept his house and cooked for him. His job was hazardous, but judging by the way he lived, his pay reflected that accordingly.

Sorak luxuriated in a heated bath while his clothes were taken to be cleaned. As he washed, Ryana relaxed by the fireplace and enjoyed some herbal tea and fresh-baked biscuits with kank honey. Soon afterward, the ferry captain arrived, bringing Sorak a change of clothing, which he had borrowed from one of the mercenaries.

"I think these should fit you," he said, laying them out while Sorak bathed. "Your own clothes should be clean and dry by tomorrow morning."

"That was considerate of you, Captain," Sorak said. "Thank you."

"It was nothing. And please, call me Tajik." He sat on a wooden chair while Sorak bathed. "You will pardon my curiosity, but I can see you are not a full-blooded elf. Yet, you look different from most half-elves I have seen."

"My father was a halfling," Sorak said. "Half-elves are part human. I am an elfling."

Tajik's eyebrows went up. "Indeed? I had heard something of the sort, but thought it merely a fanciful embellishment."

"Embellishment?"

"Of the song," said Tajik. "The Ballad of the Nomad."

Sorak rolled his eyes and shook his head. "It hardly seems possible it could have spread so quickly," he said.

Tajik chuckled. "Bards travel widely and steal each other's songs as readily as they compose new ones. Tell me, is it true you single-handedly saved a caravan from a host of marauders?"

"Nothing quite so spectacular, I fear," said Sorak with a wry grimace. "I merely learned of a marauder plan to ambush a caravan from Tyr and passed on a warning to the merchant house."

"I see. And what of the tale of your crossing the Stony Barrens and rescuing a princess of the royal house of Nibenay?"

"That one is true," admitted Sorak.

"Really? Then the Shadow King is in your debt?"

"Hardly," Sorak said. "The princess in question had taken preserver vows and been exiled as a result. An ambitious nobleman from Gulg had seized her and planned to force her into marriage so he could lay claim to kinship to the royal house of Nibenay. The girl asked for my help, and as a fellow preserver, I could not refuse."

"And so you stole her from the nobleman and fled across the Barrens?" Tajik asked.

Sorak nodded.

"Incredible," said Tajik. "They say no one has ever tried to cross the Barrens and survived."

"It was not an experience I would care to repeat," said Sorak.

"And what of the nobleman?"

"He died," said Sorak simply.

"And the princess? What became of her?"

"She returned to Nibenay and joined the Veiled

Alliance."

"So that part of the story is true, then," said Tajik. "I would never have believed it. A daughter of the Shadow King enlisted in the Veiled Alliance!" He shook his head in amazement. "That must have made the old dragon king absolutely furious."

"He does not hold me in very high regard."

"And this does not frighten you?"

Sorak shrugged. "There is no love lost between preserver and defiler. Simply being what I am has made me the enemy of the dragon kings. I knew that when I chose to take my vows."

"Yes, but taking preserver vows is not the same as making a personal enemy of the Shadow King."

"Perhaps not," said Sorak. "But there is little use to being afraid. Nibenay has tried to kill me several times. As you can see, I am still alive, so perhaps the dragon kings are not all-powerful, as they would have everyone believe."

"Still, being marked for death by a sorcerer king is the sort of thing that would terrify most men."

"Perhaps, but I should think that I would find your job much more dangerous," said Sorak. "Nibenay's primary concern is to complete his dragon metamorphosis. I may have aroused his ire, but he will not spare much energy to snuff out the life of one insignificant preserver. You, on the other hand, face death every time you board your ferry. So which of us has more to fear?"

Tajik smiled. "I have always thought the rewards of my job justified the risks. What justifies the risk for you?"

"Well, to put it in dwarven terms," said Sorak, "the satisfaction of staying true to my focus. Accepting the risk and living with it is a sort of compromise."

"I suppose we all make compromises and take the good with the bad," said Tajik, taking the hint and not pressing his inquiries. "Well, I shall let you finish your bath. I will have some more water heated for Ryana. She did not go swimming in the silt, as you did, but I am sure she would appreciate a good, hot soak. And then you shall be my guests for dinner, and afterward, I hope you will accept the hospitality of my home for the night."

"That is very generous of you," Sorak said. "But it is really not necessary to go to so much trouble."

"Do not concern yourself. It is no trouble at all. I rarely have company and will enjoy showing you my village. We may not have the luxuries of a city such as Tyr or Balic, but we do know how to entertain our guests."

After they had both bathed and dressed, Tajik took them to dinner at an eating house that boasted "the best larder in South Ledopolus." It was a short walk from his home in the center of town, and Sorak marveled at the difference between the streets of South Ledopolus and those of Tyr or Nibenay. In most towns and cities, and even in most villages, there was no shortage of beggars. Not so South Ledopolus. Since the town was situated on a caravan route, and well isolated from any other settlements except North Ledopolus, the only transient traffic was that brought by the caravans, and beggars could not afford to book passage.

The streets of the village were also remarkably clean, reflecting a dwarven obsession with neatness and order. Even though the streets were hard-packed dirt, Tajik told Sorak with a sense of pride that they were regularly swept and graded by kank beetles pulling weighted drags through town once every two weeks and after each rain. There was a narrow ditch for runoff at the side of each street, and well-planed wooden sidewalks had been constructed on both sides of the street, shaded from the desert sun by overhangs made from wood planks or cactus ribs.

The buildings were freshly plastered, painted in muted tones of reds and pinks and tans. Tajik told them that the owners of the buildings were responsible for maintaining a clean facade. Chipped or flaking exteriors resulted in fines levied by the council. It was a remarkably pleasant looking village, with gently winding streets and well-groomed pagafa trees providing shade and color. With its tidy shops and inviting hostelries, it did not look at all like the rollicking, wide-open caravan town Sorak had expected.

On the other hand, the mercenary presence was very evident. Everywhere he looked, Sorak saw lean and muscular, hard-bitten and well-armed men mixing with the dwarven population. Some were human, some were half-elves, but all looked tough. Sorak wondered about the women. Men such as these had needs to satisfy, and they often liked to satisfy them without any encumbrances. Yet, he saw no women of easy virtue wandering the streets. It probably meant that there were pleasure houses where such things were kept discreetly out of sight.

The ferry captain was clearly respected in the community. He was were greeted effusively and given the best table in the house. The whitewashed adobe walls were painted with murals of desert scenes, and the tables were covered with clean white cloths, unusual even in cities. The dwarven staff gave them prompt and courteous attention, and Tajik suggested that they order braised erdlu steaks with herb sauce and wild rice and baked, honey-glazed gava root. He flushed and immediately apologized, realizing his error.

"Forgive me," he said, glancing at Ryana awkwardly. "I had forgotten that villichi priestesses do not eat flesh. I did not mean to give offense."

"None was intended, and none taken," Ryana replied with a smile. "I am not offended by others eating flesh. For myself, I would prefer some simple vegetables. The wild rice and gava root sound perfect."

Tajik looked relieved. "In that case, may I also suggest the spiced bread, which they do very well here, and the mulled ale, which is excellent."

"It sounds delightful," said Ryana.

"And what of yourself, my friend?" asked Tajik, turning to Sorak. "Do you also abstain from meat?"

Ordinary, Sorak would have answered yes.

Though elves were omnivorous and halflings were carnivorous, even to the extent that they often ate human flesh, he had been raised in the villichi convent and had always followed the villichi ways. However, his other personalities had remained true to his origins. They had craved the taste of meat, which he had forsworn. To avoid a conflict, he had reached a compromise of sorts with his more predatory personalities. Though he had refrained from eating flesh, after he went to sleep, his other personalities would assume control of his body, and would go out to hunt. They would stalk and make their kill as halflings did, consuming the flesh still raw and bloody.

Though divested of his other personalties, Sorak felt an unfamiliar craving brought on my the smells from the kitchen. Since leaving Bodach, he had eaten only wild desert plants and a mixture of nuts and dried fruits. Though he had taken vows as a preserver, those vows did not specifically prohibit him from eating meat. Ryana's vows as a villichi priestess did, and though she had broken those vows by leaving the convent, she still kept to the spirit of them. He was neither priest nor villichi. He knew that his body had eaten meat regularly in the past, though he had no memory of it.

"I think I shall try the erdlu."

Ryana glanced at him curiously, raising her eyebrows.

"Excellent choice," said Tajik, beaming.

Ryana pursed her lips and said nothing.

When the meal came, it was delicious. Sorak ate

ravenously. His first taste triggered a craving for more. He had never felt anything like it before.

"You must have been hungry," Tajik said with a grin, watching him eat. "Here, try some of this ale."

"Thank you, but I prefer water," Sorak said.

"*Water?*" Tajik said with surprise. "You prefer *water* to ale?"

"I do not drink spirits," Sorak said.

"Not even wine?"

Sorak shook his head. "I have no taste for it."

"Pity," Tajik said, shaking his head sadly. Like most dwarves, he loved to drink, and he quaffed the ale as quickly as the serving girl refilled the pitcher. Sorak had heard that dwarves could outdrink anybody, and watching Tajik swill the ale, he believed it.

"So, have you come to South Ledopolus in search of employment, or are you just passing through?"

Sorak hesitated. "I have not yet decided," he replied after a moment.

"Ah. Well, if you choose to stay, for however long, perhaps I could be of assistance. I am not without influence here, and would be pleased to give you a recommendation."

"Thank you. I appreciate that," Sorak said. "But for the present, we would simply like to rest from our journey before making further plans."

"Where were you traveling from?" asked Tajik. "Most people come to South Ledopolus by way of the caravan route, yet you came across the estuary.

Don't tell me you walked all the way from the Mekillots?"

"That is the way we came," said Sorak, which was the truth, though not the whole truth.

"A long, hard journey," Tajik said. "But not really a surprising one, for two people who had crossed the Barrens. You came from Salt View then?"

Ryana nodded. "Yes, we spent some time there." Which was also true.

"The gaming houses of Salt View are not the sort of place one would expect to find a villichi priestess," Tajik said.

"Our pilgrimages take us all over the world," Ryana replied. "Besides, why preach to the converted? Wherever there is hope of spreading the preserver cause, that is where you'll find us."

Tajik nodded, apparently satisfied, but Sorak had a feeling the ferry captain suspected they were withholding information. Without his telepathic personalities, though, Sorak could not know. He saw no reason to distrust Tajik, but prudence advised against being completely frank with him.

"What can you tell me of a mercenary named Kieran?" Sorak asked, to change the subject.

Tajik frowned and shook his head. "The name is not familiar to me."

"He was the one who gave me his water on the boat," said Sorak.

"Ah, the one dressed like a walking catalog of rare hides?" asked Tajik.

"That's him," said Sorak.

The ferry captain shook his head. "I noticed him. Who could not, with clothes like that? But I have never seen him before. His name is Kieran, you say?"

"Yes, that was the name he gave me."

"Hmm. Well, I could ask around. Is there a particular reason for your curiosity?"

"He offered me employment," Sorak said. "He said he was on his way to Altaruk to accept a position as captain of the guard with the House of Jhamri."

"Indeed?" said Tajik, raising his eyebrows. "That speaks highly of his capabilities. Jhamri hires nothing but the best for senior officers. If this Kieran has offered you employment, perhaps you should accept. You will not find anything in South Ledopolus that could compare with the salary you would receive working for a merchant house in Altaruk."

"I told him I would consider it," said Sorak. "But I should like to know something of a man's background before I agree to work for him."

"Quite understandable," said Tajik, nodding. "Well, I know where we can probably find out. If he has been recruited for such a post, he must have a reputation. His fellow mercenaries would know, and since most of them have just been paid, I know where we can find a good sampling to ask. But perhaps we should escort Ryana back to my home first."

"Why?" Ryana asked, puzzled.

"Because the Desert Damsel is not the sort of place to take a priestess," Tajik replied.

"And why is that?" she asked again.

Tajik cleared his throat. "Well . . . the Damsel is a pleasure house, the most popular attraction in South Ledopolus, where women dance and, uh, artfully remove clothing. One can go there simply for the show, but there are also rooms upstairs where, for a price, one can enjoy a, uh, 'private dance,' if you get my meaning."

"How very interesting," Ryana said. "I would like to see it."

Tajik looked scandalized. "You *would?*"

"Yes, very much. Can we go there after dinner?"

Tajik swallowed hard. "I . . . uh . . . really do not think it is a proper place for a lady like yourself."

"Why not?" Ryana asked.

Tajik glanced at Sorak, helplessly.

"Don't look at me," said Sorak. "Ryana makes her own decisions."

"I have never seen a pleasure house," Ryana said. "I'm curious to know what it is like."

"It is much like any other place where mercenaries drink, only much more so," Tajik said. "I don't think you would enjoy it much."

"I should like the opportunity to judge that for myself," Ryana said.

Tajik sighed with resignation. "Well, if you insist. . . ."

* * * * *

"It is a rather rowdy crowd tonight," said Edric as he came into the dressing room, rubbing his temple where a thrown bottle had struck him. It had shattered and cut the skin, and a thin trickle of blood ran down the side of his face. The spot was already swelling, and there would be a nasty bruise.

Cricket was up out of her chair at once. "Here, let me see," she said.

"It's of no consequence," said Edric. "This is my last night."

Cricket moistened a clean cloth and gently washed the cut. "Those brutes," she said vehemently.

Edric winced as she cleaned the cut. "Well, they did not come to hear my ballads. I do not know why Turin even bothered hiring me."

"To build up their anticipation," Cricket said. "He likes a dull act to open the show." And then she realized what she had said and bit her lower lip. "Forgive me. That came out wrong. I did not mean that I found you dull myself."

Edric chuckled. "No, I understand. The pleasure of your company has been the only thing that has made this engagement bearable. And you have been a most appreciative audience, for which I thank you."

"I cannot wait to leave this place," said Cricket. "I've booked passage on the caravan. I only wish it would leave tonight."

"Tomorrow will be soon enough," said Edric. "Turin still does not suspect your plans?"

"I do not think so," Cricket said. "If he does, he's shown no indication of it. Still, I would not put it past him to attempt something to make me stay."

"What could he do?"

"Hire some mercenaries to detain me while the caravan departs," she said. "He probably wouldn't even have to pay them. He would merely offer them inducements."

"Mmmm, yes, I can imagine what sort of inducements he would offer," Edric said. "Still, he can't force you to dance."

Cricket shook her head. "I don't know," she said. "I have wanted to leave here for so long, it hardly seems possible that the time has come at last. I keep thinking something will go wrong."

Edric patted her shoulder. "Nothing will go wrong," he said. "By this time tomorrow, we'll be on our way to Altaruk."

"I want it to be now," she said anxiously.

"Try to put it out of your mind," said Edric. "You don't want Turin to wonder why you seem distracted. Go out there and put on a good show. It'll be the last time they'll ever see you in this pestilential dump. Give them something to remember."

She smiled. "That I can do."

* * * * *

Walking into the Desert Damsel was like entering another world. Outside lay the quiet, picturesque and orderly dwarven village of South Ledopolus, with its immaculate streets and well-tended shade trees and desert gardens. Inside was the raucous South Ledopolus the Wanderer had described in his journal.

Tajik, Sorak, and Ryana entered through a small antechamber where a dwarf seated at a high podium collected the cover charge of ten coppers, which included a token for one drink. He also gathered all weapons, in exchange for numbered tokens that would allow the owners to claim them on the way out. Just past the podium was an arched, curtained entry where a muscular human bouncer stood at his post, thick arms folded across his bare, barrel-shaped chest.

Tajik led them through the beaded curtain and into the interior of the Desert Damsel—a single, large, open room with booths built around the perimeter and small round tables with wooden chairs filling the space beside the long bar against the right wall. Behind the bar and in the center of the room, at the rear, were two large stages with four smaller stages on square risers on the right and left sides of the room. No matter where one looked, there was a stage in view, and atop each of those stages, including the one behind the bar, nearly naked women danced.

There was a small band playing, set up on a small stage at the right rear corner of the room, just beyond the bar, and a woman gyrated on the stage in front of the band, as well. The band consisted primarily of drummers, bell ringers, and cymbal players. The melody, what there was of it, was carried by several flutists, but the music was mostly beat and the jangle of bells and cymbals.

The place was packed, mostly by mercenaries, though there were also some dwarves and humans who came in on the caravan from Balic. The lighting was dim, provided by a few lanterns hanging from the ceiling above the stages. The tables were full, and there were stools around each stage, as well.

Men crowded the edges of the stages, staring up at the undulating dancers and shouting encouragement as they held out coins. The dancers would gyrate over to the men and take the coins in some creative way, either bending over backward and grabbing them with their teeth or allowing the men to slip them inside their girdles. Each dancer carried a small coin purse tied to her belt, and presumably at the end of each dance, she would empty the purse so it could be filled afresh.

As Tajik, Sorak, and Ryana stood at the entrance, a fight between a couple of mercenaries broke out in front of them. Before more than a few blows could be exchanged, several large human bouncers separated the combatants and promptly escorted them outside.

"Fascinating," said Ryana, looking around. "The atmosphere seems . . . primitive and energetic."

"Well, I suppose that's one way of putting it," said Tajik. "Come, let's sit at the bar. From there, you can see the entire room."

An attractive young human female wearing practically nothing came up and led them to the bar, then departed with a smile.

"Greetings, Tajik," the burly barkeeper said, leaning over and raising his voice above the music. "It's been a while. What'll you have?"

"A tankard of your best ale, Stron," said Tajik. He turned to Ryana.

"I'll have the same," she said.

"Some water, please," said Sorak.

"What?" the barkeeper said, as if unsure he had heard correctly.

"Water," Sorak repeated.

"*Water?*"

"Yes, please. Water."

"I'll have to charge you for it," said the barkeeper.

"I will be glad to pay," said Sorak. "How much?"

"Stron . . . just give my friend some water," Tajik said.

"Well, seeing as how he's a friend of yours . . ."

"Thank you, my friend," said Tajik.

"Water," repeated the barkeeper, shaking his head and grimacing. "Two ales and one water, coming up."

Sorak glanced up at the stage behind the bar. The woman dancing there wore nothing save a skimpy girdle that consisted of a thong and a piece of cloth no bigger than an eye patch. Her long red hair cascaded down her shoulders, framing a large and perfectly shaped pair of breasts. She came down a short flight of wooden steps leading to the bar from the stage, moving slowly and swaying her hips.

She stepped down onto the surface of the bar and the patrons hurriedly moved their drinks to give her room. As they held out their coins, she knelt on the bartop before them, with her back to them. Most of the customers were apparently well familiar with her routine. They placed the coins between their teeth as she bent over backward, leaning back so that her face was just below theirs, then they bent their heads down so that she could take the coin from them in her own teeth. As the exchange was made, their lips barely brushed hers, then she straightened, turned around, and gently caressed each man on the cheek or ran her fingers through his hair. She would finish by looking at each man suggestively as she briefly slipped the coin inside her girdle, then dropped it into her purse before moving on.

One customer became a bit carried away and spat the coin out before she could take it from him, then crushed his mouth to hers. Instantly, two large and muscular bouncers appeared behind him and carried him away as the others cheered and shouted.

"This is what men like?" Ryana asked, raising her eyebrows.

"Some men, apparently," said Sorak.

"Not you?" she asked.

"I would never put money in my mouth," he said.

"Yes, one has no way of knowing where it's been," Ryana replied dryly.

The barkeeper brought them their drinks and then the dancer moved in front of Sorak. She stood over him atop the bar, swaying her hips in time to the music, and slowly came down to her knees before him, facing him. Sorak looked up into her eyes. She smiled, parted her lips, and ran her tongue around them. He shook his head slightly and placed a coin down on the bar. She raised her eyebrows, then glanced briefly at Ryana. She mouthed a kiss at her, glanced briefly back at Sorak, picked up the coin, dropped it in her purse, and moved on.

"I think she likes you," Tajik said with a grin.

"I think she likes his money," Ryana replied.

"I wasn't speaking to *him*," said Tajik with a slightly mocking smile.

Ryana cleared her throat uncomfortably. "I thought we came here to find out some information."

"I thought you came because you were curious to see a pleasure house," said Sorak, keeping a perfectly straight face.

"Well, now I've seen it," she said.

"Oh, you haven't seen the best part yet," said Tajik. "You haven't seen the star attraction."

"I can hardly wait," Ryana said with a grimace.

The music stopped, and the dancers left the stage, then a red-haired dwarf stepped up in front of the musicians as everybody clapped and shouted. Raising his voice above the din, the dwarf called out, "Are you ready for more?"

There was a resounding chorus of assent.

"Well, more you shall have!" the dwarf shouted. "Remember, the girls dance for your enjoyment, and for your tips, so please be generous! They all have sick old mothers to care for!"

There was laughter and shouting, then the dwarf raised his hands for silence, which he didn't get. "Don't forget," he shouted over the noise, "you can ask your favorite girl for an exclusive, private dance, and she will be happy to oblige! They are all very obliging!"

There was more laughter and the dwarf signaled the musicians. They started a new song, which sounded much like the previous one, and a fresh shift of dancers took the stages.

Tajik saw someone that he knew and waved him over. A mercenary joined them at the bar and greeted Tajik with a hearty back slap that made the ferry captain's teeth rattle.

"Tajik, you old scoundrel! Why aren't you home counting your money?"

"Because I'm here, buying you a drink," Tajik replied.

The mercenary threw an arm around his shoulder. "That's the kind of talk I like to hear! Barkeeper! Ale!"

The barkeeper set a drink in front of the mercenary, and Tajik paid.

"I hear you had some trouble earlier this evening," said the mercenary.

"Yes, an encounter with some giants," Tajik said. "It was close. They almost sank me this time."

"So they say," the mercenary said. "Everyone is talking about it, exaggerating as usual. I even heard some ridiculous nonsense about one of your passengers jumping overboard and killing a giant with his sword."

"Neither ridiculous nor nonsense," Tajik replied. He pointed to Sorak. "This is the very passenger. He saved all our lives."

The mercenary turned to stare at Sorak. "Truly? You killed a giant, hand-to-hand?"

"I was fortunate," said Sorak.

"Well, then let me shake your hand, stranger," said the mercenary.

"Sorak, Drom," said Tajik, performing the introductions, "and the lady is Ryana."

As the somewhat inebriated mercenary focused his gaze on Ryana, his eyes grew wide. "Gith's blood!" he said. "I'd like to see you up there on the stage!"

"Mind your manners, you great oaf!" said Tajik, sharply. "Are you so blind drunk you can't see she is a priestess of the villichi sisterhood?"

The mercenary's jaw dropped, then he blushed, bowed his head, and stammered an apology. "F-forgive me, my lady. I—I am a fool. Truly, it was not drink but your beauty that had blinded me."

"Nice save," said Sorak, lifting his goblet to his lips.

"Tajik is right, I am an oaf," the mercenary said. "I have offended you both. How may I make amends?"

"Well, perhaps you can help with some information," Tajik said.

"Yes," said Sorak, "do you know of a mercenary by the name of Kieran?"

"Kieran of Draj?"

"I do not know where he hails from," Sorak replied, "but he is a blond, good-looking man, blue eyed and clean shaven, about my height, very muscular, and dresses expensively, in rare hides."

"That sounds like him," said Drom, nodding. "He carries iron weapons, a sword and two stiletto daggers, the hilts wrapped with silver wire?"

"That's the man," said Sorak. "What do you know of him?"

"Good blade," said Drom emphatically. "One of the very best. A seasoned campaigner. Served with the Drajian army—joined up as a boy, they say—and worked his way up through the ranks to regimental commander. Might have made general, too."

Sorak frowned. "What happened?"

"I'm a little dry," the mercenary said, rubbing his throat. Sorak took the hint and ordered him another ale. When it arrived, Drom was distracted for a moment by a dancer who stopped before him on the bar and reached out with her foot to brush her toes against his chest. Drom kissed her foot and tossed her a coin, which she caught adroitly. She bent down and pecked his cheek lightly, then moved on. "Where was I?"

"Why did Kieran fail to make general?" Sorak prompted.

"Ah, yes. Well, he killed a Drajian nobleman."

"You mean he murdered him?" Ryana asked.

"No, it was a duel," said Drom.

"Let me guess," said Tajik. "They quarreled over a woman."

"You might say that," Drom replied, "but it isn't what you think. The girl was the nobleman's daughter."

"Ah," said Tajik. "And Kieran's attentions were unwelcome?"

"They were more than welcome," Drom replied. "They were in love and planned to marry. But the girl's father disapproved. He refused to allow his daughter to wed a soldier, and a commoner at that. The way the story goes, she argued with her father, and he beat her. When Kieran learned of it, he publicly called the man a craven coward—and a few other names, besides—and struck him. Well, that was enough right there to put an end to his career, but the nobleman lost his temper and challenged him on the spot. Kieran killed him, for which he was arrested and sentenced to death. When the girl heard of it, she took her own life by swallowing poison."

"How awful!" said Ryana.

"How did Kieran survive the sentence?"

"Friends interceded for him," Drom replied. "And his regiment threatened mutiny. The death sentence was commuted to exile for life, and his estate was confiscated. When Kieran left Draj, without a copper to his name, almost a third of his regiment left with him. The rest had families and other ties, or else they might have gone as well.

They formed their own company of mercenaries and hired out to whatever kingdom needed fighting men to fill out their armies for campaigns. In time, attrition thinned their numbers until only a few were left. Eventually, the ones who survived all went their separate ways."

"You seem to know a great deal about him," Sorak said.

"I should," said Drom. "I served with him in the army of Raam during the war with Urik. By then, he had only half a dozen men from the original regiment. They were fierce fighters, to a man, and intensely loyal. Where did you encounter him?"

"He met him on my boat," said Tajik. "Kieran was there when Sorak slew the giant. He offered him employment."

Drom looked surprised. "Kieran, here? In South Ledopolus?"

"He said he was on his way to Altaruk, to accept a post as captain of the guard for the House of Jhamri," Sorak said.

"Ah," said Drom. "Well, they can afford him, certainly. But it is a pity to see a top blade such as Kieran reduced to service with a merchant house guard. Truly, it is a waste of talent. Ah . . . it seems my goblet's empty."

"Another round for my friend," said Sorak, to the barkeeper.

"Well, if Kieran offered you employment, you must have made a strong impression," Drom said, as another drink was set before him. "You could do far worse. I would accept the job if I were you.

You will be paid well, and you will learn much in the bargain."

"Thank you," Sorak said. "I appreciate the advice."

"When you see him, tell him Drom of Urik sends his regards. Most likely, he'll not remember me. I am not a memorable man."

"I will be sure to pass on your regards," said Sorak.

Drom nodded, suddenly looking depressed. "Thank you for the drinks, friend," he said. "And for the conversation. Sometimes, it is good to remember the old glory days." He belched. "And sometimes, not so good." He turned to Ryana and bowed, unsteadily. "My lady . . ."

Sorak watched him stagger off.

"He used to be a good man," said Tajik as he watched Drom weave away into the crowd. "But drink has got the better of him. He fought in over a dozen wars, and now he guards the construction of a bridge in a small village stuck out in the middle of nowhere. Think on that, my friend. The trade of mercenary can be rewarding for a young man with some skill, but do not remain in it too long."

The music stopped and the dwarf took the stage again, raising his arms for silence. "I know what you've all been waiting for!" he shouted. "The time has come! The Desert Damsel proudly presents . . . the lovely, the incomparable . . . Cricket!"

The crowd roared, and the drummers rattled off a fast tattoo, then stopped abruptly and started a slow and steady, gently rolling beat, accentuated by the bells and cymbals. The crowd fell silent as the beaded curtain at the back of the main stage parted, revealing the backlit silhouette of a tall, slender, beautifully proportioned woman in a sheer, transparent gown.

She moved sinuously in the backlight, swaying slowly to the beat, tantalizing the audience with the silhouette of her body showing through the gown, then she stepped into the light, and Sorak caught his breath. She was breathtakingly beautiful, a young half-elf girl with long, dark, silver-streaked hair almost to her waist; a heart-shaped face with slanted, dark eyes; delicately arched eyebrows; high, pronounced cheekbones; full lips and a slightly pointed chin. Her body was slender yet curvaceous, with a slim and narrow waist and long, exquisite legs. The other dancers had all been greeted with raucous shouts and cheers when they came on, but Cricket's entrance brought utter silence as the men watched, mesmerized.

"*That's* the star attraction," Tajik said softly.

Unlike the other girls, who writhed provocatively and assumed seductive poses in time to the music, Cricket *danced.* Her muscular control was impressive as she undulated her upper body in time to the music, her belly rippling like the surface of a gently flowing stream and her arms stretched over her head moving languidly, like the wings of a graceful bird. Slowly, the musicians picked up the tempo and she began to whirl, bumping and twisting her hips in time to the beat, moving on tiptoe as she twirled and spun. She sank down slowly into a perfect split, her upper body swaying, bending over first to touch one leg and then the other. Then she twisted on the floor and crouched upon her knees, slowly bending backward until she touched the floor with the back of her head, her arms raised over her chest and intertwining like snakes coupling as her hips rose and fell rhythmically. It was beautiful, sensuous, and blatantly erotic.

"Worth the wait, eh?" Tajik said with a grin.

Sorak glanced over at him and saw Ryana watching him curiously.

"I . . . uh . . . have never seen anyone dance like that," said Sorak.

"Nor have I," Ryana said in a neutral tone. "She's very beautiful, isn't she?"

"Yes," said Sorak, turning back toward the stage, "she is."

Cricket slowly raised herself up and got to her feet, and the gown fell away from her as if removed by unseen hands. Somehow, she managed to shrug free of it without ever appearing to remove it, allowing it to slowly slip down her body until it was bunched at her feet. Gracefully, she stepped out of it, now dressed only in the smallest of girdles and a halter consisting of thongs and two tiny pieces of lizardskin. She wore a thin silver chain around her waist and another around her left ankle, with a tiny silver bell hanging from it. Around her thigh, she wore a lizardskin garter with a small pouch sewn into it, only large enough for one coin at a time.

As the men crowded the stage, holding out their coins, she pirouetted toward each of them, stopping and undulating her stomach muscles as she put one leg forward, bent slightly at the knee, her bare foot arched gracefully with only the toes touching the floor, and the men would slip their coins into the garter pouch. A few of them tried to run their hands up her leg, or kiss it, but she twisted away adroitly, snatching up the coins with her hand as she spun away, then turning back toward them and smiling with a slight shake of her head.

Sorak glanced at some of the other dancers. Some of the women were gazing at her with obvious envy or resentment. Others watched her with open and undisguised lust. And those were just the women. She drove the men absolutely wild. Half a dozen were carried out as they tried to climb up on the stage, and the rest were shoving and elbowing each other, trying to get closer.

"She's pulling out all the stops tonight," said Tajik, shaking his head as he watched her dance. "If she doesn't watch out, she'll start a riot."

The music reached a crescendo, though it was barely audible in the roar, and with a graceful flourish, Cricket finished and curtsied low, bowing to the crowd. Coins rained upon the stage. The overworked bouncers moved in to restore order, pushing the crowd back.

"A round of drinks for everyone, courtesy of the Desert Damsel!" the dwarf shouted, and he looked relived as everyone immediately surged toward the bar.

Cricket started picking up the coins. As she crouched by the lip of the stage, a hand snaked out and grabbed her by the wrist.

"How about a private dance, my lovely?" a powerfully built mercenary said.

"I do not perform private dances," Cricket replied. "Please, let go."

"Come on, now, I've already paid for the room."

"Then ask one of the other girls," said Cricket. "Now let me go."

"You're the one I want," the mercenary insisted. "Now get down here." And he yanked her right off the stage onto the floor.

At once, two bouncers moved in, but without letting go of Cricket's wrist, the mercenary kicked out at the first one, breaking his knee, and smashed the second one in the jaw. Both men went down, the first one screaming with pain, the second unconscious.

Sorak started to rise from his stool, but felt Tajik's hand on him. "Keep out of it," the ferry captain said. "Turin pays these men well for their pains, and they know their business."

Indeed, they seemed to, for even as Tajik spoke, Sorak saw three more bouncers move in, this time with three-foot agafari fighting sticks.

The brawny mercenary knew his business, too. He released Cricket, shoving her against the stage behind him and turned to meet the bouncers. As the first one came in with an overhanded blow of the fighting stick, the mercenary took it on crossed forearms, catching it on the muscle rather than bone, and then deftly wrenched the stick out of the bouncer's grasp while kicking him in the groin. Without pause, he pivoted, sidestepped a blow from the second bouncer, and cracked the stick against the side of his head.

As the second bouncer went down, the mercenary quickly dropped to the floor and swept the third bouncer's legs out from under him. He, too, fell, and the mercenary brought the heel of his booted foot down hard on the man's throat, collapsing his larynx and trachea. The bouncer made a horrible gargling sound and thrashed several times, then choked on his own blood.

Moving swiftly and smoothly, the big mercenary got back to his feet, snatching up the third bouncer's fighting stick as well, so that he now had one in each hand. Cricket tried to crawl away, but he saw her and hooked a stool with his foot, sending it crashing against the stage, just missing her. She cried out and stayed huddled where she was. Two more bouncers moved in, and by now the crowd had gathered round, watching and cheering the combatants.

The fighting sticks whirled in the mercenary's hands as he met the two remaining bouncers and, moments later, both were lying senseless and bleeding on the floor.

The crowed cheered, and the mercenary dropped the sticks and turned back to Cricket. He grabbed her arm and hauled her to her feet.

Sorak got up off his stool, shaking off Tajik's

hand, and Ryana rose beside him.

"I'd say I've earned a lot more than just a private dance," the big mercenary said. And as he turned to drag her upstairs, he found Kieran blocking his way, standing there with his arms folded across his chest.

Sorak paused, holding out his arm in front of Ryana. The crowd fell silent.

"You're in my way," the big mercenary said to Kieran.

"Yes, I suppose I am," Kieran replied.

"Move."

"I don't believe I will."

"Well, well," the big mercenary said, derisively. "So you want to play the gallant, eh? You think the whore is worth it?"

"Oh, I'm not doing it for her," said Kieran, casually. "I'm doing it for you."

The big mercenary stared at him. "*What?*"

"It's for the benefit of your education. You require a lesson in manners. You seem pretty good with those sticks. You want to find out just how good you are?"

The big mercenary grinned unpleasantly and shoved Cricket back to the floor, then picked up the two fighting sticks he'd dropped. "You're the one who's going to get a lesson," he said with a sneer, as he twirled the fighting sticks in his hands.

Kieran bent to pick up one of the fighting sticks, but before he could grab a second one, the big mercenary moved quickly and kicked it away into the crowd.

"Kieran!" someone in the crowd shouted, and in the next instant, a fighting stick came sailing toward him.

Kieran snatched it out of the air and glanced to see who had thrown it. He spotted the man and nodded his thanks, then smiled.

"It's been a few years," he said. "The war with Urik, wasn't it?"

Sorak saw Drom break out in a surprised grin.

Kieran looked down and experimentally hefted the sticks. "These really aren't balanced very well," he said, and in that moment, the big mercenary struck. Kieran raised his sticks, almost casually, without even seeming to look, and they moved in a rapid blur, with an accompanying *rat-a-tat-tat* of wood as he blocked the mercenary's blows. The big man retreated quickly, and Kieran looked up, as if with surprise. "Oh, have we started?"

The big mercenary snarled and came back at him. The sticks moved so quickly it was almost impossible to make out the individual blows as both men struck and parried, crossing their arms in front of them as it they were batting away insects, and the clatter of the sticks against each other sounded like a rapid drum roll. Then they sprang apart as the crowd cheered in approval of the display.

"You're good, I'll give you that," the big mercenary said grudgingly.

Kieran shrugged. "I'm a little out of practice."

With a growl, the mercenary came at him again. There was a blur of sticks, a clattering tattoo of wood on wood, and then one of the mercenary's sticks flew from his grasp. The big man sprang back, shaking his hand with pain.

"You dropped something," Kieran said. He pointed with one of his sticks. "It's over there. Go on, pick it up. I'll wait."

The mercenary stared at him with loathing, then went to pick up the dropped stick.

Kieran shrugged his shoulders several times, rolling them as if working out some kinks. "Bit stiff, but I think I'm starting to warm up."

"You bastard," the mercenary said, and moved in again. The sticks whirled, clattered, moving with blinding speed, and then there was the sharp crack of a stick on bone and the mercenary cried out and staggered, bringing one of his hands, still clutching the stick, up to the side of his head.

"Sorry," Kieran said. "Clumsy of me."

Roaring, the mercenary charged him. Kieran sidestepped the rush, simultaneously sweeping the mercenary's legs out from under him and rapping quickly on his head as he fell.

"Watch out for that spilled ale," he said. "It makes the floor slippery."

Stunned, the mercenary slowly got back up to his feet, pure murder in his eyes. With a sudden motion, he hurled one of the sticks at Kieran, who raised both his sticks and, with a quick flourish, batted the missile away.

"You want to use just one?" he asked, then shrugged. "Suits me." And he tossed one of his sticks away.

The mercenary screamed with rage and charged once again, bringing his stick down in a vicious, sweeping blow. Kieran parried with a circular motion and hooked his stick under the charging mercenary's arm as he sidestepped and somehow the man was suddenly flipped and flying through the air. The crowd parted quickly as he landed on his back with a loud crash on a table, which broke under his weight. The crowd broke out in cheers and applause.

Kieran looked at the motionless figure of the mercenary for a moment, shrugged, and tossed his stick aside, then went over to Cricket and offered her a hand, helping her up. Turin came rushing up to them.

"Magnificent!" he said, effusively. "Truly magnificent! I have never seen anything like it! Whatever you wish, it's on the house tonight! And I'm sure Cricket will be happy to give you a private dance in one of our comfortable rooms upstairs, won't you, Cricket?"

"No, I won't," she said, firmly. "I quit!"

Turin chuckled awkwardly. "There, there, now, you're upset, and I can certainly understand, under the circumstances, but this gentleman has just fought on your behalf and surely you wouldn't be so ungrateful as to refuse him?"

"The lady owes me nothing," Kieran said. "Scum like that give my profession a bad name. I acted on my own behalf."

"Well, it is very gallant of you to say that," Turin replied, "but I am certain once Cricket gets over her shock and has some time to think things over, she'll want to be properly appreciative."

"Do not misunderstand," Cricket said to Kieran, "I *am* very grateful for what you did, and if there is some way I can repay you, I will try. But not . . . that way. I . . . I cannot."

"I understand," said Kieran. "I would never wish a woman to lie with me out of a sense of obligation. And, as I said, I did not do it for you. You owe me nothing."

"I owe you my thanks, at the very least," said Cricket, "but I am leaving this place tonight. The caravan is departing for Altaruk tomorrow and I am going with it."

"Then I will look forward to the pleasure of your company. We shall be traveling together."

"Now, Cricket, there is nothing to be served by making hasty decisions," Turin said. "You're upset now, and—"

"I had already booked passage before this happened," Cricket interrupted him. "I am leaving, Turin, so don't try to stop me. I am already packed."

Turin's jaw dropped. "Is this how you repay me, after all I've done for you?"

"After all *you* have done for *me?*" said Cricket angrily. "I have made you a great deal of money, Turin! I have earned every copper I have made in this place, and more, but at least I have done it without compromising my virtue!"

"Your *virtue?*" Turin said. "Oh, really! Isn't it a bit ludicrous for you to put on the airs of an affronted virgin?"

"I *am* a virgin!" she shouted at him.

Everyone fell silent. Turin simply stared at her with shock.

"Damn you, Turin," she said softly as tears flowed down her cheeks.

"May I escort you home, my lady?" Kieran asked, offering her his arm.

"I . . . I have to get my things," she stammered.

"I will bring them to you," an elven bard said, stepping up beside her. He patted her on the shoulder. "Go on, now," he said, handing her his cloak. "It will be all right." He smiled. "You've certainly given them something to remember you by."

She smiled through her tears. "Thank you, Edric," she said, kissing him on the cheek. "Please," she said to Kieran, "I want to go home now."

The crowd parted for them as they turned to leave.

Behind them, the big mercenary regained consciousness and sat up groggily. His gaze focused on Kieran, and he reached behind his neck, pulling a stiletto from a concealed sheath on his back, under his tunic. He drew his arm back . . .

"*Kieran, look out!*" Drom shouted.

Kieran spun around just in time to see a ceramic bottle come flying through the air and shatter against the big mercenary's temple. The man grunted and collapsed, dropping the knife. Kieran looked quickly to see who had thrown it. His gaze fell on Sorak. Sorak simply nodded at him.

Kieran smiled. "That's two I owe you, Sorak," he said. "My thanks. I won't forget."

Edric turned to stare at Sorak intently.

"Well, I think I've had enough entertainment for one night," Ryana said.

Sorak offered her his arm. "In that case, my lady, will you allow me to escort you home?"

She took his arm and snuggled up against him. "Would you like a private dance, as well?"

"I didn't know you could dance," said Sorak with surprise.

"I can't," she replied, batting her eyelashes.

"Tajik," Sorak said, "we're leaving now."

"Well, I must say, it's certainly been an interesting night," said the ferry captain as he led them toward the door. Behind them, Edric continued to stare at Sorak. Then he turned to Turin. "I will return for Cricket's things," he said.

"Aah, do as you like, and good riddance to you both," said Turin, sourly. But Edric was already heading for the door.

FIVE

"That girl was very beautiful, wasn't she?" Ryana asked.

Sorak ran his fingers lightly down her bare thigh. "Yes, she was."

They lay together wrapped in a blanket on a rug in front of the fireplace. After they had returned to Tajik's home, the captain had diplomatically withdrawn, saying he would see them in the morning. The servants had prepared a spare room for them, lit a fire, and brewed a pot of tea, then retired to their own quarters, wishing them goodnight. And Sorak and Ryana had made love.

Though they had known each other almost all their lives, they were still only recent lovers, still discovering things about themselves in their new physical relationship. The first time they made love, in Sanctuary, it had been a gentle, tentative, profoundly emotional experience. This time, it had been passionate and energetic. Ryana had showed a side of herself Sorak had never seen before. And he thought he knew why.

"Did you find her desirable?" Ryana asked, her face inches from his own as they lay with legs intertwined.

"I was affected by her beauty," Sorak replied.

"And her dancing?" asked Ryana.

"She was very good," said Sorak.

"You found her exciting."

"Yes. She was beautiful, and I thought her dancing very sensual and seductive."

Ryana sighed. "At least you're honest. I wish I could dance for you like that."

"You don't have to," Sorak said, kissing her.

"But I'd like to," she replied. "I saw the way you were watching her."

"I've seen women dance before," said Sorak, "but never like that. She's very skilled. She has a gift."

"Do you recall her name?"

"Cricket."

"I was going to call you a liar if you claimed not to remember," said Ryana wryly.

"I would never lie to you." He kissed her lips and squeezed her leg between his own. "Besides, it's an unusual name."

"And I suppose that is the only reason you remembered it."

"Are you jealous?" he asked, raising his eyebrows.

"No," she replied. Then grimaced and said, "Yes."

"You have no reason to be," Sorak said. "Besides, she left with Kieran."

"Mmmm. He's very handsome, isn't he?"

"Yes, I suppose he is."

"And a great body."

"I agree."

"And he's very dashing."

"I can see that, yes."

"A girl could do far worse."

"Undoubtedly."

"Damn you," she said, poking him.

Sorak chuckled. "I have no reason to feel jealous. I do not doubt your love. Do you doubt mine?"

"No," she said, snuggling against him and kissing his neck. "But I still wish I could dance for you the way she did."

"I would enjoy seeing you dance."

Ryana made a face and shook her head. "My body would not move like hers. I am too muscular and lack the flexibility. Besides, I do not have her skill. If I tried, I would look foolish and clumsy. You would only laugh at me."

"Never."

She sighed. "In a way, it was easier before, when your female aspects prevented you from lying with a woman. I knew you could never lie with me, but neither would you lie with others. Now, I cannot help but wonder if I will be enough for you."

"You are more than enough woman for me," said Sorak.

"But I'm the only woman you have ever been with."

"And I'm the only man that you have ever been with," he replied. "Unless there's something you have kept from me."

She poked him again. "You know better. But it's different with a man. A woman loves. A man has appetites."

Sorak frowned. "Who told you that?"

"It's what the sisters always said."

"Ah, and they, of course, are vastly experienced in such matters," he said in a gently mocking tone.

"They are not all virgins. You know that."

"Yes, I know," he agreed, "but those who are not have experienced only the physical side of love, and that merely as a curiosity. When it came their turn to make a pilgrimage, they took the opportunity to find a man and satisfy their curiosity, and they did so in a manner that only validated their preconceptions."

Ryana frowned. "I don't understand."

"What prevented me from experiencing physical love before is what helps me understand it better now," he said. "I used to resent the interference of my female aspects, but in a way, I'm grateful for it now. I wanted you, but my female aspects would not allow it, because if I made love to you, they would have experienced it with me. They would have been repelled by it, as I would have been had one of them made love with a man. Well, perhaps not all of them would have been repelled. Kivara always found the possibility intriguing."

"Yes, I remember," said Ryana with a smile. "She was always a creature of sensation, entranced with excitement, attracted to the unpredictable."

"And so, through her, I knew that side of female behavior," Sorak said. "With the Guardian, I knew the stable, maternal, nurturing side. The Watcher taught me yet another side of women, that which observes and protects and evaluates. I may be male, but because of them, I also know what it's like to be female. To say that women love while men have only appetites is to deny that women also have appetites and men can also love. And the sisters stand as living proof of that."

"They do?" Ryana asked, with surprise.

"Of course," said Sorak. "If a sister goes out on a pilgrimage and takes a man to bed to satisfy her curiosity, then is that love? Or is it not an appetite she is indulging?"

"But . . . doing it merely to find out what it's like, that is not really lust," Ryana said.

"Perhaps not, but if curiosity must be indulged and satisfied, then it's an appetite, just as lust is. And if you were to take a man to bed without loving him, merely to satisfy your curiosity, then how would that be any different from my taking Cricket to bed simply because she aroused me with her beauty and her dancing? Those sisters who spoke to you of men so knowledgeably, did any of them ever say they were in love?"

"No, they didn't," Ryana admitted.

"So, if women love and men only indulge their appetites, then what were *they* doing?"

"I never really thought of it that way," Ryana said. "I never questioned it."

"If I were a young girl, listening to my older sisters, I probably would not have questioned it, either," Sorak said with a shrug. "But I was a young boy, and though the sisters never spoke to me of such things, I heard them talk among themselves, and saw them give me sidelong glances, and it did not sit well with me. So I consulted with my female aspects, especially the Guardian, for she was the oldest and the wisest. And she helped me see that what the sisters said was not entirely true."

"How did she do that?" Ryana asked.

"Well, she rather irritably pointed out that I could have seen it for myself if I had only thought more clearly," he replied. "I loved you long before I ever felt desire for you, not because I wanted you, but because of who you are. I felt frustration and regret because I believed my love for you could not be consummated, but I still loved you nonetheless. The Guardian said an appetite diminishes with satisfaction, but love never does. If it is truly love, then it grows stronger. And now I know that she was right. And, in a way, so were you. You will never be enough for me. I shall always want more . . . of you."

"I love you," said Ryana, hugging him.

The fire flared abruptly, unnaturally. The thick wood normally burned steadily, but slowly. Even when the flames hit pockets of the resinous sap, they did not normally flare up, they merely sparked and burned a little faster, with a crackling and popping sound. But the flames in the adobe brick fireplace shot up suddenly with a whoosh, several feet high, turning a bright blue and licking up the chimney, and a cloud of blue-green smoke appeared, shot through with tiny, shimmering lights. It did not go up the chimney, but hovered over the brightly burning flames, then moved out into the room and started to spread out like mist.

Sorak and Ryana sat up as the cloud hovered over them, sparkling with dancing pinpoints of energy. As they watched, a brightly glowing shape appeared within the cloud, indistinct, shifting and transparent. It started to resolve into a face, then flowed and shifted once again, moving and sparkling with bright lights, like tiny stars, only vaguely suggesting features. The glow emanating from it was too bright to make out any detail. And then a voice spoke.

Sorak . . . The voice spoke with a ghostly echo, and it seemed to come from all around them. It was a voice Sorak knew, though it had never spoken to him before. He felt the familiar ethereal presence, serene and powerful. Several times before, it had descended on him and possessed him, but now it served the Sage.

"Kether," he said, softly.

You are needed in Altaruk, Sorak. Go there. Contact the Alliance. Waste no time. They are in grave danger. Guard yourself. Trust no one. Death comes across the desert. Go. For the avangion.

The glow faded and the cloud started to dissipate.

"Kether, wait!" said Sorak, but even as he spoke, the cloud dissolved until there was only a sprinkling of bright pinpoints in the air, like fireflies seen from a distance, and then those, too, were gone. The flames in the fireplace burned normally once more, and all was as before.

"What was that?" Ryana asked.

"A message," Sorak said. "A message from the Sage."

"But . . . I heard nothing," said Ryana.

"You did not see the glowing cloud? You did not hear Kether speak?"

"I saw the cloud, but I heard no one speak."

"Strange," said Sorak.

"What was the message?" Ryana asked, staring at him.

"That I must go to Altaruk and contact the Alliance. They are in danger. Death comes across the desert."

"What does that mean?" she asked.

He shook his head. "I do not know. But it seems I shall be accepting Kieran's offer, after all. We will go and see him first thing in the morning. We must be on that caravan when it departs."

* * * * *

Edric the bard stood out in the street, staring at the house. All was quiet. He had seen them go in, and then he had found out whose house it was. It belonged to Tajik, captain of one the dwarven ferries that plied the estuary. He had heard some of the mercenaries talking in the club earlier that night, about how the giants had attacked Tajik's boat and how one of the passengers had saved everyone aboard with an incredible feat of bravery.

Could he be the one?

That mercenary who had gone with Cricket called him Sorak. *Sorak.* Elvish for nomad. And he traveled with a villichi priestess.

For a long time, Edric simply stood out in the street and watched the house. He was tempted to go and knock upon the door, but could not bring himself to do it. What could he say? "Are you the one? Are you the Nomad? Are you the one they call the Crown of Elves?"

What would he be doing in a place like South Ledopolus? Perhaps he came to join the caravan to Altaruk. Yes, that had to be it. And if he had crossed with Tajik from North Ledopolus, then he must have come across the desert, from the Great Ivory Plain. What would he be doing out there? There was nothing . . . unless he came all the way from the Mekillots. A long, harsh journey. Yet, there was nothing else out that way except . . .

Bodach. The city of the undead.

Edric swallowed hard. Only fools would go to Bodach. Only fools . . . or heroes. What could be in Bodach that the Crown of Elves would want? Edric moistened his lips as he stood there, thinking. The lost treasure, obviously. That was the only reason anyone would go to Bodach, and even so, they would have to be insane. No one in his right mind would willingly face an army of undead.

But the Nomad was said to be no ordinary man. Part elf, part halfling, and the living embodiment of an ancient prophecy. A prophecy the fulfillment of which might be hastened if he had the lost treasure of Bodach to finance it.

Edric leaned back against a wall, thinking. Perhaps he was jumping to conclusions. He thought about how he had sung the Song of Alaron for Cricket only the previous night. He had always liked the myth, the charming sentiment of it, but he had never believed in the prophecy. That a Crown of Elves would arise to reunite the tribes after all these years . . . it did not seem even remotely possible.

The elves had been scattered for too long. Few were even tribal anymore, and those that were competed violently among themselves. It was the way of survival in the desert. The rest all lived in towns and cities now, and each year, more and more interbred with humans. Cricket was a lovely girl, but half-elves weren't really elves. Full-blooded elves looked down on them, even in the cities, where they had fallen from the old ways and were merely shadows of their ancestors.

Most elves had no use for a king. Not anymore. Still, there were many who believed the myth. Or wanted to believe it. It gave them hope. And now that this Nomad had appeared. . . .

Was it really possible that the prophecy was

true? Or was it more likely that this Nomad was merely some adventurer who chose to take advantage of it? No, thought Edric, he would be no *mere* adventurer. To put a scheme like this into effect required boldness of an unprecedented nature. And if only half the things they said of him were true, then he had more than amply demonstrated his courage and abilities. But then, it would take someone like that to even consider such an audacious scheme. Especially given the odds against its succeeding.

Galdra. What of Galdra? He would need a sword to pass off as the legendary blade of elven kings. That would be no easy task. The legend gave a good description of the sword, so that part would be no problem, but it also said the blade was made from elven steel, which had not been seen in over a thousand years. At the same time, however, that very fact would make it easier to fake. Who would know the genuine article anymore?

With a steel blade that could be passed off as Galdra, what remained was the getting of a reputation. Some daring feats would have to be performed to capture the imagination of the people—feats such as rescuing a princess of the Royal House of Nibenay and taking her across the Barrens and back to Nibenay, where he could tweak the noses of the templars and their city guard in a very public way. Yes, it certainly required boldness, perhaps even a death wish, but if the plan succeeded . . .

What could be his final goal? Was it possible that he really aspired to reunite the elves under his kingship? No, thought Edric, that would be insane. Even if he could accomplish such a thing, which did not seem possible, it would take many years, and the dragon kings would never stand for it. Then he would truly bring down their wrath. So it couldn't possibly be that. What then?

And then it hit him. Of course. The lost treasure of Bodach. It all came back to that. If this Nomad had somehow stumbled on the secret of the treasure's location, he would need help in removing it. He would never be able to do it by himself. Even a heavily armed party would risk death. The only way it could be done would be if he knew exactly where the treasure was. Then he could go in with a party large enough to load it and remove it, working swiftly during the daylight hours so they could be out again before then sun went down, when the undead of Bodach would attack with a frightening, unrelenting fury.

And to be sure of success in such a task, he would have to be certain of the loyalty of those he took with him, because the treasure would tempt anyone to seize it once it was safely removed from Bodach. And how better to command such loyalty than to go in with a small army of elves who had been duped into thinking he truly was the king the prophecy foretold?

He could tell them that the treasure would be safely hidden, or perhaps invested with a merchant house to grow in value and finance the coming kingdom. Something like that, anyway. And then the riches would be his, converted into merchant bonds he could take anywhere on Athas and use to buy himself a title and a palace and private guard of mercenaries to protect him from those whom he had duped.

It was plausible, thought Edric, but could that really be what he intended? If the Nomad joined the caravan—well, of course he would do that; why else come here—Edric could observe him. And when they arrived in Altaruk, if he went directly to one of the great merchant houses. . . .

The treasure. It came back to that again. If he really knew where the treasure was hidden, he would have brought out some piece of it to show the merchant houses. Which meant that he was probably carrying it with him.

Edric took a deep breath and exhaled slowly. He could be wrong, of course. All this was merely supposition. But what if he was right? The trip to Altaruk just might let him find out for sure. Perhaps he could arrange for some distraction somewhere along the way, so he could examine what this Nomad carried with him.

He hurried back to the Desert Damsel to fetch Cricket's belongings. The caravan would be leaving in the morning, and it promised to be a very interesting journey.

SIX

Shortly after sunrise, Sorak and Ryana arrived at the camp on the outskirts of the village. The campsite was already a bustle of activity. The caravan captain had been up for several hours before dawn, cracking the whip and having the roustabouts light the cookfires for breakfast, then mustering the kank handlers and making sure the giant beetles were well fed before the journey.

Kanks were docile creatures, especially those raised in captivity, and were the preferred means of caravan transport. Otherwise, the merchant houses employed large and fully enclosed armored wagons drawn by mekillots, usually in paired teams. Each mode of transport had its advantages and disadvantages.

With the kank beetles, a caravan could make

much better time, but the caravan crew and passengers were exposed to the elements and were more vulnerable to attack. Consequently, a larger force of mercenaries was usually employed to guard a kank caravan against desert predators and raiders.

The armored wagons drawn by mekillots were large enough to hold the complement of the entire caravan, in addition to the cargo, and they were nearly impregnable to attack. However, the huge, six-ton mekillot lizards that pulled the heavy armored wagons—the only creatures on Athas capable of such a task—were slow moving and difficult to control.

Only skilled handlers adept at psionics could deal with the beasts, and their job was the most hazardous of all, for the giant lizards had long and powerful tongues that could snare a handler for a snack if his control slipped even for an instant. The passengers and crew were well protected, but even with the roof vents of the wagon open, the heat inside became oppressive, and the stench of sweaty bodies crammed together inside the dark enclosure made for a very long, unpleasant journey.

Kanks, on the other hand, could manage a surprisingly rapid pace for creatures of their size, even loaded down with cargo, but they grew stubborn and recalcitrant when they were hungry. Getting a four-hundred-pound beetle to move when it didn't want to was not only difficult, but potentially hazardous. Kanks were vegetarian, and domesticated ones did not attack, but they indicated their hunger by clicking their powerful pincers together, and if an unwary handler happened to come too close, he could be severely injured, or even killed. Consequently, the welfare of the kanks was the first priority of the caravan captain, after the safety of the cargo. The passengers came last.

It took several hours to feed the kanks, and while the handlers were seeing to that task, the roustabout crew loaded up the cargo pouches, strapping down the large hide bags and cinching them tight on the chitinous backs of the creatures. Others worked at taking down the camp, furling the tents and packing all the gear away for travel.

Once he had issued orders to feed the kanks and strike the camp, the captain of the caravan mustered the guard. The supply clerk took careful inventory as the cargo was loaded, making sure none of it had gotten sidetracked since the previous night's inventory. If any of the cargo turned up missing, the guards who had been on watch the night before would have to answer for it, so they stood anxiously by the supply clerk, making sure each item on the manifest was systematically checked off.

The few hours before the caravan moved out were profitably used by the captain to make sure all his men were present and accounted for, which sometimes took a bit of doing, particularly when a caravan stopped at a place like South Ledopolus. Mercenaries were drifters by nature, and despite the high salaries paid by the merchant houses, they sometimes drifted off before the caravan reached its final destination. Others had gotten deep into their cups the previous night and had failed to make the muster. If some of the guard turned up missing, the captain sent a flying squad through town for a quick check of the taverns and the pleasure houses and the back alleys in their immediate vicinity.

If the missing guards were found, the flying squad would sweep them up and return them to the campsite. If they were not found, or were discovered too injured or hung over to make their way back to the camp, then they were simply left to fend for themselves, and new men were recruited from among those who got up before the crack of dawn and gathered at the campsite in the hope there would be vacancies they could fill.

It didn't take long for Sorak to find Kieran, who was conversing with the caravan captain when they arrived. As the new captain of the house guard for the House of Jhamri, Kieran would be the caravan captain's superior when he arrived in Altaruk to assume his duties, so the caravan captain's desire to impress was evident in his posture and demeanor. As Sorak and Ryana approached, they saw the captain nod to Kieran and clap his right fist to his left breast in salute, then hurry off to resume his duties. Kieran turned and, when he saw them, grinned broadly.

"I was hoping you would come," he said, holding out his hand in greeting. "So, you've decided to accept my offer?"

Sorak clasped forearms with him, in the mercenary fashion. "Well, it's a tempting offer, and I have no other prospects at the moment. But before I give you my answer, I would like to know a little more about the terms and conditions of my employment."

"Fair enough," said Kieran, nodding. "I will be your immediate superior. A man of your courage and abilities should not be wasted in the ranks, so if you accept, I shall make you my lieutenant. I pride myself on being a good judge of character, and you strike me as the sort of man I can depend on. You will draw an officer's pay of one hundred silvers a month."

"One hundred silvers? That is very generous."

"The House of Jhamri can afford to pay its soldiers well," Kieran replied. "However, you will not be paid for the first two weeks of your employment. You'll receive those wages at the termination of your service. This is to discourage you from leaving the service of the house without giving adequate notice. Should you choose to leave without serving two weeks notice, those wages will be forfeit."

"That seems fair," said Sorak. "But what if I am short of funds during those first two weeks?" He did not wish to give the impression he had money. The last thing he wanted was for Kieran to know what they carried in their packs.

"As an officer, you will be paid an adequate allowance for your room and board, in excess of your wages, which you may draw upon as soon as we arrive in Altaruk," said Kieran. "If you are reasonably frugal, it should allow you to secure comfortable lodgings and enjoy three meals a day, if at least one of those meals is a light one. The enlisted men live in the barracks, but I think you would prefer private quarters." He said this casually, with no obvious inference regarding Ryana. "Besides, I do not approve of officers living in the barracks with enlisted men. It encourages familiarity."

"Room and board *and* one hundred silvers?" Sorak was impressed.

"As I said, the House of Jhamri pays its soldiers well. But they do not do so merely out of the goodness of their hearts." He grinned. "Merchants have no hearts. The high salaries they pay ensure that they attract top men and keep their loyalty. Should you fall ill during your service, or become wounded, you will have free access to a healer. Should you become crippled in the service of the House, you will receive a pension that should keep you from resorting to the beggar's cup. And should you die while in the service of the House, a one-time cash benefit shall be paid to your assigns, or they may accept the equivalent value in House shares."

"With such terms, it is amazing they have any vacancies at all," said Sorak sincerely.

Kieran indicated a large group of men milling around near the entrance to the camp. "As you see, there is never any shortage of applicants. However, the work can be hazardous, as I am sure you know, and while the terms are generous, the conditions are equally strict. After leaving service with the House of Jhamri, you may not enter into service with a competing merchant house for at least five years."

Sorak frowned. "I suppose I can understand the reasoning, but how could they enforce that?"

"Violating that condition of your employment results in a bounty placed upon your head," said Kieran. "A bounty lucrative enough to ensure that you will be looking over your shoulder for the remainder of your days, as there is no time limit to the bounty. Once offered, it is not rescinded."

"I see," said Sorak.

"This is to discourage you from accepting a better offer with another merchant house and, in the process, divulging any secrets you may have learned," said Kieran. "Still interested?"

"Continue," Sorak said. "Anything else?"

"Yes, one more thing," said Kieran. "The word of your superiors is law. Pure and simple. In other words, *my* word. The punishment for disobedience to orders, whether direct or indirect, can be quite severe."

"How severe?" asked Sorak.

"That is entirely up to my discretion as captain of the house guard," Kieran said. "It could be as mild as extra duty and a dock in pay, if I felt the infraction a minor one and unintentional, or as severe as fifty lashes, possibly even death."

"What sort of offense would merit a sentence of death?" asked Ryana.

"Murder; desertion or direct disobedience to orders in the field or under conditions of combat;

sabotage or espionage for a competing merchant house; and striking a superior officer in the field or under conditions of combat. Under other circumstances, the normal penalty is fifty lashes. However, it is possible to die from that, as well. Those are the rules of the House of Jhamri. I have a certain amount of latitude in how I choose to interpret them."

"Which means?" said Sorak.

"Which means I consider fifty lashes for striking a superior officer an excessive penalty," said Kieran. "I can easily imagine conditions under which an officer might well deserve to be struck. I would judge such matters under individual circumstances."

"And if someone under your command struck you?" asked Ryana.

"Under conditions of combat, my lady, I would kill him instantly," said Kieran. "Otherwise, I would simply strike him back. Repeatedly." He glanced at Sorak. "Have you a problem with any of those conditions?"

Sorak shook his head. "No, they seem straightforward."

"Good. Then you accept?"

"I accept," said Sorak with a nod.

"Excellent! Raise your right hand."

Sorak did so.

"Repeat after me," said Kieran. "On my oath and on my life, I hereby swear to abide by the terms and conditions of service with the House of Jhamri, which have been explained to me and which I fully understand."

Sorak repeated the words.

"That's it," said Kieran. "You are now the executive officer and my second-in-command of the House Guard of Jhamri. Congratulations, Lieutenant. Henceforth, except in private, you will address me as Captain."

"Second-in-command?" said Sorak, with surprise. "But . . . we have only just met! You barely even know me!"

"I know what I need to know," said Kieran. "Your past does not concern me. In the present, you have demonstrated your courage and saved my life not once, but twice—once indirectly, on the boat; and once directly, in the Desert Damsel. And I feel confident that in the future, I shall not regret my decision."

"But . . . with all due respect, Captain," Sorak said, "is this wise? Surely, there is already a senior officer in service with the house guard whom my appointment will displace. Will this not incur resentment?"

"It is a commander's privilege to appoint his own second-in-command," said Kieran. "Every officer knows and understands this, or should. If not you, then I would have recruited a new man from outside the house guard for this position."

"May I ask why?" said Sorak in a puzzled tone.

"Certainly. A senior officer already in place will inevitably have certain prejudices or predispositions, and an established relationship with those under his command. When taking a new post, I always prefer to start fresh, with a man I do not have to break of old habits and routine, and one who has not yet established any sort of a relationship with the rank and file. A new broom sweeps clean, in other words. And a man who has already killed a giant in single combat is not likely to be regarded as unqualified by those under his command."

"I see," said Sorak. "Well, I shall try to justify your confidence in me."

"No, Lieutenant, you shall not *try*," said Kieran. "You will *do* it. Understood?"

"Understood, Captain," said Sorak with a smile.

Kieran clapped him on the back. "Good. And now that you have been sworn in, your first two weeks of service begin as of today. You will have no duties to perform until we reach Altaruk, but in the meantime, we can discuss what will be expected of you, and this way, you will not have to wait as long to draw your pay. And since you have already joined my command, you will receive free passage on the caravan, and I shall be honored to extend the same courtesy to you, my lady."

"Thank you. That is very kind of you," Ryana said.

"I would do so in any case," Kieran said, with a slight bow, "out of respect to any cleric or priestess."

"Even a templar?" asked Ryana.

"Especially a templar," Kieran said. "It is wise to show respect to any cleric, whether preserver or defiler. And since templars exert considerable influence of a political nature, it is prudent to be politic with them."

"And where do your own sympathies lie, Captain?" Ryana asked.

"Close to my vest, my lady, which is where I prefer to keep them," Kieran replied. "And now, if you will permit me, it would please me if you would join me for some morning tea. Our caravan captain strikes me as an able fellow, and I am sure he would be relieved to go about his duties free of the concern that I am watching him. I seem to make the poor man nervous."

Before long, they were ready to get under way. It was normal for a caravan to travel with a string of spare kanks, and Kieran had the chief handler select one for them. Some caravans traveled with light carriages drawn by kanks, a luxury afforded to well-heeled passengers and dignitaries, for a carriage offered a more comfortable ride and shade from the searing sun, but this caravan lacked such amenities. There were no aristocrats among the passengers, and the caravan captain had not wished to burden himself with carriages when he could make better time without them. As a result, the passengers and roustabouts all rode mounted in pairs upon the backs of kanks, as did about half the mercenary force. The outriders rode solo upon crodlu.

The lizard-hide kank saddles were specially crafted for the merchant houses, providing some welcome padding between the hard, chitinous shells of the beetles and sensitive posteriors. They also had high backs that provided support, allowing the riders to lean back and relax with the slightly rolling gait of the giant, six-legged beetles. Sorak found it a much more comfortable way to ride than bareback.

He found the crodlu mounts of the mercenaries of greater interest. They were large, bipedal, flightless birds, covered with reddish-gray scales instead of feathers. Their cousins, erdlu, were raised for their large eggs, one of the staple foods of Athas, and their scales were used for shields and armor. The birds were also slaughtered for food when they became mature, and erdlu meat prepared in tenderizing marinade was regarded as a delicacy.

Erdlus weighed up to two hundred pounds and stood around seven feet tall, with long yellow necks and small heads with large, wedge-shaped, powerful beaks. Their rounded bodies had small, vestigial wings which were kept folded to the sides and which the erdlu flared when they grew agitated. Their long legs ended in four-toed feet with strong, razor-sharp claws. If threatened, the birds defended themselves with powerful kicks which were easily capable of killing a man; but domesticated, herd-raised erdlu were mostly passive creatures that rarely became aggressive. Crodlu were a rather different breed.

Crodlu were specially bred for aggression by a small group of master herdsmen. Their eggs still made a good food source, though they were smaller, and their powerful beaks and claws were often fashioned into spearheads and daggers.

Crodlu scales were stronger and thicker, so armor made from them was more expensive, and it was readily identified by its darker, brick-red color. But primarily, crodlu were valued as fighting mounts.

Unlike the gentler erdlu, crodlu did not spook easily and in an attack they were more than merely mounts. A trained crodlu would kick upon command, and they would strike opponents with their deadly beaks at any opportunity. Erdlu could run very quickly, sprinting for up to half a mile, but crodlu had greater powers of endurance and could run much faster. For this reason, the mercenary outriders were all mounted on these birds, and Sorak was hoping he would have a chance to try one out.

The dark sun was quickly warming up the desert as the caravan prepared to set off. For protection from the sun's potent rays, the riders wore loose, hooded cloaks, and most also wore turbans with extra lengths of cloth hanging down that could be used as veils to protect their faces. Each passenger carried his or her own waterskin, slung from the saddle, and there were spare skins strapped to the cargo kanks, as well, but the caravan captain made it clear the water would be rationed, so the passengers would be responsible for conserving their supply between stops. Those passengers mounted in front on each individual kank could control the reins if they wished, but there was no real need: the kanks instinctively followed those in front of them, and the kanks leading the caravan were ridden by handlers, who also rode the cargo kanks and those bringing up the rear.

"It's the first time I have ever traveled with so large a caravan," Sorak said, glancing down the line of huge, restive black beetles. Kieran had insisted that they ride together, and he rode at the front, mounted on a crodlu, just behind the handlers who rode point. "Does it present many problems on the trail?"

"It actually presents fewer problems than with smaller caravans," said Kieran. He turned and pointed. "To keep things organized, the captain has the formation drawn up five abreast, with the cargo kanks positioned single file in the center, a file of passenger-bearing kanks to either side and the two outer ranks of kanks bearing mercenaries and roustabouts.

"This way," he continued, "the formation is kept closely grouped, except for the mercenary outriders, who range out ahead and to the rear, as well as scouting to the left and right for a mile or more, always within sight of the caravan. They ride the faster crodlu, of course, so they can quickly return to the main body and give warning in case they spot any raiders or natural hazards such as dust storms or rampaging antloids."

Ryana frowned. "But the instincts of the kanks, even domesticated ones that have been raised by herdsmen, are to organize into hives, with a hierarchy of soldiers, food producers, and brood queens. Unless they're separated, as in the case of kanks used as individual mounts or to draw light carriages, large groups of kank beetles that remain together for any length of time tend to fall into the organization of a hive."

"You are quite correct, my lady," Kieran replied, inclining his head toward her, "which is why food producers and brood queens are invariably used as cargo bearers, with young soldier kanks used as mounts for the mercenaries and older ones for passengers. Since the natural instinct of the soldier kanks is to protect their brood queens, that means they will never stray far from the cargo and will fiercely fight away predators or raiders."

"That makes good sense," said Ryana, "but what prevents the brood queens from nesting?"

"The interruption of their cycle," Kieran said. "Brood queens used as cargo bearers are sterilized. It does not cause them any harm, and actually increases their life span and renders them more manageable. The food producers and soldiers cannot tell the difference, and so they continue to react the same way to the sterile queens as they do to fertile ones." He saw the caravan captain ride out to the side of the formation, giving it one last check. "Ah, it seems we are about to get under way."

The captain raised his baton, from which several bright red streamers waved, symbolizing the House of Jhamri. "Out-ri-*ders!*" he called, stretching it out into three syllables. "Move out!"

The mercenaries taking the first shift of outrider duty prodded their crodlu into a fast trot and moved out to take their posts on the flanks, while the forward scouts rushed to the head of the main caravan. Sorak noted that all the mercenaries in service to the House of Jhamri wore red turbans, except Kieran, perhaps because he had not yet officially assumed his duties.

The caravan captain raised his baton once more. "*Car-rah-vannnn* . . ." he called out loudly in a sing-song voice, ". . . *ho-ohhhhh!*" He circled the baton over his head and wheeled his kank as the point riders urged their mounts forward and the caravan moved out.

They started down the trail, leaving the campsite and South Ledopolus behind, and gradually picked up speed. The caravan captain, mounted on a crodlu, rode out along the flanks, keeping an eye on things and making sure the formation did not string out. Ryana looked behind her to see how far the caravan was stretching out and spotted Cricket some distance back, sitting astride one of the passenger kanks, behind the elf they had seen in the Desert Damsel.

Ryana glanced over at Kieran. Riding at the very front, behind the two point riders, they had no cargo kanks between them, so they could converse easily. "I see your dancer friend made good her threat to leave."

"Yes, surprisingly," said Kieran.

"Why surprisingly?" Ryana asked.

"I did not really expect to see her," Kieran said. "Despite whatever resolutions these girls may make, they rarely leave such places as the Desert Damsel. And Cricket was the star attraction, after all."

Ryana frowned. "But if the conditions were unpleasant . . ."

"The money usually is not," Kieran replied. "A dancer in a busy pleasure house may easily make in one night what it would take me a month to earn. They become seduced by the money. They may tell themselves they will only do it until they can get out of debt or put enough aside to move on to a better life, but it rarely happens."

"Why?" Ryana asked.

"Because they don't save their money," Kieran said. "They spend it on expensive jewels and costumes, trying to outdo one another in competing for the attention of the customers, or else they start treating themselves to luxuries they could not afford before, better housing, better clothing, more expensive meals, some drugs to induce short-lived euphoria. . . . They tell themselves they deserve it, because they work hard and besides, they're making plenty of money. Before they know it, they're spending everything they make and become caught up in the life. And it is not much of a life."

"It does not seem so difficult," said Sorak.

"No, the job itself is not so difficult," Kieran agreed, "but the longer they remain, the more it wears them down. They come to think less and less of men, because they always see them at their worst, and because they expect men to behave badly, they often wind up with men who take advantage of them . . . or else give up on men entirely and seek the company of women. One day, they wake up and find that drugs have ruined their health and their appearance, or else they have simply gotten older and no longer appeal to the customers as much as the younger, prettier ones . . . and there are always younger, prettier ones.

"They start doing things they would not have done before," Kieran continued, "and as time goes on, they do them for less money. What little self-esteem they may have left soon dissipates and, unless they're fortunate enough to find some man to take them, before long they are no longer attractive enough to keep their jobs and often wind up on the streets. It happens all the time. The young ones see it happen to the older girls, but don't learn. Who knows, Cricket may be different, but chances are she will only go back to the same thing after we arrive in Altaruk."

"You don't seem to have a very high opinion of her," said Ryana. "And yet, you went home with her last night."

"I *escorted* her home," said Kieran. "And I have no particular opinion of Cricket, one way or the other. I acknowledge that she is young and beautiful and a skilled dancer. Otherwise, I know nothing of her. She claimed to be a virgin, which seems unlikely, but I did not dispute the issue. Neither did I press it. I walked her home, then said good night and took my leave. So you may spare me your disapproving looks. I have done nothing to deserve them."

"I stand corrected," said Ryana. "It is just that men often lack respect for women, yet that does not prevent them from enjoying their favors."

"Just as women often lack respect for men, yet still eagerly accept the contents of their purses," Kieran replied. "Cricket may indeed be what she claims, and she may have chosen her occupation out of sheer necessity, but mark my words, she will yet cause trouble on this journey."

"What makes you say that?" Ryana asked.

"Experience, my lady. There isn't a roustabout or mercenary on this caravan who hasn't seen her dance. Now she travels with them, with no bouncers to look out for her, and that limp-wristed elven bard she rides with will not be much protection."

"Is it not part of your duties to keep order among your men?" Ryana said.

"Officially, I have not yet assumed my duties," Kieran replied with a shrug. "And keeping order on this journey is the caravan captain's job, not mine. But if it were up to me, I would have left her behind."

"Would you have left me behind, as well?" Ryana asked.

"No, my lady. An attractive, unescorted woman on a caravan is always trouble," Kieran said. "You have an escort, and a highly capable one, at that. Aside from which, you are a priestess, commanding respect, and the fighting prowess of villichi are well known. A woman like Cricket, on the other hand, commands little respect, if any, and is unable to protect herself. And her chosen escort is scarcely better than nothing. So . . . there will be trouble. Now, if you will excuse me, I think I will ride down the line and observe the captain's disposition of his guard."

He wheeled his crodlu and urged it to a fast trot, leaving the formation.

"What an infuriating man!" Ryana said.

"I thought you said he was handsome and dashing," Sorak replied, with a hint of amusement in his voice.

"He is all that," Ryana conceded grudgingly, "but he is also very irritating."

"He merely speaks his mind," said Sorak. "And I cannot say I disagree with anything he said."

"So you think a woman is merely an encumbrance unless she has a man to protect her?"

"That is not quite what he said," Sorak replied. "He said that an attractive, unescorted woman on a caravan brings trouble. Roustabouts and mercenaries are a rough lot, and they are not known for their gallantry."

"So women must be penalized for men's failure to control their impulses?"

"I admit it is unfair," said Sorak, "but that is the way of things."

"Spoken like a true male," said Ryana with a grimace. "I never thought to hear you of all people speak like that."

"I do not think that is the way things should be," Sorak replied, "but regrettably, it is the way they are. Certainly in Cricket's case. After all, she makes her living by arousing men."

"Then it's all her fault, is that it?" Ryana said irritably. "You are beginning to sound like Kieran.

What would the Guardian have said if she could hear you speak like this?"

"I suspect she would have said that Cricket made her own choices. She was born with the gift of beauty, and she chose to exploit it by dancing in a pleasure house."

"What if she had no other choice?"

"There are always choices," Sorak said. "They may not be pleasant ones, but they exist. Suppose you had not been born villichi. You are also beautiful, and your family was poor. Knowing how much money you could make at a place such as the Desert Damsel, would you have chosen to work there?"

"No," Ryana replied at once. "I would dance for you, if I knew how, but that is hardly the same thing."

"I do not dispute that," Sorak said. "But what might you have done, instead?"

"I would have found a job that I could do without taking off my clothes for strangers and then I would have searched for some way to improve my lot in life."

"Even if it only paid a small fraction of what you could make by dancing in a pleasure house?"

"Even so. I would not wish to spend my days with men leering at me and offering me money to gratify their lusts."

"Then there are other choices," Sorak said. "Not easy ones, perhaps, and not as profitable, but choices nonetheless. I do not hold men blameless, mind you. If there was no demand for pleasure houses, then they would not exist. But at the same time, so long as there are women willing to work in such places, the attitude men have toward them will not change."

"You mean as long as there are women who need money, it is all right for men to exploit them?"

"I never said that," Sorak replied. "It seems to me that both men *and* women are exploited in such places. The women exploit the baser instincts of the men, and the men exploit the beauty of the women. But in the long run, I think the women get the worst of it."

"I wish I'd never gone to that place," said Ryana. "I was curious to see it, but the more I think about it, the more angry I become."

Sorak nodded. "For a short time, before you joined me after you left the convent, I worked in a gaming house in Tyr. The Crystal Spider, you remember?"

"In the elven quarter?"

Sorak nodded. "I was hired to keep watch for cheats and cardsharps, but gaming was not their only trade. There were girls like Cricket there, as well. People went there for a good time, but there was a feeling of desperation in the air, and hunger." He shook his head. "A lot of money changed hands in the Crystal Spider, but I don't think it ever made anybody happy."

They made good time the first day, without any misadventures, stopping at midday for a rest break and a meal, then continuing on until they were about halfway to the oasis called Grak's Pool. The oasis was at the midpoint of their journey from South Ledopolus to Altaruk, a distance of about one hundred miles, though the caravan had already traveled an equal distance to South Ledopolus from Balic.

The plan was for the caravan to stop at Grak's Pool for one day, to allow the passengers and their mounts to rest, relieve the cargo kanks of their burden for a while, and take on more water. But Grak's Pool was still another day's journey away, and they camped that night within sight of the banks of the estuary, which the trade route followed all the way to Altaruk.

They stopped about two hours before sunset to allow light to pitch the tents, post the watch, and light the fires before darkness fell, and as the roustabouts pursued their tasks, Kieran asked Sorak what he thought of the caravan captain's disposition of the camp.

"He has placed us with the estuary at our rear," said Sorak, "which I would not do with troops, but it strikes me that for a caravan, it could have advantages."

"How so?" asked Kieran.

"Is this a test?" asked Sorak.

"Merely an informal one," replied Kieran with amusement. "I am curious to hear your opinion."

"Well, we are not likely to encounter an opposing army," Sorak said. "If we did, there would be no choice but to surrender. Raiders would be the most immediate concern, and we would not be able to outrun them. We would have to stand and fight. It is doubtful there would be enough of them to push us back into the silt, which would not be their intention, in any case. They would want the cargo. By disposing us with the estuary at our rear, the captain eliminates the possibility of raiders attacking from that quarter."

"Good," said Kieran. "What else?"

"He has placed the cargo in the center of the camp, where it can be most easily protected, and the passengers' tents are pitched between the cargo and the estuary, with the roustabouts and mercenaries in the front and on the flanks."

"Why?" asked Kieran.

"I can think of two reasons," Sorak replied. "One is that with the passengers disposed behind the cargo, they cannot get in the way in the event an attack must be repelled, and the second is that if an attack takes place and the raiders happen to break through, they will reach the cargo before they reach the passengers. Since it is cargo they will want, they will seize that and leave the passengers alone, unless any of them are foolish enough to interfere."

"Excellent. And what of the disposition of the watch?" asked Kieran.

Sorak looked out at the placement of the guards. "Triangular," he said. "One outpost on each flank, two at the front, to the right and left, and one at point, between them and about fifty yards advanced. It seems a practical arrangement."

"Could you improve upon it?" Kieran asked.

"I would detail roving pickets to ride along the left and right sides of the triangle, checking with each guard outpost as they pass. And I would give them watch words, as an added precaution."

Kieran smiled. "I have already made that suggestion to the captain," he said, nodding. "I see we think alike. I do not think I shall regret choosing you for my second-in-command."

"While there is still time, you may wish to reconsider that decision," Sorak said.

Kieran glanced at him inquisitively as they walked back toward the tents, but said nothing, waiting for him go on.

"For one thing, you have no evidence of my ability, or lack of same, to handle men," said Sorak. "For another, while I am not ungrateful, I have never stayed long in any one place. I have a wandering nature. It would seem to mean that you would want someone who offers . . . greater permanence."

Kieran smiled. "You need have no concern on that account," he said. "When it comes to the ability to handle men, the foremost quality required is character, and I am a good judge of that. After that, a man requires intelligence and thoughtfulness. When I asked you about the disposition of the guards, you observed, then you evaluated, and you considered before giving your reply. And I have noticed that you do not have the tendency to speak without thinking. As for permanence. . . ." He chuckled. "What is ever permanent in this world? My own appointment shall not last more than a year."

"Only a year?" said Sorak.

"That was the term of the contract," Kieran replied. "I insisted that it be subject to renegotiation every year, and they immediately agreed to it, which tells me they have no interest in a permanent appointment. For that matter, neither do I. But had they wanted me as a permanent commander for their house guard, they would have bargained for a much longer term. They also would never have agreed to my salary demands. I asked for one hundred thousand gold pieces a year."

Sorak stopped and stared at him with astonishment. "*One hundred thousand in gold?*" he said with amazement.

Kieran chuckled. "Yes, an obscene sum, isn't it? The terms of the contract are supposed to be secret. No soldier in the history of the world has ever been paid as much. I named the figure because I was certain they would never agree to it. Only they did, and I found that fascinating."

"Not to detract from your abilities," said Sorak, "but why would anyone pay such a sum?"

"That is the same question I asked myself," said Kieran. "Why? I have a well-known reputation, true, but only part of it is due to skill. Much of it was due to nothing more than luck. Even the best swordsman can fall in battle. I was merely fortunate enough to have survived more than my share. Ironic, when one considers that at that time in my life, I would have liked nothing better than to get myself killed. However, that is another story. I had retired to an estate outside the village of Salt View, and I had wealth enough to see me through the remainder of my days in reasonable comfort. I had no wish to return to the profession of arms."

"So what changed your mind? The temptation of the salary when they agreed to it?"

"No," said Kieran. "Once I had named the figure and they agreed to meet my price, it would have been bad form to turn them down. There was nothing to prevent me, of course, but my reputation was at stake. And then I was very curious. I felt certain that the House of Jhamri's agents were not empowered to agree to so outrageous a demand, even had they been inclined to do so, but when they agreed I realized that they had been instructed to secure my services regardless of the price. Oh, they tried to bargain, mind you, but when I stood firm, they finally agreed.

"Now, I may have won considerable fame in my profession, but no man is worth that kind of money. They knew it and I knew it. So, I had to ask myself what possible reason they would have for doing such a thing?" He glanced at Sorak. "What would you think if you were in my place?"

Sorak thought it over for a few moments as they walked past the cargo area and approached the tents. "The sum itself would have to be the reason," he said, finally. "The House of Jhamri must want it known that they will stop at nothing to hire the very best, and that they can afford to pay so high a sum. But then you said the terms of the contract were supposed to be kept secret." He shook his head. "It makes no sense."

"It does if they never intended it to be a secret," Kieran said. "Obviously, they plan to leak the information. That way, it will not be seen as ostentatious posturing on their part. But there is surely more to it than that. There has to be. Only for the life of me, I could not imagine what."

"And so you took the job to find out."

Kieran nodded. "I could not resist the mystery. And then, of course, there is the money."

"Yes, there is that," said Sorak with a grin. "You will be known as the highest paid mercenary in history."

"I have just enough vanity to like the sound of that," said Kieran, with a smile. "But something is surely afoot in Altaruk, an intrigue of some sort in which I am meant to play a key role. And it shall not take long to develop, because not even the House of Jhamri would pay me such a salary for a second year. Yes, something interesting is going on there, and I have to find out what it is."

"They say curiosity killed the kirre."

Kieran glanced down at his kirreskin breeches. "Yes, well, I plan to keep my own skin intact. It's possible that someone may want me for a trophy for some reason. I have made my share of enemies. But they will find this cat difficult to skin." He clapped Sorak on the shoulder. "Especially with a good fighter at my back."

"Ah, so now it becomes clear," said Sorak. "I am an insurance policy."

"Paid for by the House of Jhamri," Kieran said.

"But with the money they are paying me, I can easily afford to add a bonus. You keep your eyes and ears open, my friend, and watch my back. I will make it worth your while."

"Well, now you have me curious," said Sorak.

Kieran smiled. "I told you that we think alike."

SEVEN

It was almost midnight, and outside the mansion headquarters of the House of Ankhor, most of the town slept. There were a few gaming and pleasure houses that stayed open all night, mostly catering to mercenaries and travelers passing through on their way to one of the seven city-states of the Tablelands. But for the most part, the residents of Altaruk went to bed early and rose early. The desert nights were cold at this time of the year, and there were few people on the streets. The night seemed quiet and peaceful.

Ankhor stood out on the open, moonlit veranda outside his private quarters on the fourth floor, in the west wing of the mansion. As he gazed over the town, it struck him once again just how much it had grown the last few years. Without turning, he spoke to the dark-robed guest standing behind him, in the shadows.

"You know, as a boy, I hated growing up here," he said. "I dreamt of running away to one of the large cities, such as Tyr or Nibenay or Balic. Back then, Altaruk was little more than a fortress outpost in the middle of nowhere, at the tip of the estuary, a tiny, rough-hewn settlement sheltered by the mountains.

"But it was a choke point for caravans," Ankhor continued. "South from Urik, southeast from Tyr, toward Balic, Gulg, Nibenay, from Raam and Draj—all these caravans had to pass this outpost."

"It has grown quickly," said the dark-robed figure in a deep and throaty voice hoarse with age.

"And is growing still," said Ankhor, looking out over the town. "It went from being a miserable outpost fried by the sun and buffeted by windstorms to being a thriving village.

"My father—Lord Ankhor the Elder—saw the opportunities in Altaruk. His gaming house in Tyr bought him a merchant empire here—the House of Ankhor. He accomplished with grit and luck what young aristocrats did with blue blood. Aristocrats like the Jhamris."

"And so began the famous rivalry," the dark-robed figure said.

"Yes," said Ankhor, turning to face his guest. "It grew as Altaruk grew, a rivalry between a commoner and an aristocrat. And that rivalry drove all other merchant houses in Altaruk into penury. My father had won himself a peerage, but the Jhamris never allowed him to forget his humble beginnings.

"By the time I was born, Lord Jhamri had also sired a son. They had competed even in that, striving to bear the first heir. But fate mocked them, for both Father and Jhamri repeatedly fathered daughters. The Elder Jhamri had eight, by three different wives, and I have seven older sisters. My father's first wife gave him four daughters and died in childbirth with the last, and my mother gave him two more daughters before finally giving birth to me. I was given my father's name as a sign of pride in the achievement, but by then, Jhamri's third wife had already given birth to a son, a year earlier. And the two us were raised from childhood to loathe each other."

Ankhor turned to look out over the town once more, with a proprietary air. "Both founders are old and frail now, unable even to get around without assistance, but the old hatred still burns between them. It is all my father ever talks about. The old rivalry."

"You seem fond of it, too."

"Yes," said Ankhor, "we heirs both have taken over the management of our respective houses. But while the elder Jhamri was a shrewd and calculating trader, young Jhamri is merely arrogant and smug, confident in his superior wealth and position. He has never regarded the House of Ankhor as a serious threat.

"In part, that is because I have publicly played the part of the dissipated sensualist," Ankhor said, turning back to face his guest. "I am seen in gaming and pleasure houses, drinking excessively and spending lots of money. I sport with women of low class while young Jhamri has married well, taking to wife the daughter of Viscount Tomblador, cementing a firm alliance with that house. And while Jhamri immediately set about getting his young wife pregnant, to insure an heir, I have remained single and childless, apparently more interested in spending my father's wealth than building on it.

"So young Lord Jhamri regards me with condescension and contempt, thinking me weak and indolent. The alliance we have signed, with the House of Jhamri as the senior trading partner, has only furthered Jhamri's opinion. And that is exactly what I want him to think."

"To lull him into a false sense of security," the robed figure said, nodding.

"Precisely," said Ankhor, leaning back against the parapet. "I am still young, and there will be plenty of time to think about finding a suitable wife and starting a family . . . after I've destroyed my rival. And I shall settle for nothing less than that, total destruction. First, I'll topple his house and humiliate him, make him crawl to me on hands and knees."

"And then?"

"Then I will kill him." Ankhor said it plainly, simply, as if he were merely making an observation about the weather. Then he smiled, disarmingly. "When we were children, my loving sisters used to say our father was raising me as a serpent, feeding me on hatred and spite. They said it to tease me, but I always had a fondness for that metaphor. Serpents are sly and deadly. Serpents strike quickly and without warning. Serpents are survivors. I shall add the figure of a serpent to our standard after Jhamri is destroyed, to commemorate the event.

"So . . . are you satisfied as to my sincerity?"

The dark-robed figure stepped forward into the moonlight. The hood of the robe was thrown back, revealing a gaunt, fine-featured face, deeply lined with age, and the clean-shaven skull of a templar. Around her head was a thin, hammered gold chaplet bearing the royal crest of Nibenay, the Shadow King.

"His Majesty was concerned you might not follow through," she said. "That at the last moment, you might lack the necessary resolve."

Ankhor smiled. "Oh, please, Livanna," he said, "spare me the fiction that the Shadow King has the slightest interest in anything we do here."

He went past her, heading back inside through the open veranda doors. With a frown, she followed. He went over to a carved sideboard and poured them both some wine.

"I know perfectly well that Nibenay has ceased caring about anything but his metamorphosis," Ankhor continued. "We may be far removed from the centers of power here in the provinces, but I am not without my sources." He handed her an exquisitely crafted silver goblet. "The Shadow

King's senior templars have taken over the ruling of his realm. Nibenay has outgrown his cares about the city that bears his name. I will not venture to say just what he has grown into, but all things considered, I would much rather conduct business with his templars, whose concerns are more, shall we say . . . material?" He smiled and raised his goblet to her.

"You are impertinent," Livanna said.

"And ambitious," Ankhor added. "And given the scope of my ambition, along with the benefits that you can reap from it, I am sure my impertinence is something you can tolerate."

"To a point," Livanna said.

Ankhor raised his eyebrows and gave her a slight bow. "Well, I shall try to keep that in mind."

"Do," said Livanna curtly. "Our interests happen to coincide, but that does not make you indispensable."

"Altaruk shall one day be a defiler city, with me or without me, I know," said Ankhor. "I have seen the writing on the wall. However, that day will come much sooner with my help than without it. And you know that very well, or else you would not be here to insure that it is Nibenay who will rule in Altaruk rather than Hamanu of Urik or the Oba of Gulg." He smiled. "We both want an edge on the competition."

Ankhor took a sip of wine and settled comfortably into his chair, an action that would have been an insufferable affront to the senior templar in her home city. Her nostrils flared slightly, but otherwise, she showed no reaction.

"Let us understand each other, Livanna," Ankhor said. "I am not one of your subjects. At least, not yet. You need me now, and when Altaruk falls under the Shadow King's domain, you are going to need me even more. With Jhamri out of the way, I will control Altaruk's economy. The revenue Nibenay will receive from the House of Ankhor in taxes alone, to say nothing of the profits from investments, gratuities and outright bribes, will not be insignificant. No government can survive without the merchant houses. We both know that. At the same time, we both know that you could easily destroy me. I have no knowledge of magic, whereas you bear the awesome power of the Shadow King. But if anything were to happen to me, the House of Ankhor would collapse.

"Not even my minister of accounts knows all the intricacies of our dealings. My father is much too old to run the business now, and my sisters lack the necessary skills. Five of them have been profitably married off, and the remaining two are merely awaiting their turn. They have been raised to be fine ladies of distinction, not merchant traders.

So you see, Livanna, I am indispensable. I am the House of Ankhor. Stop trying to intimidate me with your powers and your lofty status as a templar and accept that we are equal partners in this venture, or else stop wasting my time. I could manage this without you. It would be inconvenient and would involve delays, but it could be done."

Livanna gave him a hard stare. "I am sure Lord Jhamri would be happy to make time for me."

"No doubt," said Ankhor. "If you like, I will have Lyanus arrange an appointment for you first thing in the morning."

For a moment, the templar said nothing, then she smiled. "No, I do not think that will be necessary," she said. "Are you like this in all your trade negotiations?"

"No," said Ankhor. "Sometimes, I find it necessary to be firm and uncompromising."

Livanna chuckled. "A serpent would, indeed, be an appropriate device for your standard. I will be pleased to report to our elder council that we have the right man in Altaruk."

"You had decided that before you arrived," Ankhor said. "So, shall we get down to business?"

"You have arranged for suitable quarters for our recent acquisition?"

"*My* recent acquisition," Ankhor corrected her. "The full amount of the purchase price came out of my pocket, as you will recall, and it was not inconsiderable."

"But are we not partners in this enterprise, as you just said? After all, I am providing the transportation, free of charge," Livanna responded, "and at a considerable cost in energy to myself."

Ankhor shrugged it off. "Which you will immediately recover by defoliating a garden or two or else killing some hapless drunk wandering through the streets."

"Nevertheless, I am saving you the time and

trouble it would take to arrange for transport all the way from Balic, and in secret, too. And then there is the matter of the time and effort I shall invest in the enterprise from this point on."

"Which will be offset by the intelligence I will provide, through contacts I have gone to great trouble and expense to develop and skilled agents I have placed in key positions." Ankhor frowned. "What is the point of all this dickering?"

Livanna smiled. "I merely wanted to see if I could out-bargain you. Apparently not."

Ankhor chuckled. "Not a bad effort, though. For a templar. But right now, I am more interested in seeing what you do best."

"Well, then . . . prepare yourself," Livanna said. She threw back her robe and raised her arms, shutting her eyes in concentration as she mustered her energies for the casting of the spell.

Ankhor felt a subtle change in the atmosphere of the room. It was nothing he could put his finger on, but he felt it, growing, raising goosebumps on his flesh and making the hairs on the back of his neck stand on end. He was no stranger to magic; he had seen it used before, but never on this level. The sorcerer kings imbued their templars with power, and even at this distance, the Shadow King's power was mighty.

Livanna had been trained since childhood, and she was now a very old woman. It was impossible to guess her age. She looked about seventy, but she was a senior templar, which meant she had to be at least twice that age or even older. She had not yet even cast her spell, and already the room was thrumming with energy.

Ankhor nervously moistened his lips and gripped the arms of his chair to keep his hands from trembling. As a trader, he had learned never to reveal uncertainty and always act as if he was in the superior position, but it was not until that moment that he truly understood just what kind of power Livanna had at her command. He swallowed hard. He could not afford to reveal weakness, but he felt afraid.

With her back to him, Livanna softly spoke the words of the spell, mumbling them under her breath. Ankhor could not make them out, and doubted he could have understood them even if fully audible. The old spell scrolls so jealously guarded by adepts were written in old languages, more guttural and sibilant, harsher to the modern ear. And the more complex the spell, the more complex the incantation.

As Livanna spoke the spell, the room became tenebrous and the air crackled with thaumaturgic discharges, jagged little bolts of energy that surrounded her, fine as spider webs. Ankhor had seen adepts cast spells before, both preservers and defilers, but Livanna was no ordinary adept. She was a senior templar of the Shadow King, with several human lifetimes worth of training and experience, and the power that flowed through her came from Nibenay himself. An ordinary adept would never have survived it.

A wind rose within the room, billowing her

robes and snuffing out the candles. Ankhor tightly gripped the arms of the chair, gritting his teeth as he felt all the nerve endings of his body start to tingle. Then bright blue bolts of thaumaturgic energy lanced out from Livanna's palms, converging on a spot about ten feet in front of her, in the center of the room.

Where the twin beams met, an aura formed, growing brighter and expanding slowly as Ankhor watched, shading his eyes against the glare. It was as if a hole had opened in the air, a brightly glowing tunnel through space and time, and through that tunnel came a figure, a dark silhouette surrounded by the pulsating blue aura that illuminated every corner of the room.

Ankhor felt his breath quicken as the figure stepped into the room. A large, powerful shape, it was outlined by the glare—a figure at least six and a half feet tall. And as the glow diminished and contracted, until it was no more than a fading, faintly sparkling aura surrounding the massive form, Ankhor's eyes slowly readjusted, focusing on the rippling, corded muscles of the naked figure.

"*Kah,*" he said softly.

It was a little over a year ago that he had first seen her fight in the arena of Balic. It had not been the first time he had witnessed gladiatorial combat, nor even the first time he had ever seen a mul fight in the arena, but it had been the first time he had ever seen a female of the breed. Female muls were rare. It was far easier to breed males, and both genders had to be specially bred, for all muls were born sterile.

An artificial crossbreed of dwarves and humans, muls did not occur in nature. Dwarves and humans could not breed together, and the secret of producing them had been discovered many years ago by a demented apothecary named Mulak. Working in his laboratory with vials and magnifiers and beakers, he had somehow found a way to stimulate the fertilization of a female dwarven egg by human sperm, producing a viable egg that he had then implanted in a human female slave, theorizing that a dwarven female would have been too small to bear the offspring. He was more than correct in his conclusion. The resulting birth was so traumatic that it killed the human mother, and ever since, no human female had ever survived the process that gave birth to the creatures that bore the name of their creator—muls.

The conception occurred in an apothecary's laboratory, and female human slaves then bore the child—if such it could be called—to term. Ankhor wondered what it must be like for the hapless women consigned to such a fate. Was it even possible that they could feel any spark of a maternal instinct toward the unnatural creatures quickening within them, knowing that their birth would bring about an agonizing death? He shuddered at the thought as he stared at the large figure looming before him in the darkness.

Livanna made a pass with her right hand, and the candles all reignited in the lamps, bringing light back into the room.

Ankhor swallowed hard as he stared at the coppery-golden skin of the mul standing before him. Her head was completely bald, accentuating the pointy, swept-back ears that lay close against her skull. Her eyes were yellow-gold, deeply sunken and hooded by a prominent ridge of brow. Her mouth was wide and thin-lipped, her chin slightly pointed, and her cheekbones high and unusually pronounced. Her nose was not as wide as that of most male muls, and it was blade straight. Though Ankhor had seen her fight before, he had never seen Kah up close, and he was surprised to find that she was beautiful—in a terrifying way.

Her shoulders were almost twice as broad as his, and her chest thick with muscle, making her breasts look small. She had almost no fat on her at all. Her powerful back muscles fanned out from her sides like wings, accentuating a narrow and extremely muscular waist. Her abdominal muscles stood out in sharp relief, and her long arms were corded with thick muscle. Her thighs and calves looked as if someone had taken a chisel to them. She lowered her head and went down to one knee before him. She did not speak, for she could not. She had been born mute.

It felt strange to see her kneel like that before him. It was perfectly right and proper, of course. He was an aristocrat, after all, and a high-ranking member of the merchant class, and she was but a lowly slave. He had bought her, and she was now his property. But she was a magnificent creature with a powerful presence, and he had seen her kill a dozen men in the arena.

The first time he had seen her, he had wanted to possess her. Not sexually, for she did not appeal to him that way, but the way one wanted to possess a fine crodlu mount or an exquisitely crafted weapon. To own a thing like that would confer not only status, but power. She was a legend in the arena of Balic, and when he saw her fight, he immediately understood why.

Kah fought with a savagery unlike anything he had ever seen. It was not the savagery of a berserker, but that of a predatory beast. Her opponents were not merely antagonists, they were prey, and when she stalked them in the arena, it was like watching an animal on the hunt.

By the time he saw her, she had already firmly established her reputation, and she no longer fought in matched pairs. She always faced several opponents, sometimes half a dozen or more, and despite being outnumbered, she struck fear into them all. And she exulted in the kill. She enjoyed killing the way most men enjoyed sex. It was both a pleasure and a release for her, and a feeling of conquest.

Ankhor had immediately sent his agents to enter into negotiations for her purchase. At the time, he had not yet formulated the plan he had in mind for her; he only knew he wanted to own her, like a dangerous pet. The arenamasters of Balic had not wanted to sell. She represented a huge investment for them, not only in terms of the original purchase from the breeder who produced her, but in all the years of training they had given her. And she was their most popular attraction. The citizens of Balic packed the arena to see Kah fight, and they had cheered themselves hoarse with her every victory. The arenamasters already had a plan for her. If she survived, and there was little question that she would, she would probably earn her freedom, and she could then become a trainer, producing skilled fighters for their games.

But Ankhor wanted her, and whenever Ankhor wanted something, he would stop at nothing to possess it. Even given the most liberal of estimates, he had paid easily ten times her worth, finally submitting an offer the arenamasters were unable to refuse. He had paid for her both in cash and stock in the House of Ankhor, thereby assuring a comfortable retirement for her masters.

Now, she was his, and it seemed incongruous to see this powerful, savage creature kneeling before him, her gaze lowered shyly, awaiting his command. It made Ankhor feel powerful.

Livanna stood leaning on a table, stooped over slightly and breathing hard. The effort of the spell had taken a lot out of her. An ordinary wizard would never have been able to accomplish it. She had magically teleported Kah all the way from Balic. It had taken extensive preparation, and she had needed to obtain samples of Kah's skin and hair in order to direct the spell. Ankhor had his agents obtain fingernail parings and loin hair from Kah, since muls were hairless everywhere else. All had been accomplished in great secrecy. No one save Ankhor and Livanna knew of Kah's arrival, or of Ankhor's purchase. The arenamasters of Balic had been paid handsomely for their silence.

"Rise, Kah," Ankhor said.

She stood, towering over him.

"Your days of fighting in the arena are finished," Ankhor said, and was gratified by the flicker of disappointment in the mul gladiator's eyes. "But never fear, I have more entertaining sport in mind for you."

She cocked her head at him inquisitively.

"Templar Livanna will explain all to you," said Ankhor. "You are to do her bidding. Understand?"

Kah nodded once.

"Ankhor, I must recuperate," Livanna said hoarsely.

Ankhor got up from his chair and walked over to the fireplace. He pressed a concealed stud behind the mantlepiece, and a section of the wall beside the fireplace swung away, revealing a secret passage.

"Take the concealed staircase and turn right at the bottom," he said. "Follow the tunnel until it branches. Take the right branch. It will lead you outside the compound and into a hidden basement of one of my warehouses. I have had chambers prepared there for you. They are not luxurious, but I think you will find them comfortable. Thereafter, whenever you leave, go back to that point where the tunnel branches. Turning left will take you back here. Continuing straight ahead will lead you to the surface, to a hidden door inside an alleyway. Can you remember that?"

Livanna nodded.

"Good. From now on, I leave things in your entirely capable hands. You know what must be done. Do not return here except after the midnight hour. On the opposite side of this hidden door, you will find a large lever and a small one. The large lever controls the door. The small one controls this obsidian statue here on the mantelpiece. You will find a tiny peephole in the door. Always check it first. If I am not alone, or if I am not present, pull down on the small lever, and the statue will turn to the right. That way, I will know you wish to see me, and I will return here at midnight the next day. Any questions?"

"No," Livanna said. "It seems you have taken adequate precautions."

"Make certain you do likewise," Ankhor said. He went over to the sideboard and picked up a small scroll. "Here is your first set of instructions. You may start tonight."

Livanna took the scroll from him and beckoned to the mul. They went through the secret passageway, and Ankhor closed the door behind them. He took a deep breath of satisfaction. Now, it would begin.

EIGHT

Sorak awoke with a start. He sat up and glanced around quickly, not knowing what had awakened him. It was several hours before dawn. The camp was perfectly still as he opened the tent flap, stepped outside, and looked around. The fires had burned down to embers, save for the watchfires tended by the guards around the cargo area, directly in front of him. Except for the quiet sounds of their conversation, nothing seemed amiss. So what had awakened him so suddenly?

He was aware of a strange vertiginous sensation, and he felt a little lightheaded. Whatever it was, it had snapped him awake with a jolt, and he was apparently feeling its aftereffects. It hadn't been a nightmare. He had been sleeping soundly for a change, after a long day on the trail. He rubbed his forehead, moist with sweat.

"Sorak?" Ryana poked her head out of their tent. "What is it? Is something wrong?"

He frowned, shaking his head. "I don't know," he said in a puzzled tone. "Something woke me up, but I have no idea what it was. It was as if—" Suddenly, the jolt came once again, even stronger this time, and he staggered, as though struck from behind. For a moment, his vision swam, and he shook his head and blinked to clear it. When his gaze focused again, the campsite was gone.

He stood motionless, feeling confused and disoriented. One moment, he was looking at the caravan tents and the watchfires by the cargo, and the next, he was standing in the middle of a street in an unfamiliar town.

Neat rows of one and two-story adobe buildings lined both sides of the dirt street, which curved away from him around a bend. The time of day had not changed, but everything else had. He stood frozen to the spot, startled and unable to comprehend what had happened. It was as if he had suddenly been transported to another place.

He spun around, looking for Ryana, but though she had stood just behind him a moment earlier, she wasn't there. The tent was gone, as well. What he saw instead was the dark mouth of a narrow alleyway between two buildings . . . and just inside the alleyway, he saw a large figure standing in the shadows, partially concealed from view.

From behind him came the sounds of footsteps. He turned around again and saw another figure, wrapped in a dark cloak and walking down the hard-packed dirt street, heading directly toward him. The stranger's path would take him right past Sorak, the mouth of the alleyway, and the shadowy figure waiting in ambush.

Sorak opened his mouth to speak, to warn the approaching man, but no sound came forth. The man kept on walking steadily, right toward him. He gave no sign of being aware of Sorak's presence, just as he was completely unaware of the ambusher. He was only several feet away now and coming straight at him. Again, Sorak tried to speak, but no sound came out. The man in the cloak passed right by him, mere inches away, but apparently without seeing him. And as he drew even with the alley, it happened.

A powerful arm snaked out and grabbed the man's cloak, jerking him back into the shadows of the alley. Sorak heard a startled gasp of surprise, followed by a brief cry, and then the sickening crunch of the man's spine being snapped.

The body collapsed to the ground, lifeless. No, it hadn't simply collapsed, the killer had *thrown* it, tossing it into the street at the entrance to the alleyway. The murderer stood over the hapless victim, but Sorak could not see the killer clearly. He was dressed in a long, ankle-length black cloak with a voluminous hood that completely concealed his features. The killer reached inside his cloak, and Sorak saw something white flutter down on the body. A veil.

Abruptly, the killer turned, and Sorak thought

he was about to see his face, but his vision blurred again, as if he were looking through shimmering heat waves, and the peculiar falling sensation came over him once more.

Sorak shook his head and blinked, and when his vision came back into focus, he saw several guards sitting around the watchfire, talking quietly among themselves. He was back at the caravan campsite, and someone was shaking him.

"Sorak! *Sorak!*"

It was Ryana. He turned toward her, a confused expression on his face.

"Sorak, what's wrong?"

"I . . . I don't know," he said slowly. He shook his head to clear it. "What just happened?"

"You seemed to go into a trance," Ryana replied, looking at him with concern. "You stumbled and grabbed your head, as if you had been struck. You looked as if you were about to fall, only you didn't. You simply stood there, motionless, staring off into the distance. I spoke to you, but you acted as if you couldn't hear me. Your eyes were open, but it was as if you couldn't see me, either."

"I was standing right here all this time? I didn't . . . go anywhere?"

She stared at him, puzzled. "What are you talking about?"

He took a deep breath and let it out slowly. "I just saw a man killed," he said.

"*What?* Where?"

"I . . . don't know," he replied, frowning with confusion. "One moment, I was standing here, looking at the watchfire, and then the next . . ." He told her what he had seen. "It was like a dream, only I was awake . . . or was I?"

"You had a vision," said Ryana.

He frowned. "How can that be? I am not villichi. I do not have the gift of Sight."

"One does not have to be villichi to have the Sight," Ryana said. "Anyone can have the talent, but it is very rare, even among villichi. I have never had it, nor did any of the other sisters, but Mistress Varanna said she had it sometimes, though she could not control it. She said no one can. It simply comes upon you. You saw something that has happened somewhere else . . . or is about to happen."

"I tried to warn the man," he said, "but I could not speak."

"You were not there," she said. "You couldn't have warned him. It was a vision. You were right here all this time."

He shook his head. "But it makes no sense. How could something like this happen all of a sudden? I thought people who had the Sight were born with it."

Ryana shook her head. "No, it comes when a child starts to mature."

"But I am not a child."

"No, but you *have* changed. The spell that took away your inner tribe may have left something of them behind . . . or perhaps given you something else. We both know what you were, but there is as yet no way of telling what you have become."

Sorak frowned with confusion. "Perhaps, but if

my grandfather had bestowed the gift of Sight upon me, why wouldn't he have told me? How long was I . . . gone?"

"Only a moment," she said.

"It seemed longer." He rubbed his forehead. It ached slightly. "I don't know what it means."

Ryana's eyes grew wide, and she gasped. "Sorak . . . *look!*"

She was staring at him, pointing at his waist. He looked down.

Galdra.

The broken blade was tucked into his belt. He drew it out, staring at it with astonishment. As he touched the silver wire-wrapped hilt, a faint, sparkling aura of blue thaumaturgic energy crackled briefly around the blade.

"How can this be?" he said with wonder. "You saw me throw it into the pool back at the oasis!"

She nodded.

"We both saw it sink!"

She nodded again. "It has come back to you," she said. "It is an omen."

"Of what?" he said, with dismay. "I don't *want* the cursed thing!" He tossed it aside on the ground.

Ryana picked it up. "That won't do any good," she said. "You threw it into a bottomless pool and it came back to you. What makes you think you can simply throw it away now?"

"I don't understand any of this," said Sorak. "I thought the spell was broken."

"Broken it may be," Ryana said, "but there is

still magic in the blade. Apparently, much more than you knew." She offered it back to him.

"No," he said, shaking his head. "I don't want it."

"Take it," she insisted.

"You take it."

"It is not for me to carry," she replied. "Galdra was meant for you."

"Then leave it. Throw the damned thing away."

"If you really want me to, I will," she replied, "but I'll wager it will only come back to you again. It served you well, Sorak. It was wrong of you to dispose of it in the first place. Galdra is part of your destiny. That much is clear."

"What does it *want* from me?" he asked irritably.

Ryana shook her head. "I do not know that it is capable of wanting anything. It does not live. It merely *is*."

"It has to be the Sage," said Sorak, with a grimace. "He must be responsible for this."

"Whether he is or not," Ryana said, "it seems you are stuck with it." She offered him the blade again. "Take it. Things like this do not occur without a reason."

"But why must they happen to *me?*" he asked, throwing his arms out in exasperation.

"Because you are Sorak, and it is your fate. Mistress Varanna knew that when she gave you the blade."

Sorak sighed and took the broken blade from her reluctantly. "All it brings is trouble."

"What sort of trouble?" asked a voice from

behind them.

They turned to see a figure coming toward them, silhouetted against the light from the watch-fire behind him.

"It is only I, Edric the Bard," he said as he came closer. "I did not mean to intrude. It seems that I was not the only one who could not sleep tonight." His gaze fell on the blade. "What have you there? A dagger?" He held his hands up, palms out. "There is no need for that, my friend. I am unarmed, as you can see."

Sorak glanced down at the blade in his hand. "Sorry," he said, tucking it away into his belt. "It was not meant to threaten you." He wished he had his cloak to cover it, but he had left it back inside the tent. He saw Edric staring intently at the blade.

"You carry a broken sword?" asked Edric. "Why?"

Sorak shrugged, wishing the bard would go away. "It has sentimental value to me."

"It looks like steel!" said Edric, still staring at the broken sword in Sorak's belt. "And those are elvish runes upon the blade, are they not?"

Sorak was growing impatient. The last thing he wanted was to pursue this conversation. "Are all you bards so curious?" he asked in a surly tone.

"Forgive me, I did not mean to pry," said Edric, placating. "But there is an old legend about a sword made of elven steel, with runes upon the blade—"

"It is merely a broken sword and nothing more," said Sorak. "It is an heirloom of my family, scarcely worth the price of a few drinks now that it is broken, but I have an attachment to it." Or, more to the point, it has an attachment to *me,* he thought.

"How is Cricket?" asked Ryana to change the subject.

"Sound asleep, my lady," said Edric. "She is not accustomed to riding such long distances and was complaining that her legs and seat were sore."

"She seemed fit enough to me," Ryana said.

"Well," said Edric, "perhaps one uses different muscles for dancing than for riding." He shrugged. "I know little of such things. She will doubtless be a bit stiff in the morning, and there will be some soreness, but another day or so and she should work it out. In the meantime, I can put up with her whining and complaining." He grinned. "Bards are accustomed to that sort of thing, you know."

"Perhaps I could be of some assistance," said Ryana. "I have some skill at healing."

"I am certain she would be grateful for your help, my lady," Edric said with a slight bow. "I will pass on your kind offer. Well, I have intruded on your time enough. There is yet some time until dawn, and I think I shall go stretch out for a while before the camp is abustle." He shook his head. "Never could get used to keeping normal hours. Good night to you, or perhaps I should say good morning. Well, you know what I mean."

He gave them a slight bow and left.

Sorak scowled at his retreating form. "I don't like that elf," he said in a low voice.

"He seems harmless enough," Ryana said.

"He has a duplicitous streak," said Sorak. "He recognized Galdra, all right. He knew exactly what it was. It was as if he dared me to deny it."

"And deny it you did," she said. "So who was being duplicitous?"

"I had no wish to get into a long, drawn out debate about the legend of the Sword of Alaron and the Crown of Elves," said Sorak. "That was why I tried to dispose of Galdra in the first place."

"Well, he did not press you on the subject."

"Only because you diverted him. But he was rather easily diverted, wasn't he?"

"Maybe it's my charm," Ryana said with a smile.

"I doubt your charms would work upon the likes of him," said Sorak. "It was no accident Cricket picked him to ride with. He's probably the only male in the caravan that she can trust not to take advantage."

"Including you?" Ryana asked innocently.

"You know what I mean," said Sorak. "Still, there's something about him that bothers me. And I am not referring to his manner or his tastes."

"What then?"

Sorak shook his head. "I don't know. I wish I still had the Guardian to help me look into his mind and find out what he's really thinking."

"You really do distrust him, don't you?"

Sorak nodded. "I do not think I would want to turn my back on that one."

"Then maybe you should follow your intuition," said Ryana. "A part of you *was* the Guardian, remember. Maybe you cannot read his mind, but you seem to sense something about him."

"And you do not?"

She shrugged. "He seems a bit elaborate, but then he's a bard."

Sorak shook his head. "It's been an ill-omened night, all around," he said. "And I understand none of what is happening. I only know I do not like it."

"Well, there's no point in trying to go back to sleep," Ryana said. "Why don't we take a stroll around the camp and talk about it while we stretch our legs a bit? We have a long ride ahead of us."

"I have a feeling there will be trouble before it's through," said Sorak. "And something tells me Edric will be part of it." He sighed. "I just wish I knew *why* I felt that way, and why I had that vision. I used to wonder what it would be like not to be a tribe of one, to be just one individual, like everybody else. Well, now I am. And I've never felt so much uncertainty."

Ryana smiled. "You'll get used to it," she said. "But you must stop thinking that you've been diminished somehow by the loss of your inner tribe. They may not be with you anymore, but they were a part of you for a long time, and you shared what they knew. Remember what they taught you. And remember what you learned back at the convent. You are almost villichi, and that is no small thing."

"No, it's not," he agreed. "Thank you for reminding me."

She put her arm around him. "You're welcome. Now, tell me again about that vision, and we'll see if we can't make some sense of it."

* * * * *

Edric did not return to his tent, as he had said he would. Instead, he furtively headed away from the cluster of tents toward the rear of the encampment. There were no guards posted back there and no fires lit, since the banks of the estuary guarded that edge of the camp. Silt monsters did not venture ashore, and the camp was well away from any habitation of giants. Neither would desert raiders attack across the silt. Raiders did not use boats; they depended on speed, and boats were slow. So all that lay in wait along the estuary shore were deep shadows in the moonlight, and as Edric approached the silt, one of those shadows moved.

Edric stopped. "Shadows have talons."

"Talons have claws," came the low response.

Edric glanced quickly over his shoulder, then hurried toward the small rock outcropping from which the voice had come. A tall, lean, dark shape rose from the ground beside the outcropping. It was an elf, dressed all in black, from head to toe. Black boots, black breeches, black tunic covered with a smooth black breastplate of kank armor, black gloves, black veil, and black hooded cloak. His sword was sheathed in a black leather scabbard, as were his knives, and the hilts of all the weapons were black-stained pagafa wood. Even on a moonlit night, he could blend so artfully with the shadows from which his tribe took its name, the Shadows. Not even Edric would have seen him had he not moved, and if Edric had not spoken the proper phrase identifying himself, he would have been instantly, efficiently, and silently killed.

"You had no trouble getting past the guards on the flank outpost?" asked Edric softly.

The black-clad elf snorted with derision. "You must be joking. I came so close to one of them that I could have reached out and touched him, but he was none the wiser."

"When is the attack planned?" Edric asked.

"The night after the caravan leaves Grak's Pool," the black-clad elf replied. "Will they tarry long?"

Edric shook his head. "I doubt it. This captain is in a hurry to reach Altaruk. They're carrying large profits from their trip to Balic, in addition to a new shipment of cargo, and the captain's new superior is among the passengers. He is a mercenary named Kieran, journeying to Altaruk to accept a post as captain of the Jhamri House Guard."

"Does he bring troops with him?"

Edric shook his head. "No, there is only the normal complement of caravan guards and roustabouts."

The black-clad elf smirked. "They shouldn't be much trouble."

"Watch out for Kieran," Edric said. "He knows his business. You cannot miss him. He's a tall, strapping blond man who dresses in rare hides. Do not dismiss him for his flamboyant costume. He's deadly. I've seen him fight."

"A well-aimed arrow will put an end to that."

"Just be careful of him. But there's something else, perhaps even more important," Edric said. "Among the passengers is an elfling who rides with a villichi priestess."

"An *elfling?*"

"A half-breed," Edric said. "Elf and halfling."

"Disgusting! I did not know such an abomination was even possible!"

"Never mind that," Edric said. "His name is Sorak. Or so he styles himself."

"The Nomad?" said the black-clad elf.

"He may have adopted the persona from the ballad, for reasons of his own," said Edric, "but he carries a sword that has been broken, so that a little less than half its length remains. I saw it. It is made of steel."

"Steel!"

"And engraved with elven runes," said Edric, "though I was not close enough to read them."

"Are you saying it is *Galdra?*" the black-clad elf asked with disbelief.

"At the very least, it seems meant to pass as Galdra, though when I questioned him about it, indirectly, he said the blade was merely an old heirloom of his family, something he carries for sentimental reasons only."

"But you said it was broken."

"That could be part of his ruse," said Edric, "to explain why the enchantment does not work. According to the legend, if the Sword of Alaron is touched by a defiler, it will shatter and the enchantment will be broken."

"And the prophecy with it, I should think," the Shadow replied.

"Perhaps," said Edric. "Or perhaps not. The legend is vague upon that point."

"So this Nomad is passing himself off as the so-called Crown of Elves?"

Edric shook his head. "No, not at present, anyway. He appears to be posing as a mercenary. Perhaps he really is, I do not know. He seems to have struck up a friendship with this Kieran. But then, that would be logical, if he intends to strike a bargain with the House of Jhamri."

"What sort of bargain?"

"I am not sure," said Edric, "but I have an idea. He joined the caravan in South Ledopolus, as I did, but he came from across the estuary. I suspect he may have come from Bodach."

"Bodach!"

"Both he and the priestess carry heavy packs," said Edric. "I have not had an opportunity to examine them, but I believe it's possible they may contain some of the lost treasure."

"That would be very interesting if it were true. What makes you think so?"

"A hunch," said Edric. "I have heard some stories of this Nomad's exploits. And if those stories are true, it may be possible he has discovered the secret of the lost treasure's location. He may have gotten his hands on a small part of it, but he could never hope to remove it all alone. That would take an army."

"An army of elves, perhaps?"

"Exactly," Edric said, nodding. "And what better way to recruit such an army from among the desperate elves and half-elves of the cities than to pose as the embodiment of one of their most cherished myths? The Crown of Elves will lead an army to secure the lost treasure of Bodach and finance the coming kingdom."

"And where does the House of Jhamri fit into all of this?"

"What better custodian for the lost treasure? Who better to invest it for him?"

"Ah," the Shadow replied. "So he brings the treasure to the Jhamris, cuts them in for a share to convert it into ready assets, and then disappears with his profits."

"Those were my thoughts, precisely," Edric said.

"A bold and risky venture," said the Shadow. "Aside from the risks involved in stealing Bodach's treasure, if he proclaims himself the Crown of Elves, pretender or not, he still risks the wrath of the sorcerer kings, who would see him as a threat."

"Not if he moved quickly enough," said Edric. "If he absconded with the treasure, there would be no elvish king to threaten anyone. Merely a bold rascal who had cheated his gullible followers and then disappeared."

"A fascinating theory," said the Shadow. "But you have no proof that this is what he plans."

"Why else would he adopt so dangerous a pose?

The rewards would have to be significant. Either way, the talonmaster must be told. If the Nomad can be taken alive, we can get the truth from him. If he really does know where the lost treasure of Bodach can be found—"

"Then we can take it for ourselves," the Shadow finished. "I will pass on what you've told me. The talonmaster will decide what is to be done. Meanwhile, see what else you can learn. Do they suspect you?"

Edric snorted. "Not a chance. I have laid the groundwork for my part too well. They all discount me as an effete, limp-wristed bard en route to Altaruk to sing songs. I have even taken up with a gorgeous half-elf dancing girl, who shares a tent with me and treats me like an older sister. She does not suspect the truth, of course, and it helps maintain the fiction. However, it is all I can do to keep my hands off her. And that is another thing. She is not to be harmed in any way. Her name is Cricket, and she may have fallen on hard times, but she was tribal once."

"I will make it known," the Shadow replied with a smile. "So, Edric, have you lost your heart, then? I did not think you even had one."

"Keep your jests to yourself, little brother. If you saw her, you would understand."

"No doubt. I am looking forward to it."

"Well, I'd best get back," said Edric. "It will soon be sunrise, and we will making ready to get under way. I will look for you at Grak's Pool tomorrow night."

"Until tomorrow then, my brother."

They clasped arms, and Edric headed back toward camp. He glanced back over his shoulder once. His brother had disappeared. Edric smiled. No one moved as silently or as swiftly as the Shadows. And no one was more adept at espionage, assassination or intrigue.

The Crown of Elves? The elfling half-breed who called himself the Nomad would soon discover what a real elf was, not the pathetic, weak-willed elves who lived among the humans in their cities or the half-savage desert wanderers the remaining tribal elves had now become, but elves who still retained the former glory of their ancestors and bowed to no one save the grand master of the talons. The Shadows would teach the Nomad a lesson he would not soon forget—assuming he survived it.

NINE

It was about two hours before sunset when they reached Grak's Pool, a small oasis roughly midway between South Ledopolus and Altaruk. For a "fast" caravan, their progress seemed annoyingly slow to Sorak. If this was how a fast caravan traveled, he could easily do without the experience of a slow one.

Of course, he reminded himself, it was an unusually large caravan. A smaller one would have made much better time. However, they would still have needed to stop several hours before sunset to make camp and unload all the cargo, then feed the kanks and crodlu while the cookfires were lit and the guard outposts were established. And while it wouldn't have taken a smaller caravan quite so long to get started in the morning, they would still have needed to take down all the tents and roll them up, then load them with the cargo, take a head count of the guards and roustabouts to make sure none had deserted in the night—not that there was anything to be done about it if they had—get the kanks fed once again and line up the formation, then send outriders ahead before moving out behind them. And then, of course, there was the midday break. . . .

They averaged between fifteen and twenty miles a day, depending on the terrain. Good time, all things considered. The caravan route was not a road, of course; it was merely familiar terrain. Yet, in the Athasian desert, the exact features of the terrain were never quite the same from one trip to another. Windstorms and monsoons worked changes on the landscape, and an area that had been easily passable three weeks earlier could be crisscrossed with windblown dunes or washes. Rarely did their course take them in a straight line. Considering his task, the caravan captain was doing an outstanding job. Even Kieran seemed impressed, though his presence was doubtless a strong incentive for achievement.

Grak's Pool was more than merely an oasis. According to *The Wanderer's Journal,* it was a vital stop along the caravan route, the only place between South Ledopolus and Altaruk where they could take on water. But the water wasn't free.

There was a settlement of sorts at the oasis, a large mud-brick fortress that was home to about fifty mercenaries under the command of an enterprising half-elf named Grak, who had established the remote stronghold and laid claim to the oasis. The number of mercenaries in residence at the fortress varied; they came and went. Grak did not sign them to any contracts. Neither did he pay them. What Grak provided was a haven for fighting men of all types and descriptions, a place where they could find free accommodations, albeit of a rough sort, without any questions asked. And since his stronghold controlled an oasis on a busy caravan route, it attracted mercenaries in search of work, as well as criminals on the run from the authorities in one city or another. Grak cared nothing about who his men were or where they came from. Whether soldier or outlaw—sometimes both—they were welcome to stay as long as they accepted his authority. But anyone who challenged that authority found that the penalties could be draconian in the extreme.

As they passed through the heavy wooden gates in the outer wall, Kieran rode up beside Sorak and Ryana.

"If you have anything of value, such as weapons, coins, or jewels, keep it close to hand," he cautioned them. "I shouldn't think we would have anything to fear from Grak's men, but there are those among them who are light-fingered. And the caravan guard will be too busy keeping an eye on the cargo to spare much attention for the passengers. If anything is stolen from you, complaints here will be of no avail."

"Thank you, we'll keep that in mind," said

Sorak.

"There will be some limited accommodations in the fortress for the passengers," said Kieran. "If you wish to bathe or sleep in a bed rather than your bedroll, it will cost you a copper or two, but I'd advise against it. The attendants will doubtless go through your clothing and possessions while you bathe, unless you keep them within sight, and even that is no guarantee. Some of these people could steal the hair right out of your nose. And the beds are liable to be lice-ridden."

"How charming," said Ryana. "What's the alternative?"

"We will make camp by the pool, within the outer walls, and pitch our tents and light our cookfires. There is a tavern in the main building of the fortress, and we can pay it a visit if you like, but I would recommend keeping one hand on your purse and another on your weapon. If you like, you may leave your packs within the captain's tent. He will remain within the camp along with the guards on duty. Your belongings will be safe with him. It would be a great embarrassment to him if I asked him to watch your things and something turned up missing."

"Yes, I imagine so," said Sorak with a smile. "But perhaps it would be best if we simply remained within the camp."

"Suit yourself," said Kieran, "but you may find it interesting. I intend to go pay my respects to old Grak. I haven't seen the rogue in years, and he's an entertaining scoundrel. Few things go on in these parts that he is not aware of. He will be sure to have all the latest news from Altaruk."

"Well, in that case, you should go," Ryana said. "I'll remain in the camp with our things. I would just as soon rest, anyhow."

After they made camp, Sorak accompanied Kieran to the main building of the fortress. It was situated on a small rise, just above the pool of the oasis in the center of the walled enclosure. It was a large, rectangular, three-story structure, like an elongated keep, constructed of roughly mortared brick with four open sentry towers at each corner of the building. The narrow, rectangular windows had heavy wooden shutters, and the large front doors were made of thick wooden planks. It was the crudest of workmanship, but appeared very sound and solid.

The main hall of the keep had been turned into a tavern, with crudely made wood tables and benches placed all around the large, open chamber. The floor was rough, mortared stone and there a long bar lined the far left side of the room. Torches in blackened sconces and thick candles on the tables lit the place. Scantily-clad human and half-elf serving wenches circulated through the crowded room, carrying trays of drinks and food. Kieran stopped one of them and asked for Grak. The half-elf server pointed out his table, set against the back wall.

Grak was seated among a group of travelers and mercenaries, holding court. He was an immense man, especially for someone with elven blood.

Elves were usually tall and lean, but Grak was part human, and the most human thing about him was clearly his appetite. He stood about six feet tall and weighed at least three hundred pounds, but there was a solid layer of muscle underneath the fat. His arms were thick and powerful, his chest barrel shaped, his shoulders wide and muscular, his neck thick and strong. Most half-elves could not grow facial hair, but Grak had a luxuriant mustache, the ends of which dangled below his chin. He had sharply arched eyebrows like an elf, but they were uncharacteristically thick and bushy. His iron gray hair hung down almost to his waist in two thick braids from below a well-worn, wide-brimmed leather hat of janx hide. He wore a old brown leather vest over his bare chest, which was covered with gray hairs and festooned with amulets. He barked out a sharp laugh when he saw them approaching.

"Hah! Look what the wind blew in!"

"Hello, Grak, you old scoundrel," Kieran said in a friendly tone. "You grow uglier each time I see you."

"And you grow prettier," said Grak good-naturedly. "You were but a fetching girl, and now you've grown into a fine and handsome woman! Put a dress on you, and you've got a strapping countess! Gith's blood, it's good to see you! Sit down, sit down. Make room, you dolts, make room for Kieran of Draj!"

At the mention of his name, the other mercenaries at the table gazed at him with interest and respect. As they sat down, Grak flagged down a serving wench.

"Drusilla! Bring two tankards of ale for my friends!"

"Water for me, please," Sorak said.

"Water?" Grak said, scandalized. "*Water?*"

"If you don't mind," said Sorak. "I have no taste for ale or wine."

"Strange company you keep," Grak said to Kieran. He turned back to Drusilla. "Water for this youngster, who's not learned to drink like a man."

"He may not drink like a man, but he fights like one," said Kieran. "He slew two giants, one with a bow, one with his blade. This is Sorak, my new lieutenant. Sorak, meet Grak, an old compatriot of mine."

They clasped forearms across the table. Grak's hand was a vice. "Sorak, eh?" He looked him over. "You have elvish blood, but uncommon features for a half-elf."

"That is because I am an elfling," Sorak said. "My mother was a elf, my father a halfling."

"So. I have heard of only one such rarity. You must be the one called the Nomad."

"That is the elvish meaning of my name," said Sorak.

"The word is you're a troublemaker," Grak said. "Is that true?"

"I suppose it would depend on who relates the word," Sorak replied.

Grak chuckled. "Well spoken. I see you've found

yourself a lieutenant with a reputation, Kieran."

"So it would seem," Kieran replied, "though I was not aware of that when we first met. I hired him because of his abilities. Unlike you, Grak, my friend does not regale everybody within earshot with tales of his exploits."

"Hah! You should have more respect for your elders, stripling," Grak replied. He turned to Sorak. "They say you bear a most unusual blade," he said. "Might I see it?"

Sorak hesitated, then drew the sword he had been given by Valsavis and placed it on the table before him. Grak glanced at it and frowned. "That is not the blade I heard described," he said.

Sorak simply shrugged.

"It is the only one I have ever seen him carry," Kieran said.

Grak pursed his lips, thoughtfully. "Well, perhaps the stories were mistaken," he said.

"I have yet to hear any of these stories," Kieran said, glancing at Sorak.

"I thought you said a man's past was of no consequence to you," said Sorak.

"True enough," said Kieran. "But I must admit to being curious."

"You have no other blade?" asked Grak.

Sorak shrugged again. "Only short ones," he replied truthfully, feeling Galdra tucked into his belt at his side, concealed by his cloak.

"Hmm," said Grak. "Strange. My sources are seldom wrong."

"Speaking of your sources," Kieran said, "what

do you hear of the goings on in Altaruk?"

"You have business there?"

"I have accepted the post of captain of the house guard for Jhamri," Kieran said.

Grak raised his eyebrows with surprise. "You? Isn't that a bit beneath your capabilities? Besides, I had heard you were retired."

"Their offer was most generous," said Kieran. "I found I was unable to refuse."

"They must have paid you a king's ransom," Grak replied. He frowned. "Now why would they want to do that, I wonder? They could easily have found men qualified for such a post for much less money than they must have offered you."

"I was wondering the same thing myself."

"Curious," said Grak. "I cannot imagine why they would have wanted you for such a post except for bragging rights. And Lord Jhamri scarcely needs to brag. His recent partnership agreement with the House of Ankhor, bringing that house into subservience to his, makes his the most powerful merchant house in Altaruk, and one of the largest on the Tablelands."

"Lord Ankhor is now a partner with the House of Jhamri?" Sorak said.

"A junior partner, yes."

"I see," said Sorak.

"What is it?" Kieran asked, noting the expression on his face.

Sorak cleared his throat. "I think it would be wise if you found yourself another second-in-command."

Kieran frowned. "Why? You have some grievance against Lord Ankhor?"

"More likely, he has a grievance against me," Sorak replied. "We had occasion to meet several times before. The first time, I saved him from being cheated by a cardsharp in a Tyrian gaming house. But the last time we met, I stole a princess from his caravan."

"Hah! A daughter of the Royal House of Nibenay!" said Grak, slamming his fist down onto the table. "That story is true, then!"

"You did *what?*" asked Kieran. He glanced from Sorak to Grak and back again.

"Have you never heard the Ballad of the Nomad?" Grak asked him. "Where have you been? It is being sung by every elven bard across the Tablelands!"

"I'd like to find the one who sang it first," said Sorak with a grimace.

"How goes this ballad?" Kieran asked.

"I would be glad to sing it for you," Edric said, coming up to their table with Cricket on his arm. "Assuming I would be allowed to pass my hat, of course."

"Whatever they may offer you, I will pay you double not to sing it," Sorak said.

"Well, now I *am* intrigued," said Kieran.

"I must admit, that is the first time anyone has ever offered to pay me *not* to sing," said Edric with amusement. "I think I should feel insulted."

"Grak, allow me to present one of our passengers, Edric the Bard, late of South Ledopolus, and

Cricket, whose beauty is surpassed only by her skill at dancing."

Edric bowed, and Cricket curtsied gracefully.

"Well now, I would much rather see her dance than hear him sing," said Grak.

"Now that is one sentiment I can wholly understand," said Edric. "Allow me, then, to make the choice a simpler one. I shall briefly summarize the story of the ballad, for the benefit of our friend Kieran, and then perhaps Cricket will honor us with a performance."

"Done!" said Grak. "But make the tale short, good bard, so that we may get on with the dancing."

Edric sighed and glanced at Cricket. "A warm-up act again," he said with resignation. "Well, if I could trouble you for some libation with which to lubricate my throat. . . ."

Grak bellowed for a tankard of ale, which arrived promptly, and Edric began to tell the story of the ballad, glancing around at all of them, but paying particular attention to Sorak.

"The first few verses of the ballad retell the tale of the fall of Alaron and the dissolution of the elven kingdom," he began. "Alaron, the last king of all the elves, was said to bear a magic sword of elven steel. Its name was Galdra, and no other weapon could withstand it. In the hands of the true king, it would cause even steel to shatter. Upon his death, Alaron gave the sword to a shapechanger for safekeeping, to keep it from the hands of the defilers, whose touch would cause the magic blade to break and shatter its enchantment.

'One day,' said Alaron with his dying breath, 'a future king will come to reunite the elves, and when that hero appears, then he will bear the sword.'

"Many years then passed," Edric continued, "and the elves fell into decadence. The story of Alaron and his enchanted blade became remembered only as a myth. Until, one day, a wanderer appeared, a nomad from the Ringing Mountains, a pilgrim who bore a sword the like of which no one had ever seen. It was made of elven steel, the crafting of which had been lost for centuries, and it had a curved hilt wrapped with silver wire. The blade itself was curved, as well, forged in a shape that combined the forms of a cutlass and a falchion, and on that blade, engraved in elven runes, was the legend, 'Strong in spirit, true in temper, forged in faith.'

"The ballad then goes on to tell some of the exploits of this wanderer," Edric continued, watching Sorak as he spoke. "It tells of how he foiled a defiler plot to seize the government in Tyr, and how he saved the city from a plague of undead. Then it tells of how he set off across the Tablelands, in company with a beautiful villichi priestess, and of how he stole a princess of the Royal House of Nibenay from a nobleman who was holding her against her will. Having taken the vows of a preserver, this daughter of Nibenay had been exiled by her father and had appealed to our hero to rescue her and return her to her home. This the Nomad did, taking her across the dreaded

Stony Barrens, which no man had ever crossed before. The nobleman pursued him and the Nomad slew him in fair combat, then brought the princess back to Nibenay, where she joined the Veiled Alliance to help them carry on their war against her father's templars.

"In retaliation, the Shadow King sent an army of half-giants to destroy the Nomad, but he fought them valiantly and made good his escape, disappearing from the city and mysteriously vanishing into the desert with his beautiful villichi priestess by his side.

"What has become of him? Is he, indeed, the Crown of Elves, which the legend has foretold? Will he be the one to reunite the tribes and return them to their former glory? Has the age-old prophecy come true at last? Throughout the world, defilers tremble. And among all the elves of Athas, spirits rise in hope. They all look for the wanderer who calls himself the Nomad, and wonder where he will next appear. And so the ballad ends, on a tantalizing note of mystery and questions unresolved. But it really does play rather better when sung."

"Well, well," said Kieran, gazing at Sorak with look of both interest and amusement. "I had no idea I had recruited such a celebrated figure. At the price, it seems I got a bargain."

Sorak sighed and shook his head. "Bards have to sing of something, I suppose. And imagination is their stock in trade. They seize upon some small thing and exaggerate it out of all proportion."

"Mmm," said Kieran with a look of mock disappointment. "Pity. I have never had a king for a subordinate."

"So then the story is untrue?" asked Cricket, staring at him intently. "As we approached I thought I overheard something about your stealing a princess from a caravan."

"Yes, I'd like to hear more about that," said Kieran.

"I'd like to see the lady dance!" said Grak, smashing his fist down on the tabletop.

"There is no music," Cricket said.

"It just so happens I have brought my harp," said Edric, producing it from beneath his cloak. "For a small sum, I could be induced to play."

Grak threw a handful of copper coins onto the table. "For your music, bard," he said, "and for the song we cheated you of singing. And now, my lady, we shall see you dance." He stood up and bellowed for silence. "My friends! My friends! We have a lovely lady who will dance for us! Make room!"

Tables and benches were quickly cleared from the center of the room, and as Cricket took her place inside the circle they created, everyone in the tavern crowded around. As Edric plucked out chords on his harp, she began a slow, sinuous dance. Sorak took the opportunity to slip away.

He cursed Edric as he left the building and headed back for camp. It had seemed as if the bard had been purposely taunting him by telling the story of the ballad. He hadn't cared about singing it at all, Sorak realized. He had just wanted to recite the story so that he could see his reaction.

They had not even reached Altaruk yet and already things were going wrong. Lord Ankhor had entered into partnership with the House of Jhamri . . . from whose caravan he had helped Princess Korahna escape. As a result, they had been pursued across the Stony Barrens by the Viscount Torian, Lord Ankhor's friend and business partner, and far from slaying him in single combat, Sorak had, at best, an indirect role in his death. Rather than submit to defeat, Torian had taken his own life, to deny Sorak the final victory. However, the only ones who knew that were Sorak and Ryana and the Princess Korahna herself, who had witnessed it.

When Korahna had returned to Nibenay and joined the Veiled Alliance, the members of that underground resistance movement could not have failed to see the potential benefits in making it known that a princess of the Royal House of Nibenay had taken the vows of a preserver and joined them in their struggle. The daughter of a dragon king, betraying her own father, made for a valuable weapon in their arsenal. They must have spread the story, and from that, some bard had been inspired to compose the Ballad of the Nomad—to Sorak's everlasting regret.

He stopped by a spreading pagafa tree on a small rise overlooking the pool of the oasis. The tents of the caravan were pitched there, just a short distance away, and the cookfires were lit. Ryana was down there, resting, watching their packs and waiting for him to return. She had such faith in him. She had left the convent for his sake, broken her vows for his sake, faced all manner of danger and hardship for his sake. She trusted him and believed he knew what he was doing. He wished he shared that trust.

"What do you want from me, Grandfather?" he murmured as he leaned back against the tree. "What am I supposed to do? Put a sword in my hand and give me an opponent. That I can deal with; that I can understand. But this game of intrigue . . ." He shook his head. "I do not even understand the rules."

The jolt hit him suddenly with a force that made his head spin. His vision blurred, and if he had not been leaning back against the tree trunk, he would have fallen. He spun around, clutching at the tree trunk for support as everything started to spin. The walled enclosure surrounding the oasis vanished. The tents disappeared from view. The quarter moons cast a dim light over the darkness of the desert as the watchfires of the camp burned low. In the distance, perhaps thirty or forty miles away, rose the foothills of the Estuary Mountains, curving gradually to the northwest. The caravan was no more than a day's journey from Altaruk.

He saw the guards sitting at their posts, gathered around their watchfire, tossing dice. Then, abruptly, one of them jerked and clutched at his neck as a black arrow sprouted from his throat. Another rose quickly to his feet, only to be felled instantly by an arrow through his chest. A third cried out an alarm and started running toward the camp, but before he had run four steps, an arrow struck him between the shoulder blades, and he fell sprawling, facedown on the ground.

From out of the darkness, like specters in the night, Sorak saw them come, black-clad riders in dark robes thundering out of the night on their crodlu, their jet-black kank armor gleaming in the moonlight.

"*Sorak!*"

His vision blurred as he saw them descend on the camp, dozens of them, riding at top speed—

"*Sorak! Sorak, what is it? What's the matter?*"

He was lying on the ground, at the base of the pagafa tree, and as his vision focused, he saw Kieran crouching over him, looking down at him with concern.

"Sorak, are you all right? What is it?"

He swallowed hard and took several deep breaths as Kieran helped him up to a sitting position.

"Sorak?"

"I am all right now," Sorak said. His head ached, and he felt a slight residual dizziness.

"What happened? Are you ill?" asked Kieran.

"We are going to be attacked," said Sorak.

"Attacked? When? By whom?"

"Tomorrow night, I think," said Sorak. "Raiders. Dressed in black . . . I . . . I saw them. I saw it happen."

Kieran stared at him, then nodded. "Very well, then. We'll be prepared for them."

"You believe me?" Sorak asked with surprise.

"I have learned not to question someone with the gift of Sight," Kieran replied.

"How did you know?" asked Sorak, startled.

"I have seen this sort of thing before," said Kieran, helping him to his feet. "General Trajian of Draj employed a soothsayer with the Sight. He never knew when it would come upon him, but when it did, he reacted much as you. And his visions were never false. You know, my friend, I am beginning to believe the stories of that ballad are not far exaggerated. I was going to speak with you about that."

"Is that why you followed me?" asked Sorak. "I am flattered. Not many men would pass up an opportunity to watch Cricket dance just to talk with me."

Kieran grinned. "I notice that you passed it up. You left rather suddenly."

"I had no wish to answer questions about that ridiculous ballad," Sorak said.

"Not so ridiculous, I think," said Kieran, pulling aside Sorak's cloak to reveal Galdra tucked into his belt. "The blade is broken, yet otherwise it matches the description, right down to the inscription. The runes for 'Strong in spirit' remain."

Sorak glanced at him with surprise. "You can read elvish?"

"And I can speak it, fluently," said Kieran. "I also know dwarven. And I speak a smattering of halfling. A knowledge of languages can be a great benefit in my trade."

"I am impressed," said Sorak.

"That *is* Galdra, is it not?" asked Kieran. "I am familiar with the elven prophecy."

Sorak merely nodded.

"So," said Kieran. "Elven steel. I have heard of it, but never seen it before. May I?"

Sorak drew the blade and handed it to him. As he touched it, a sparkling blue aura briefly played around its edge, but when Kieran put his hand upon the hilt, it faded.

"It still holds magic," Kieran said, staring at it with fascination. "And I have never seen so fine a blade, with the steel folded so many times. . . . How did it break?"

"A defiler touched it," Sorak said. "That part of the legend was true."

"I take it the individual concerned is now no longer with us," Kieran said.

"No," said Sorak. "I bear his blade now." He drew the sword he had earlier shown Grak and the others. "He bid me take it as he died."

"A gallant gesture," Kieran said. "That does not sound much like a defiler."

"He was a defiler only by association," Sorak explained. "A soldier like yourself, but in the service of the Shadow King. In some ways, he was an admirable man. In others, one to be despised. He was no longer young, but he still had the strength of ten, and he was the finest swordsman I have ever seen."

"Valsavis," Kieran said.

Sorak shook his head. "You never cease to surprise me," he said. "How could you possibly have known?"

Kieran smiled. "I am a professional, my friend. And, by reputation, whether deserved or not, one of the finest blades alive. Valsavis was the other. The Shadow King's personal assassin. Oh, I knew of him, all right, but I never met the man. I had always wondered which of us would be the best. I suppose now I shall never know. But you . . . you bested him?"

"It was hardly a fair fight," said Sorak. "He was gravely wounded when we fought, and he had lost a hand. Despite that, I was still no match for him. I was merely lucky."

"I would like to know how lucky," Kieran said. "We shall have to cross swords sometime, in practice. But in the meantime, there are some other questions I would ask."

"Certainly," said Sorak.

"If you truly are the Crown of Elves, why accept a post as soldier of a merchant house?"

Sorak shook his head. "I never claimed to be a king of any sort, and have no wish to be. Galdra was a gift to me from the high mistress of the villichi, into whose safekeeping it was given by a pyreen many years ago. If she knew of the elven prophecy, and if her gift was prompted by it, she never mentioned it to me. And once the blade was broken, I had no further use for it. It served me well, but came with weighty baggage. I threw it into a deep pool at an oasis not long before we met. And the other day, it magically returned to me. It seems I'm stuck with it. As for why I took the job you offered me, I had to get to Altaruk, and it seemed a good way to be in the center of things."

"I see. And what takes you to Altaruk?"

"I cannot say."

"Cannot or will not?" Kieran asked.

"I have no wish to lie to you," said Sorak. "I must go to Altaruk in the name of the preserver cause, but beyond that, I know nothing. And do not ask me how I know I must go. That I will not tell you."

Kieran nodded. "Frankly spoken." He gave Sorak back the blade, and as Sorak touched it, it briefly glowed. "So. Where does that leave us?"

"I suppose you will require a new second-in-command," said Sorak.

"You have not yet even begun your duties. Are you resigning already?"

Sorak frowned. "But . . . surely, now that you know—"

"I have heard nothing to make me think I made an error in offering you the post. If you no longer want it, that is another matter. And if what you must do in Altaruk places us at cross purposes, I will trust you to resign at that time. If I should be placed in a position where I must do something in response, I will promise you twenty-four hours before I act. Do I have your hand upon it?"

Sorak gave him his hand. "I hope the day when we are at cross purposes never comes."

"So do I," said Kieran. "Now, tell me more

about this vision that you had just now."

Sorak described what he had seen, in as much detail as he could recall. When he was finished, Kieran nodded.

"Dressed in black from head to toe, eh? With black breastplates and black arrows. You are sure about the arrows?"

Sorak nodded. "Is that important?"

"It is the trademark of the Shadows," he said.

"Who are the Shadows?" Sorak asked.

"You do not know? I am surprised. It is a tribe of elves, one of the oldest in existence, but the Shadows are no ordinary tribe of nomads. Once, many years ago, they were, but they have since evolved into a society as dark and secret as their name. Little is known about them, other than that they are masters of espionage, extortion, theft, and assassination. Especially assassination. They are divided into groups called talons, each led by a talonmaster. Each talonmaster commands a group of subcommanders known as shadowmasters, each of whom leads a smaller group known as a claw. Each claw has its own specialty. Some claws are devoted solely to magic, others to theft, assassination, raiding. . . . And in command of all is the grand shadowmaster. Who that may be is anybody's guess. If the raiders you saw in your vision are indeed Shadows, we'll have our hands full."

"Perhaps Grak may be of help," said Sorak.

Kieran snorted. "Oh, I doubt that," he said. "I would not even bother asking."

"But he is a friend of yours," said Sorak.

"An old acquaintance," Kieran corrected him. "But Grak's first loyalty was and always shall be to Grak. He might consider lending us some mercenaries to escort us into Altaruk, but he would insist on a share of the cargo in payment, and I am not authorized to make such a bargain. I doubt Lord Jhamri would approve."

"Would he rather lose the entire shipment?"

"No, he would rather I protect it," Kieran said. "And it would make a poor beginning if I started my new job by admitting I could not do it properly, which is how he would see it. No, we shall have to take care of this ourselves."

"You may count on me," said Sorak. "And on Ryana."

"I did not doubt that." Kieran frowned. "The Shadows are a cut above ordinary raiders," he said. "And even common raiders usually attempt to place at least one agent in a caravan, to learn the nature of the cargo and the disposition of the guards."

"Edric!" Sorak said abruptly.

"The bard?"

"I had a strong intuition about him from the start," said Sorak. "I thought, at first, I just disliked him, but I could not help feeling he was up to something."

"You may be right," said Kieran. "He joined the caravan in South Ledopolus, and who would suspect a mincing bard traveling with a dancer? You think Cricket may be in on it as well?"

Sorak shook his head. "I don't know. Somehow I doubt it."

"Well, there is one way to find out," said Kieran. "Let us go see your friend, the priestess. If you're right, we'll know for sure before the night is out."

TEN

It was shortly before dawn when they saw Edric leave his tent and make for the oasis pool. He walked casually, with no appearance of stealth, sauntering slowly with his cloak draped over his shoulders and a short clay pipe clamped between his teeth. He looked as if he had simply risen early and was out to enjoy a short walk and a smoke and refresh himself at the pool. Sorak and Kieran followed at a distance, staying low and keeping to the shadows, mindful of the fact that elves had good night vision.

If Edric was concerned about being watched, he gave no outward sign. He simply continued down the slight slope to the pool, where he stopped by a stand of pagafa trees and broom bush at the water's edge. He crouched and gently tapped out his pipe with the heel of his palm, then set it on the ground beside him. On his knees, he leaned forward with hands cupped and splashed some water onto his face, then dried off with his sleeve, took a drink, and sat back to refill his pipe from a small, rolled pouch. Just an early riser taking his ease.

"There!" whispered Sorak, grasping Kieran's upper arm as they lay beside each other on the ground, watching from about thirty yards away. He pointed. "By the broom bush. Do you see?"

Kieran shook his head. "Your elfling eyes are better than my mine," he said in a low voice. "What do you see?"

"A dark form crouches in the bushes to the bard's right," Sorak said. "Well concealed, but I can just make him out. Edric isn't looking at him, but I think they're talking."

"As I thought," said Kieran. "A final conference before the attack."

"Very bold," said Sorak. "The raider managed to get inside the walls and sneak right up to the camp."

"Not as bold as you may think," said Kieran. "Grak will allow anyone within the walls, so long as they pay the toll and cause no trouble. He probably came in just after we arrived and mingled with the crowd."

"There, he's moved," said Sorak. "Can you see him now?"

Kieran squinted, staring intently. "Yes, I see him now. But if I didn't know just where to look, I'd never spot him. He's a Shadow, all right. He'll probably leave right after we depart and ride out to join his friends."

"You want to take him?"

Kieran shook his head. "No, let him go. If we take him now, the Shadows will know we've been alerted. That might prevent the attack, but I doubt it. You saw it in your vision. And unless your vision played you false, that means it will take place. Better to let them think they still have the advantage of surprise. Come on, we've seen what we came to see. You were right about the bard. We'd best go see the captain and make plans to receive our visitors."

They made their way back to the tents and found the captain already up and dressed, having a light breakfast of herbal tea and bread spread with kank honey before starting his morning tasks of preparing the caravan. He rose to his feet at once as they entered the tent, but Kieran waved him back down.

"Sit down, Captain, please," he said. "Do not let us interrupt your breakfast."

"Is something wrong, sir?" the man asked anxiously, as he resumed his seat.

"We are going to be attacked by the Shadows tonight."

"Gith's blood!" the captain swore. "The Shadows!"

"Lower your voice," said Kieran calmly. "We have been infiltrated. The bard, Edric, is one of their agents. There may be others. How well do you know your men?"

"I have had the same crew for close to a year now," the captain replied, "and some have been with me even longer. I trust them, but I cannot speak for the passengers."

"They can be watched," said Kieran. "However, there may be some last minute additions. Anyone who books passage this morning must be especially suspect."

"Then we'll take no passengers from here."

Kieran shook his head. "No, that would not be wise. There would be no reason to refuse except that we may be expecting trouble. Accept anyone who wants to go, but point them out to me."

"Understood," the captain said. "How do you wish me to proceed?"

"Your crew seems efficient," Kieran said. "We'll tell them nothing until we make camp tonight. But in the meantime, I want you to select half a dozen mercenaries and inform them individually during the day. They shall report to me at the midday stop. Now, here is what we are going to do. . . ."

* * * * *

By midday, the caravan approached the northern tip of the Estuary Mountain range. The broad Estuary of the Forked Tongue thrust deep into the desert Tablelands from the Sea of Silt, curving slightly from the coast and terminating roughly two hundred miles inland, just a few miles east of the Estuary Mountains. Where the mountain range straddled the estuary, it formed a small valley in a natural pocket, with a pass leading through the mountains to the west. It was in this small valley that Altaruk stood.

"From here on in," said Kieran as they rode together at the head of the formation, "we will be traveling with the estuary on our right flank and the mountains on our left, which makes the terrain ideally suited to an attack."

Sorak nodded. "By late afternoon, the mountains to our left will cast shadows toward us. Together with the rolling terrain of the foothills, that will make any approaching party difficult to spot. By nightfall, even if the moons were full—and tonight, they won't be—there will be little visibility."

"Precisely," Kieran said. "That means the outriders will not be able to range far from the camp without exposing themselves to danger, but bringing them in closer reduces their effectiveness."

"There seems no point in exposing the outriders," Sorak replied. "They could be ambushed before giving the alarm. It would be wise to bring them in. That way, they will not be so exposed and shall be more useful when the attack comes."

"Good thinking," Kieran said, nodding. "Did you happen to notice that three new passengers joined us at Grak's Pool?"

"Mercenaries," Sorak said. "One half-elf and two humans. But tribal elves do not accept half-breeds, and certainly not humans."

Kieran shook his head. "No, these are merely hired blades. I asked Grak about them before we left. They arrived at the oasis the day before we did. And they came in from the north, which means from Altaruk. They're going back the way they came. No one comes to Grak's Pool just for a short visit."

"It does seem rather a long way to go for a drink," said Sorak.

"Especially when Altaruk offers much better entertainment," Kieran said. "So, it seems we shall have at least four people to take into custody." He smiled. "I do hope they resist."

"What do you want me to do?" Ryana asked.

"I appreciate the offer of assistance, my lady," Kieran said. "We will require every fighter we have to ward off the attack, for we do not know how many raiders to expect. With any luck, we may learn that information shortly, but the safety of the passengers must be considered. And for all we know, there may yet be other infiltrators among them. To guard against that possibility, and to keep the others safe from harm, I would like to place you in charge of the roustabouts who will be protecting them. They are a hardy lot, but there's not a trained fighter among them."

"Some might resent taking orders from a woman," said Ryana.

"If any of them are fool enough to question the abilities of a villichi priestess," Kieran said, "then you have my wholehearted encouragement to point out the error of their thinking."

Ryana grinned. "I would be happy to."

As they stopped for their midday break, the outriders came in, and six of them came at once to Kieran. He quickly instructed them in what they were to do. As the passengers dismounted, the outriders quickly closed in on the three mercenaries who had joined the caravan that morning. Two of them took each of the three, disarmed them, and took them into custody. It was all done so quickly and efficiently that the three men never had a chance to put up a struggle. As they were being taken, Sorak and Kieran positioned themselves close to Edric, and Ryana stood by to watch Cricket, just in case.

Edric showed only the barest flicker of alarm when the three mercenaries were seized, then quickly got himself under control and turned to Kieran with a frown. "What's happening?" he asked. "What have these men done?"

"Oh, nothing—yet," Kieran replied casually. "We are merely taking your confederates into custody as a preventive measure."

Edric frowned. "My what?"

"Exactly how many Shadows may we expect in the attack tonight?" asked Kieran conversationally.

"I do not understand," said Edric, trying to brazen it out. "Shadow elves? Attack?"

"Save your breath, friend," said Kieran. "We witnessed your rendezvous this morning."

"There must be some mistake," said Edric. "I met no one this morning. I had merely gone to the pool to—" Even as he spoke, Edric launched a fast kick at Kieran's privates. Kieran managed to twist aside slightly, but Edric still caught him a glancing blow and Kieran doubled over in pain. But before the bard could do anything more, Sorak was on him, wrestling him to the ground. A moment later, two of the caravan guards joined in, pinning him down. They raised the struggling bard to his feet and one placed a knife against his throat, ending his resistance.

Gritting his teeth, Kieran straightened up, still smarting from the blow. Had the kick caught him squarely on target, there was no question that it would have incapacitated him. "I must be getting slow," he said, his voice strained. He gave Edric a look of withering contempt, and then turned to gaze briefly at the three captured mercenaries. "Now," he said, "I am going to ask you four some questions. If you cooperate, you can spare yourselves some pain, but I promise you, I *will* get answers, one way or another."

The caravan guards led their captives away as the passengers stood around, murmuring among themselves.

Wide-eyed, Cricket turned to Ryana in confusion.

"I don't understand," she said. "Why have they taken Edric and those men? What have they done?"

"You pretend you do not know?" Ryana said.

"But I do *not* know!" Cricket protested. "I have no idea!"

Her confusion and concern seemed genuine. "The Shadows plan to attack the caravan tonight," Ryana said. "Edric was their spy, and the others his confederates."

"But . . . that cannot be!" said Cricket. "I know Edric! We worked together at the Damsel! You were there! Surely, you must have seen him!"

"How long did he work at the Desert Damsel before the caravan came to South Ledopolus?" Ryana asked.

"Why . . . a week or so."

"And before?"

Cricket shook her head. "I do not know."

"He arrived in town and established his identity as a wandering bard," Ryana said. "That provided a good cover for him when he joined the caravan. You were part of it. He used you."

Cricket did not want to believe it. She shook her head. "No, you must be mistaken. What proof do you have?"

"There is no mistake," Ryana said. "Sorak and Kieran both saw him meet in secret with one of the raiders at Grak's Pool shortly before dawn this morning. He was doubtless informing him of the strength and disposition of our guard and what type of cargo we carry. He and the other three who joined us this morning were to strike at us from within when the attack occurred. They would have killed the cargo guards and handlers and driven off the beasts, then probably taken hostages among the passengers."

Cricket shook her head with dismay. "Then it was all a lie," she said in a dull voice. "His friendship, everything he told me. . . . Just when I had finally met a man I thought I could trust. . . ."

"I'm sorry, Cricket," said Ryana, putting a hand on her shoulder in sympathy.

Cricket shook it off. "Leave me alone."

⋆ ⋆ ⋆ ⋆ ⋆

Accompanied by a squad of the caravan guard, Kieran and Sorak led the captives away from the others, going off a distance and down a slope toward the bank of the estuary. The four prisoners were bound securely, their hands behind their backs. When they reached the shore of the estuary, Kieran signaled the guards to push the captives to a sitting position on the ground. Edric looked perfectly calm and composed, but the other three were clearly frightened. They were painfully aware that they were completely at the mercy of their captors.

"Now, I do not wish to waste time," said Kieran, turning to face them. He glanced over his shoulder at the sluggish brown silt. "I will ask one question. If I do not get an answer, or one that satisfies me, I will have one of you thrown into the silt, and we'll watch him drown. I will leave your legs free, so I imagine you will be able to stay up for at least a few moments, but a few moments is all you'll have before you get sucked down. Drowning in silt is not a pleasant experience. When the first of you is gone, I'll ask a question of the second. And so forth, until I have the answers I want."

Two of the mercenaries immediately began protesting that they didn't know anything beyond what they were told to do. The third simply started sobbing and wet himself. Edric alone remained calm and silent. Kieran fixed him with a steady gaze. "I'll save you for last."

"I have no wish to die or suffer pain," said Edric, meeting his gaze steadily. "These three hirelings are telling you the truth. They know nothing beyond their assigned tasks when the attack takes place. I have the information you want, but how do I know you will not kill me anyway as soon as I divulge it?"

"You do not," said Kieran. "But you know I will kill you if you say nothing."

Edric smiled wryly. "I readily concede the point," he said. "Very well then, I'll do my best to bargain from a poor position. What do you wish to know?"

* * * * *

The watchfires created small, bright spots of illumination around the camp as midnight approached. The cookfires by the tents had burned down to embers, and all was still. The outriders had been pulled in earlier, even before the caravan had camped. As the shadows lengthened in the afternoon, they were brought closer, to ride along the left flank of the column until the caravan stopped. They ranged close to the camp until the guards had been posted and the fires were lit, and then they were brought in.

The handlers had staked the beasts down, and

the roustabouts had stacked the cargo in the center of the camp. The passengers and most of the caravan crew had all retired for the night. From outward appearances, everything looked perfectly normal; the caravan had stopped to camp within less than a day's ride from its destination, taking token precautions on the last night of their journey. However, Kieran had made sure appearances would be deceptive.

He had positioned the camp within the shelter of some large, natural rock outcroppings near the banks of the estuary. The tents had been pitched near the base of the rocks, as if for protection from the wind. To the watching raiders—and Kieran was sure they would be watching—it must have looked absolutely perfect. An attack from the southeast would leave them trapped in a pocket formed by the estuary in their rear and the big rocks on their flank—caught like a fly between a hammer and an anvil. Which was precisely what Kieran wanted the raiders to think.

The handlers had staked the beasts at the rear of the camp, as usual, by the slope leading to the estuary. It was the logical place to put them, but at the same time, it served another purpose. As the passengers and crew retired for the night, gradually, in ones and twos, they entered their tents and were taken out through slits cut in the backs, then led by roustabouts between the rock outcroppings and the backs of the tents, so that they were concealed from view. They were then taken down the slope behind the beasts, where they huddled together, wrapped in blankets against the chill. In this manner, masked from any observation, all the passengers were removed from the camp and secreted by the estuary, where they were protected by Ryana and a group of armed roustabouts. All the tents stood empty.

At the advance guard outpost to the southeast, the direction from which Kieran invited attack, the three captive mercenaries sat in a circle by a watchfire. They were bent over slightly, as if gaming with dice. Only on close observation could it be seen that they were gagged and bound, with hands in front of them, staked down to the ground. Kieran nodded with satisfaction as he checked their bonds and grinned.

"Well, does this match your vision?" he asked.

Sorak nodded. "It seems to."

"Good. Let's take our places and see if it all unfolds the way you saw it."

They moved off about a dozen yards and lay down to wait behind some scrub brush. The movements of the mercenaries as they struggled to pull themselves free and their panicked shouts into their gags merely made it look as if they were going about their game. Kieran chuckled softly. "They don't seem very happy, do they?" he said in a low voice.

"No, this wasn't quite what they bargained for when they signed on for this journey," Sorak replied. "Still, I suppose it's better than being thrown into the silt."

"True," said Kieran. "You never know, one or

two of them might still survive." He shrugged.

They did not have long to wait. Shortly after midnight, the attack came with devastating swiftness, just as Edric said it would. A black arrow came whistling out of the darkness and struck one of the captive mercenaries with a soft thump. It was immediately followed by several more arrows, in rapid succession. The second mercenary was struck down. The third managed, with a desperate effort born of panic, to pull his stake free of the ground. He jumped up and started running back toward the camp, but didn't get more than several yards before an arrow in his back brought him down.

"Here they come," Sorak murmured.

They heard them first, but it wasn't until the raiders were almost upon them that they became visible. A squadron of soot-blackened crodlu came galloping out of the darkness in tight formation, bearing black-clad riders armed with bows, wooden spears, and obsidian swords. Sorak and Kieran stayed low, hidden behind the brush as the Shadows rode by, storming into the camp, confident they had the element of surprise.

Kieran peered hard into the darkness as they went past. "How many do you estimate?"

"Perhaps thirty," Sorak said, his night vision sharper than the human's.

Kieran nodded. "The bard told the truth. Well, I may have to let him live, after all. Pity." As the elves thundered past them toward the camp, Sorak and Kieran jumped to their feet and drew their blades. "*Now! Charge!*" Kieran shouted as he ran forward with Sorak at his side.

Armed men leapt up from behind shrubs and rocks where they had dug in to await the attack. They quickly closed ranks behind the raiders as the black elves charged unsuspecting into the camp. One by one, the tents burst into flame, torched by roustabouts, and the resulting blaze clearly illuminated the attackers. Archers appeared atop the rocks and started firing down at the Shadows, who suddenly realized that, rather than trap their victims against the rocks, it was they who had been trapped.

More than a dozen of the black elves fell in the first volley of the archers before they wheeled their mounts to retreat, but they found themselves cut off. Thrown spears from the caravan guards unseated about half a dozen more, and then the crodlu were rearing about in panic and confusion, the riderless beasts colliding with the others. Kieran shouted out the command to move in and finish them off before the survivors could regroup.

However, several of the elves recovered quickly and got their beasts back under control. They wheeled around and rode straight for the rear of the camp, hanging off the sides of their mounts to avoid the arrows of the archers.

They were heading straight for the passengers . . . and Ryana.

"*Kieran*!" Sorak called, and without waiting for a reply, he gave chase.

The elves swung around the kanks staked down

at the rear of the camp and headed down the slope, hoping to escape, but then spotted the passengers clustered behind the roustabouts and made straight for them.

Sorak heard the alarmed cries of the passengers from behind the line of kanks staked at the crest of the slope, and he knew he would never have time to circle the kanks, as the raiders had. Running at top speed, twice as fast as any human could, he leapt ten feet into the air and landed atop one of the kanks. As he fought to maintain his balance on the giant beetle's slippery carapace, he drew one of his daggers and hurled it.

An elf raider cried out and fell from his crodlu as the blade stuck home, but by then, the others were already atop Ryana's group.

As Sorak leapt down from the kank and tumbled down the slope, the passengers fled in panic toward the silt.

Ryana moved in with her roustabouts to meet the attack. She brought one elf down with her crossbow, then tossed it aside, drew a dagger and hurled it in one smooth motion, felling another. As she drew her second dagger from her boot, one of the mounted raiders hurled his spear at her. She twisted aside, and it missed her by scant inches. Then she threw her dagger as the elf thundered down upon her, bringing up his blade.

It took him squarely in the chest, and he fell backward off his mount. It was only by diving to one side that Ryana avoided being trampled by the riderless crodlu. She hit the ground, rolled, and came up with her blade in her hands, just as another raider closed with her. She went down to one knee and parried his downward slash, then came up and swept her blade around, opening a deep gash in the raider's leg as he rode by. He screamed, and blood fountained from the wound, but by then, Ryana was already engaging another opponent.

Several of the roustabouts had fallen, slain or wounded, by the time Sorak reached the scene. He ran straight into the melee and leapt, carrying a Shadow off his mount. He landed on top of the raider and heard the breath whoosh out of his lungs. Before the elf could recover, Sorak grabbed his large, pointed ears and twisted his head sharply.

He heard the sharp crack as the raider's neck snapped, then felt the breeze of a blade slashing down at him, missing his head by a hair. He ducked down and rolled, came up to his feet, and drew his sword, but by then the raider had already ridden past. And an instant later, Sorak saw why.

Edric stood perhaps a dozen yards away, his hands bound behind him and his ankles tied together. He had been unable to run off toward the rocks with the other passengers, but then he had not wanted to. He hopped toward the raider, and Sorak saw the black-clad elf lean down from his saddle to sweep him up.

But before Sorak could react, he heard another crodlu pounding the ground behind him and turned to meet the attack. He met the Shadow elf's blade on his own, then ducked and rolled as the raider tried to ride him down. The elf wheeled his mount, and Sorak ran up behind it, slashed the crodlu's legs. With a screeching cry, the crippled bird went down, and the raider tumbled from the saddle. As he fell, one of the roustabouts pounced on him and brought down his knife.

Sorak turned back to see that the other raider had already hoisted Edric up onto his saddle and slashed his bonds. Edric straddled the crodlu, sitting in front of the rider and bending low, grasping the beast's long neck for support. The rider urged his mount up the slope on a diagonal path, away from Sorak. There was no way to stop them. As they galloped up the slope, Kieran appeared at the crest.

"*Kieran!*" Sorak shouted. "*Edric is getting away!*"

The mercenary drew his dagger as the riders thundered by him, and he threw. The knife struck the raider between the shoulder blades, and he tumbled from his mount, but Edric seized the reins as the crodlu surged up the slope.

Sorak shifted his sword to his left hand and pulled Galdra from his belt. The broken blade glowed with a bright blue aura as he grasped it, flipped it around, and threw it with a powerful, overhand motion. It seemed to leave a blue contrail in its wake as it flew toward Edric and struck him in the shoulder. Sorak heard him cry out, but he retained his seat, slumping in the saddle. The crodlu and its rider disappeared over the crest of the slope.

Sorak spun around, looking for Ryana. He saw at least half a dozen roustabouts lying on the ground, some moving, some perfectly still. He felt a knot forming in his stomach, but then saw her, bending over one of the roustabouts and tearing a strip from his cloak to use as a tourniquet. He exhaled heavily with relief.

Then Kieran was at his side.

Sorak asked, "How goes the battle?"

"It's over," Kieran said. "A number of them got away, but at least a score won't be doing any more raiding. We'll take the bodies with us into Altaruk and present them to the Jhamris. They may wish to display them as an object lesson to other would-be raiders. Every man who fought tonight will win a reputation. There aren't many mercenaries who can boast surviving an encounter with the Shadows."

"How many of ours died?" asked Sorak, glancing back at the bodies littering the shore.

Kieran shook his head. "We've made no count as yet, but we lost some good men." He set his teeth, and Sorak saw a tic in his jaw muscles. "I should have killed that bard."

"You gave your word you would let him live if he cooperated," Sorak said. "And he did give us an accurate account of what to expect. Still, now he'll have to answer to his friends, the Shadows, and only he could have betrayed them."

Kieran nodded. "They will hold him to accounts, all right, but he's a slippery character. He may yet talk his way out of it. I hope he does, for I would dearly like to encounter him again. A pity about that special blade of yours."

"It was broken, anyway," said Sorak. "It's no great loss." But even as he spoke, he wondered. It had returned to him once before; it could yet return to him again. Only time would tell.

"We had best see to the wounded," he said, then suddenly, he staggered against Kieran as everything started to spin. He felt the mercenary catch him.

"*Sorak*! Are you wounded?"

Kieran's voice sounded as if it were coming from the bottom of a well. The sounds around him receded and Sorak's vision blurred; he gasped for breath.

Then, slowly, everything came back into focus . . . but he was elsewhere. And this time, it was not only his body that seemed to have been transported. It was his mind, as well.

He stood in a dark room, illuminated only by one thick candle standing on a wooden table. There was someone seated at that table, a robed figure cloaked in darkness. And he heard a low, raspy voice say, "He is coming. I can feel it."

The robed figure leaned forward into the light and Sorak tensed inwardly as he saw the shaved skull of a templar. It was an old woman, and on her head she wore a chaplet of beaten silver bearing the crest of Nibenay. She sat in a peculiar posture, with one arm hanging limply at her side, favoring her shoulder as if it were injured.

"It will not be long now," she said, looking up at

him, "but he will surely come. And it will be up to us to stop him."

The feeling was surreal. It was as if the templar were looking straight at him and speaking to him directly. At the same time, he felt not himself at all. It was as if his body had somehow become alien to him. It felt large, grotesque and . . . but then the templar's next words mesmerized him.

"Valsavis is dead. The Nomad has fulfilled his mission. Somehow, he must have managed to make contact with the Sage. Now, he will be truly dangerous." The templar smiled wanly. "You haven't the faintest idea what I'm talking about, do you?"

Sorak felt his head shake slowly.

"No matter. You do not need to understand. Your needs are simple. That must be reassuring. In a way, I envy you your simplicity. You eat, drink, sleep, defecate, and kill. But then, that is what you were bred for. The subtleties of life escape you, and yet it concerns you not. How refreshing, in a primitive way. Does my conversation bore you?"

Another head shake.

"No? Well, I rather doubt you would admit it if it did. Perhaps it truly does interest you in some way. I do not imagine anyone has ever bothered to converse with you before. What would be the point? You could not answer, anyway. Doubtless, the only words anyone ever spoke to you were commands . . . or pleas for mercy. And those last fell on deaf ears, of course. No one ever taught you mercy. I doubt you even understand the concept.

Still, I've come to find our one-sided conversations comforting. Do you know why?"

Brief head shake.

"Because a templar has no one in whom she can confide. Oh, when she's young, she can share confidences with her senior sisters, but as she grows older, she learns about such things as palace intrigue and political maneuvering and soon realizes she can profit best by keeping her own council. Her life becomes a maze of ritual and duty, and she becomes isolated, commanding of respect and fear and yet, a lonely woman. Do you know what it means to feel lonely?"

This time, a nod.

"Ah. Of course. I thought you would. Then perhaps you can understand. Have you ever mated? No? Not even once? Well, who knows, that may be for the best. That means you cannot have unreasonable expectations. Do you know how old I am?"

Head shake.

"I am almost two hundred years old. That surprises you. I look old, but not that old, eh? Well, I am. Magic can extend one's life, if one knows how to use it." The templar sighed. "My husband's magic. A power so great it makes me tremble, even after all these years. I was brought to him when I was just fifteen, but I had already learned something of love. Oh, I was a virgin, else I would not have been acceptable, but I was not entirely innocent, you see. There was a boy, a lovely boy of seventeen . . . I can still see his face as clearly as if he were standing right here in front of me. I can still recall our cautious fumblings, clumsy and yet tender. We swore we would always love each other, but we were afraid to go much further than sweet kisses and intimate caresses. And then I was chosen for the harem of the Shadow King and I never saw him again.

"No, not true," the templar continued, after a brief pause. "I saw him once, many years later. I chanced across him in the street. He was afraid even to look me. I imagine he found himself a fat little wife and sired fat little sons, and lived his life . . . and died. This is the first time I have even spoken of him in over a hundred and fifty years, and yet, even though his bones now molder in a grave, he has never left my thoughts. I think back to those bygone days of girlhood and wish just once, we could have had the courage to . . ."

The templar fell into a long, contemplative silence. Finally, she looked up, and the wistful look was gone, replaced by the cold, regal demeanor of a servant of the Shadow King.

"Memories. They serve no useful purpose. And we are here to serve a useful purpose."

Sorak felt an unwholesome thrill of anticipation run through him. It was not his feeling at all. It made his skin crawl, and yet, at the same time, he somehow felt what the *other* was feeling, and it repelled him.

"Let us go, my silent friend," the templar said, rising to her feet. "It is time for you to do what you do best. You will not have the sort of audience you are accustomed to, but I will be close by. An audience of one, but one who has a true appreciation of your craft. And soon, very soon, you will have an opportunity to test your skills against one who should, by all accounts, provide a proper challenge to your abilities. You would like that, wouldn't you?"

An eager nod.

"Yes. I rather thought you would. But tonight, if our reports have been correct, there will be some fine amusement for you. And by tomorrow, all of Altaruk will be abuzz with talk of your doings . . . and the Veiled Alliance will know the meaning of fear."

* * * * *

"*Sorak! Sorak! Oh, Sorak, wake up, please!*"

Ryana bent over him anxiously. He blinked several times and brought his hands up to his forehead. It felt as if his head were splitting, and he was covered with sweat.

He was lying on his back on a bedroll spread out on the ground. The first orange-tinted light of dawn was visible on the horizon as the dark sun slowly rose over the Sea of Silt. He sat up slowly, with a groan.

Kieran came and knelt at his side. "You had us worried, my friend," he said. "You were gone for a long time. Over four hours. And whatever it was you saw, it must have been a nightmare, judging by the way you thrashed and moaned."

Sorak took a deep breath and exhaled slowly, sitting with his head in his hands.

Ryana put her arm around him. "It's all right," she said softly. "Whatever it was, it's over now."

He shook his head. "No, it is not over," he said in a dull voice. "It is only just beginning."

"What did you see?" asked Kieran, gazing at him intently.

"Death," said Sorak.

"Whose?" asked Kieran, frowning. "One of us?"

Sorak shook his head. "No. I did not know them."

"*Them?*" Ryana said. "How many?"

"At least half a dozen," Sorak said. "Members of the Veiled Alliance. We must get to Altaruk with all speed," he said. "They are being butchered."

"Who is doing this?" asked Kieran.

Sorak shook his head. "I could not tell. But this time, it was different. I think it was the same killer I saw before, but this time I was seeing through the killer's eyes, feeling what the killer felt, and it was . . ." He shuddered, unable to complete the thought.

"Can you can recall any more?" asked Kieran.

Sorak nodded. "Yes. A templar. One of the senior templars of the Shadow King."

"In Altaruk?" said Kieran.

"She seemed to be directing the killer," Sorak said. "And she knew about the Shadows' attack on us. I think she was involved somehow. It may have been because of me. I'm the one they're after. But I am not the only one."

"So," said Kieran, "the defilers are making their bid to control Altaruk. And I thought this was going to be a simple, boring job. But where do you fit in? Why do they want you?"

"Because of who I am," said Sorak. "And what I represent."

"Then the bard's tale was true?" said Kieran.

"In part," said Sorak. "But there is much more to it. Have you ever heard of the avangion?"

"The myth of the preserver dragon?" Kieran said. "The legend of the Sage?"

"The avangion is neither myth nor dragon," Sorak said. "And the Sage is more than legend."

"You mean to say he actually exists?"

"He was once called the Wanderer," said Sorak.

"The pilgrim who wrote that journal of his travels? He is an adept?"

Sorak nodded. "He is also my grandfather."

Kieran exhaled heavily. "Gith's blood," he swore softly. "I knew there was more to you than met the eye, but this . . ." He shook his head. "You know where he is, don't you?"

Sorak nodded.

"Who else knows?"

"Only the pyreen elders. And Ryana, of course. It is my task to do what my grandfather cannot. Not only to serve the cause, but to make it known. And in some ways, ways that I still do not understand, he has prepared me for it."

"You mean the Sight?" said Kieran.

Sorak nodded again. "And the blade. And I do not know what else. There is much about myself I have yet to discover. It would be difficult to explain. I had hoped there would be more time, but it seems I'll not have that luxury. The Shadow King has other plans."

"More than just the Shadow King, if all you say is true," said Kieran.

"You doubt him?" asked Ryana. "I can attest to the truth of everything he says. I was there."

"Oh, I would not question your word, my lady," Kieran said. "But it does strain one's credulity. I wish I did *not* believe it, for it means you will both be targets for every defiler on Athas. You must admit, that argues against a long life, for you and anyone with you."

"You still want me for your lieutenant?" Sorak asked wryly.

"Well, it will make things interesting," Kieran replied with a smile. "I was getting bored in retirement, anyway."

"We'll make a preserver of you yet," Ryana said with a grin, punching him in the shoulder.

"We should all live so long, my lady," Kieran said. "I have no magic blade, and your friend here just threw his away."

"I did that once before," said Sorak, "but there are some responsibilities one simply can't avoid." Kieran's eyes grew wide as Sorak reached down and drew Galdra from his belt. He held the broken blade up before him, and it sparkled with a faint blue aura.

"Now that was a neat trick," said Kieran.

Sorak smiled. "Just don't ask me how it's done,"

he said. "A moment ago, it wasn't there. And then I felt it pressing against my side. It seems no matter what I do, I cannot get rid of it."

"What else does it do?" asked Kieran.

Sorak shrugged. "It makes me wish I had been born someone else. In fact, I used to *be* someone else every now and then."

Kieran frowned. "What does that mean?"

"It's a long story," Sorak said. "But we still have about a day's ride ahead. I'll tell you all about it on the way to Altaruk."

"Well then, let's ride," said Kieran. "I'd like to see just what's waiting for us when we get there."

"It's me they're waiting for," said Sorak. "You do not need to involve yourself."

"In case you have forgotten," Kieran said, "you've saved my life twice, and my caravan once. The way I see it, I'm involved."

"I did what I chose to do," said Sorak. "You are under no obligation to me, Kieran."

"That's not the way I see it. And I will brook no arguments. I am still your superior officer, if you'll recall."

Sorak smiled. "Whatever you say, Captain."

"I say we've wasted enough time," Kieran replied. "Mount up."

ELEVEN

It was, Matullus thought, a truly lousy way to start the day. His weak stomach notwithstanding, he had somehow managed to hold his gorge down when he walked into the room and saw the carnage. Perhaps he was getting used to it. And that was bad enough in itself.

The first thing that hit him was the smell. The bodies had been dead only a few hours, but in the desert, the morning temperatures rose quickly, and they were already stinking. And the blood. It was splattered everywhere. Its coppery smell commingled with the stench of bowels that had released at the moment of death. Matullus was still young and had never fought in a full-fledged campaign. He had never seen a war. But this morning, he finally understood what the old veterans meant when they said that a battlefield smelled like human waste.

Bad enough to be murdered, he thought, but to be found like this, mangled and begrimed with feces . . . if this was any indication of what it was like to die in battle, he could see no glory in it. Better to die old in bed, he thought, of a ruptured heart, wrapped in the arms of a young woman. That was a sort of glory he could understand.

The sound of flies buzzing in the room was almost as oppressive as the stench. He covered the lower half of his face with the free end of his turban and looked around.

"Gith's blood!" said one of his men behind him, clapping his hand over his mouth and nose as he came in. "What kind of animal would *do* a thing like this?"

"The kind that walks on two legs," Matullus said grimly. He stepped around and over the corpses, looking down at each one and giving it a cursory examination. "This one was stabbed in the stomach, disemboweled. This one had his throat slashed from ear to ear. Look at that stroke. It practically decapitated him. And this one had his back broken. This one had his neck snapped. The head was almost twisted right off the spinal column. This one was stabbed straight in the heart. The blade smashed right through the ribs. And this one was strangled. See the bruises on the neck? Look at this. . . ." He laid his hand across the discolorations, matching his fingers to the marks. "The killer did it with just one hand."

"Look at the white veils dropped on the bodies," one of the men said. "Just like with the last one."

"A calling card, perhaps?" Matullus asked rhetorically. "Did the Veiled Alliance kill these men, or are we supposed to believe they were killed because they were in the Alliance, themselves?"

"Lord Ankhor isn't going to like this," one of the men said.

"No, he certainly will not," Matullus agreed. "And Lord Jhamri will like it even less. This sort of thing is bad for business."

"What are we going to do, sir?" one of the younger guards asked.

"Dispose of the bodies," said Matullus. "There is little else we can do. And then we will spread out through the neighborhood and make inquires. Someone must know these men. But if they were in the Alliance, none will admit it. An admission would be self-incriminating. We may learn their names, but I doubt we'll learn anything else."

"The caravan from Balic should be in tonight, shouldn't it?" one of the guards asked.

Matullus nodded. "If they are on schedule. Our new captain is going to inherit this sorry mess. I doubt he will be pleased to start his job on such a note. And if Kieran is displeased, I fear we'll be the first to feel that displeasure."

"This isn't going to stop, is it?"

Matullus shook his head. "No. Not unless we stop it. Whoever is doing this is good at killing. The bastard likes it."

"Surely this isn't the work of one man?" one the guards asked with astonishment.

"Each of these men was killed by someone very powerful," Matullus said. "And it was done very quickly. Two of them didn't have a chance to draw weapons. And if they were adepts, they certainly did not have a chance to cast defensive spells. This one here had drawn his dagger. It's still grasped in his hand, for all the good it did him. One dagger was thrown." He pointed to where it was embedded in the wall. "I think . . . by that one, there. Obviously, he missed, and it cost him his life. The others were all disarmed before they died. And quickly, too, for the killer toyed with them." He indicated the smashed table and overturned chairs.

"One was thrown across the room, onto that table, and while he was stunned, another was disposed of. Then another was thrown against that wall there, where the spice jars have fallen off the shelf and shattered on the floor. Stun one, grab another, and so forth, like a mountain cat toying with janx. Whoever did this was incredibly strong, and burst in upon these men like a windstorm off the desert. They never had a chance."

"Six against one, and all died," a guard said in a low voice. "And not one of these men was far above middle age. Only one was on the frail side. Still . . ." The guard shook his head. "To throw men around like this, like chaff before the wind . . ."

"It isn't human," one of the guards said.

"No," said Matullus thoughtfully. "Something much stronger. A half-giant or a mul, perhaps."

"But there are no half-giants or muls in Altaruk," one of the others said.

Matullus nodded. "There is now."

"Someone like that would stand out in this town like an oasis on a desert."

"You would think so, wouldn't you?" Matullus said. "Unless someone is hiding him. And that means a confederate. Perhaps more than one." He nodded. "At least we will have something to tell Kieran when he arrives."

"What do you think he will do?" someone asked.

Matullus turned to face him. "Well, we'll soon find out, won't we? He's supposed to be the best. I expect he'll waste no time in taking charge of the situation. And that means we'll have to be up to the challenge. When he arrives tonight, I want every man in the house guard turned out clean and sharp. And woe to the man our new captain finds fault with. I will personally see to it that he regrets not being one of these corpses. Now clean this mess up. We have a great deal to do before the caravan arrives."

* * * * *

It was late afternoon when Lord Ankhor entered his private study on the top floor of the mansion. A few hours earlier, Matullus had nervously made his report about the recent killings. He was cautious in remarks, but astute in observations. He'd conjectured that the killer was a half-giant or a mul, judging by the murders, which indicated not only strength but also fighting skill. Matullus was a clever young man. Undoubtedly, Kieran would be more clever, still.

Ankhor went to the sideboard and poured himself a drink. It would not do for Kieran to resolve the situation too swiftly. That would displease the templar and undermine his plans. Jhamri needed to be suitably embarrassed by his ineffectiveness in countering the threat. And then, of course, at the proper time, the mul would be apprehended by the Ankhor House Guard. A pity to waste a property like that. She was rather an expensive purchase to discard, but it would be well worth it to see Jhamri properly humbled. Merely the first step, of course, but a significant one—the cost of doing business.

Ankhor frowned as he saw the small statue on the mantlepiece turned to one side. He had specifically told the templar to hold her meetings late at night, except in an emergency. Could something have gone wrong? He paused to lock the heavy, ornate door of his study before opening the secret panel. He stepped back in surprise as Edric came into the room.

"What in thunder are *you* doing here?" he asked, frowning. "You were supposed to be with the caravan!"

"I was," said Edric, moving to the sideboard to pour himself a drink as casually as if he were in his own home. For the first time, Ankhor noticed he was wounded. His left arm hung limp at his side, and he favored his shoulder as he moved. "I rode like the wind itself to get here ahead of them. We had some problems."

"What are you talking about?" asked Ankhor.

"The attack failed," Edric said simply.

"What do you mean it failed? How could it fail?"

"It failed because we lost the element of surprise," said Edric, tipping back his goblet. "And I almost lost my life as well, but we won't dwell on little things like that."

"What happened? What went wrong?"

"Everything," said Edric. "Those three fools you hired to join the caravan at Grak's Pool drew suspicion instantly. I told you additional men on the inside were not necessary. I would have been quite capable of handling things myself. And then, just to make things worse, I was unmasked."

"How? By whom? Kieran?"

"No, though I have a score to settle with that one. He shall have to wait his turn. There was another. A half-breed. The Nomad."

Ankhor frowned. "Sorak? *Here?*"

"You know of him?"

"We've met before," said Ankhor.

"Oh, yes, of course," said Edric. "He stole that princess from your caravan."

"Torian's loss, not mine," said Ankhor dismissively. "And the rash fool was stupid enough to give pursuit into the Barrens, which cost him his life. An inconvenience, as he was a valued trading partner, but a minor loss, all things considered. But Sorak's presence is a greater inconvenience, still."

"An inconvenience," said Edric wryly. "How quaint. We lost over a score of our tribe, and you call it 'an inconvenience.' "

"I thought the Shadows were supposed to be masters of their craft," said Ankhor scornfully. "And over a score of them were brought down by mere caravan guards? Had I known your people were so inept, I would have spent my money elsewhere."

"They were ambushed," Edric said. "You might have done better to rob your own caravan at a time when Kieran of Draj was not there to take command. He knows his trade, that one. He laid a brilliant trap. Your money was well spent in hiring him. But your timing in having him on that particular caravan left something to be desired."

"I could not control his movements," Ankhor said. "When I discovered he was coming on that caravan, it was already too late to change the plan."

"And so we paid the price for it," said Edric bitterly. With his right hand, he refilled his goblet and drained it in one gulp. "Still, but for that elfling, the plan might have succeeded. What makes it truly galling is that I was the one who told them when the attack would come. I had no choice. To resist would have been suicide, and I was not prepared to give up yet. My people are very dissatisfied with me at the moment. And they are even less satisfied with you."

"Is that a threat?" asked Ankhor.

"A statement of fact. I did not come here alone,

in case you're thinking of doing something foolish," Edric cautioned him. "I have brought some of my people with me. If I do not return, they will see to it that all of Altaruk knows who it was who hired us to rob the caravan."

"Very well," said Ankhor. "Let's get down to business. What do you want? Reparations for your losses? Name your price."

Edric considered. "Fifty thousand in gold."

"Done," said Ankhor. "Anything else?"

Edric snorted. "I should have asked for more. But yes, there is one more thing. I want the Nomad."

Ankhor shrugged. "Take him. He does not concern me."

"I beg to differ," Edric said. "He happens to be yours."

"Mine?" Ankhor frowned. "What do you mean?"

"Kieran has hired him to be his lieutenant in your house guard," Edric said. "The two of them are thick as thieves, and it would be difficult to seize him while he is under your protection."

Ankhor chuckled.

"You find that amusing?" asked Edric, scowling.

"Yes, frankly, I do," said Ankhor. He smiled. "The Nomad and I seem fated to cross paths in fascinating ways. The first time, it was to my benefit. The second, to my loss. But this time, there is more at stake. I do not want him getting in the way."

"Then we will be pleased to take him off your

hands," said Edric. "In addition to the gold, of course."

"You will have your gold," said Ankhor with thinly veiled contempt. "As for Sorak, I will make it easy for you. I'll greet the caravan when it arrives, as a show of gratitude for his assistance in foiling the attack. To prove I hold no grudge against him for the royal twit, I will offer him the use of one of our apartments in the shopkeeper's quarter. It is on the Street of Clothiers, above the shop of Lorian the Bootmaker. The house is marked with the sign of a blue boot. The entrance to the stairs leading up to the apartment is through an alley to the right of the shop. I'll see to it that Kieran is otherwise engaged tonight, with the remainder of the house guard, so they cannot interfere. The rest is up to you. Will that be satisfactory?"

Edric pursed his lips and nodded. "It will do."

"Good. And though it is not my habit to give rewards for failure, I'll arrange a discreet payment of the gold, through our usual intermediaries, as a gesture of good faith. I expect no problems with the Shadows on any future shipments in my caravans. I do not expect to be seeing you again. Our business is concluded. Feel free to have another drink before you leave."

Edric picked up the crystal decanter and carried it with him to the secret panel. "Just see to it the gold is delivered promptly."

"Of course," said Ankhor. "And in the event you should decide it is not enough to buy your silence, be mindful that any difficulties you may try to cause me will be countered by the full resources of the House of Ankhor. Should you renege on our agreement, within a month all of Athas will know the Shadows do not bargain in good faith."

"A bargain is a bargain," Edric said. "But this has been a most unhappy business, all around. Good-bye, my lord."

"Goodbye," said Ankhor curtly.

The panel opened, Eric stepped through, and it closed again behind him.

Ankhor snorted with disgust and grimaced. "It seems one cannot buy good help these days."

* * * * *

As Edric reached the bottom of the stairs inside the secret passage, he saw a dark-robed figure waiting for him in the tunnel just ahead. He paused, his right hand going to the knife tucked into his belt.

"Stay your hand, Edric, unless you wish to lose the use of *both* your arms."

Edric allowed his right arm to drop casually back to his side. "Greetings, Templar Livanna," he said. "Forgive me, I did not know it was you."

"Who did you think I was?" the templar asked.

Edric shrugged. "Some lackey of Lord Ankhor's, perhaps, bent on treachery. I expected trouble, not a chance meeting with you."

"I leave nothing to chance," Livanna said. "I felt your presence close by, even as I now feel the pain of your wound." She touched her left arm, which hung limply at her side. "I came to heal you so that I would not feel your pain. I find it distracting."

Edric's eyes narrowed with suspicion. "How is it that you feel my pain?" he asked warily.

"Have you forgotten? When we agreed to terms, you made your mark in blood," Livanna said.

"I see," said Edric. "I thought it was no more than a ritual to seal our bargain. I'll have to be more careful of that sort thing in the future."

Livanna examined his arm. "What happened?"

He told her about the failed raid. As he spoke, she listened and concentrated at the same time, grasping his arm firmly. He felt a tingling sensation at first, followed by a gradual warmth spreading up his arm and into his wounded shoulder. It grew hotter, to the point where it started to burn, and then the templar released him, and he felt the heat fade gradually. He moved his arm and shoulder experimentally. It felt as good as new.

"My thanks," said Edric. "I had no time to seek a healer before coming here. But I'm curious. What would you have felt had I been killed instead of merely wounded?"

"I would have felt your death," replied Livanna. "The sensation would have been brief: your death would have canceled the spell. How did Ankhor react to your report?"

"He was not pleased, but he took it reasonably well, all things considered," Edric replied. "After all, I could not be held entirely responsible. He had hired three infiltrators to join the caravan at

Grak's Pool, against my advice, and I am sure they raised suspicion. Then there was Kieran's presence to consider. And that miserable Nomad. I intend to make it up to him quite soon."

"I do not want the Nomad killed," said Livanna. "I want to question him. After that, he is yours to dispose of as you will. But do not make the mistake of underestimating him. He is dangerous."

"I had already discovered that," Edric replied. "And I am in no great rush to kill him. I want him to live long enough to regret having interfered with me. And once I am through with him, I will take care of Kieran."

"Do not overreach yourself," Livanna said. "What of Ankhor? Does he know anything of our arrangement?"

Edric shook his head. "No, he suspects nothing. He assumes our business is concluded. He is smug and overconfident. He believes his money can buy anything, and that will be his downfall. Just let me know when you are prepared to make your move. The Shadows stand ready. They blamed me, at first, for the ambush they rode into, but I managed to convince them Ankhor had betrayed us. They're chaffing for revenge."

"Wait until I give the word," Livanna said. "The timing must be right. For now, the Nomad is the first priority. And I want to know the moment you have him."

"Why such an interest in this elfling pretender?"

"Pretender?"

Edric said, "The Crown of Elves, indeed. His

arrogance offends me."

"Pretender or no, Nibenay wants him. Princess Korahna was exiled by her mother to protect her from her father's wrath because she had taken the vows of a preserver," Livanna said. "When Sorak brought her back to Nibenay, she joined the Veiled Alliance, and since then they have been sheltering her. They have made much of the conversion of a daughter of the Shadow King."

"Yes, of course," said Edric, nodding.

"Sorak has contacts with the Veiled Alliance in Nibenay," Livanna said. "If we can find out who they are, we can take steps to get Korahna back."

"And teach her the error of her ways?" Edric smiled. "I didn't think the Shadow King would care about one errant daughter; he has so many others. It seems we both have unfinished business with the elfling, but it will not remain unfinished long. I'll send word to you the moment we have him, but on one condition. When our business is concluded, you'll remove the spell that links us."

"When our business is concluded, I'll have no further use for it," she said. "Until then, try to exercise more caution. I have no wish to feel your aches and pains."

"Then perhaps you should have trusted me, without the spell," said Edric.

"Trust an elf?" said Livanna. "I think not. Until you have fully lived up to your part of our bargain, the spell is necessary."

"So be it, then. Are we agreed?"

"Agreed."

Edric nodded. "I thank you for the healing. I'll be in touch soon."

He turned and walked off down the corridor. Livanna watched him go. She did not and would not trust him for a moment, except where his own self-interest was concerned. He might not be as quick to betray a templar of the Shadow King as he was to betray Ankhor, but if there was enough profit in it, he would certainly consider taking such a risk. She wanted him to know just how much of a risk it was.

But if the Shadow elves could capture Sorak, it would save her the trouble of going after him herself. There was, of course, a chance that they would be unable to take him alive. That would be regrettable, for she wanted to force him to reveal what he knew about the Sage. Still, if he were dead, he could be no threat, and the Sage would lose his champion. Either way, the outcome would be favorable.

In the meantime, she had work to do. Kah was waiting.

* * * * *

A caravan coming into town was always an event, one eagerly awaited by the populace. It meant more business for the shopkeepers, more guests for the inns, and more patrons for the gaming and pleasure houses. When the dust cloud was sighted in the distance, the word quickly went out through the streets, and by the time they rode into town, a large crowd had gathered to welcome them.

Lord Ankhor himself was on hand. He greeted Kieran effusively, then listened gravely to his report of the attack, the caravan captain standing nervously by.

Uncertain how Lord Ankhor would react to seeing him, Sorak had hung back with Ryana until Kieran turned and pointed to him, apparently telling Ankhor about his heroics in their defense. Instead of beckoning him over, Lord Ankhor came to him, with Kieran by his side. There was a broad smile on his face as he extended his hand to Sorak in greeting.

"So we meet again, Nomad," he said. He turned to Ryana and greeted her respectfully. "Welcome to Altaruk, my lady. It is a pleasure to see you again, and on so auspicious an occasion." He turned back to Sorak. "It seems each time we meet, you come to my rescue."

"I fear that was not the case on our last meeting," Sorak said. He was not anxious to bring it up but wanted to know where he stood. "Are you glad to see me, even after that?"

"If you are referring to the matter of the princess you 'escorted' from my caravan, that was Viscount Torian's loss. She was his concern, not mine. I understand the matter was resolved between the two of you."

"I thought Viscount Torian was your friend," said Sorak uncertainly.

Lord Ankhor shrugged. "A business acquaintance, no more. In trade, I was obliged to extend certain courtesies to him, but his involvement with the princess was unwise, and I feared it might have repercussions. Frankly, I was relieved when she departed. Torian's demise may have made me suffer a slight, temporary reverse, but nothing like the losses I would have sustained had that raid succeeded. Once more, I am in your debt."

"It was nothing, my lord. And as Kieran had recruited me to serve, I felt it no more than my duty."

"It was rather a great deal more as far as I'm concerned," said Ankhor, "and I am pleased to display my gratitude. As it happens, my house is in partnership with that of Lord Jhamri, so you will be working for us both. And as your employer, I know you will be in need of housing here in Altaruk. A senior officer and his lady should have comfortable, private quarters, so it would please me if you accepted my offer of an apartment."

"That is most gracious of you, my lord," said Sorak, "but there is no need for you to trouble yourself on—"

"Nonsense," said Ankhor, interrupting him. "The House of Ankhor maintains a number of apartments here in town, for visiting trading partners and dignitaries. At any given time, at least half are vacant. You would find the accommodations more comfortable than you could afford, and as one of your employers, I insist you accept."

"Well, since you put it that way . . ."

"Excellent. I have just the place in mind. It is

located in the shopkeeper's quarter, on the Street of Clothiers. Anyone can tell you where it is. Look for the sign of the blue boot. It marks the shop of Lorian the Bootmaker. He will have the key. The apartment is above his shop. Once the shops close for the night, the area is quiet, and there is little traffic. I think you will find it preferable to the noisy apartments in the gaming district."

"It sounds perfect, my lord," Sorak said.

"You may as well go now and take up residence, before Lorian closes up his shop for the night," said Ankhor. "Kieran and I have several matters to discuss pertaining to his new duties, and I would prefer to speak with him privately, as I'm sure you'll understand. You may report to me at the House of Ankhor in the morning, and then we can have our talk."

"Thank you, my lord," said Sorak. "In that case, with your permission, I shall take my leave and see you in the morning."

"Until tomorrow," Ankhor said. He turned to Ryana and bowed. "My lady . . ."

"Well, it turns out there was no reason for concern, after all," Ryana said as they walked away. "Lord Ankhor bears no grudges over the incident with Korahna and we now have a place to stay without having to walk all over town in search of one. A quiet apartment over a shop sounds nice. A real home for a change, after all those nights spent sleeping on the ground." She smiled and took his arm. "It will be our first place together."

"Our first place," he said, hugging her close. "I

like the sound of that. But don't grow accustomed to the idea. There is no telling how long it will last."

They asked directions to the Street of Clothiers, only a short walk away. It did not take long before they found the shop with the sign of the blue boot hanging over the entrance. Lorian was just about to close up for the day when they came in, and after they introduced themselves and gave him Ankhor's message, he welcomed them effusively and gave them the key, telling them the entrance was through the alley to the right and up a flight of stairs.

"I know it may sound foolish," said Ryana, putting her arm around Sorak's waist as they left the shop, "because we may never be able to settle in one place for very long, but I still feel excited. This is going to be our first real home."

"It is only an apartment above a shop."

"It doesn't matter," said Ryana as they turned into the alley. "It will be ours, a place you can come home to. Home to me."

The attack came suddenly and swiftly. Sorak felt a sharp, glancing blow against the side of his head, and he went down, grunting with pain.

Instinct and years of training took over, and he rolled quickly to his feet, drawing his sword as he came up. They were rushed from both sides of the alley. Five came from behind, five from in front.

Ryana had been seized from behind by two of the attackers, but she stomped down hard on one's foot, twisted away, and flipped the other over her hip. As he fell, she drew her sword, but before she could get it clear of the scabbard, a blade took her from behind. She gave a grunting, gasping sound and stiffened, arching her back sharply with the impact.

A bloody sword tip emerged from her stomach.

"*Ryana!*" Sorak screamed, and then they were on him.

He drew Galdra with his free hand and waded into them like a man possessed. They tried to seize him and wrestle him to the ground, but he broke away, slashing one elf across the throat with Galdra and driving his sword deep into another's midsection. He kicked the elf he'd spitted off the blade, backward into three other attackers, and they went down beneath the dead weight of their comrade.

Spinning like a dervish, Sorak laid about him with both blades, screaming his rage at the top of his lungs. Within seconds, four elves lay dead, and the remainder found themselves with far more on their hands than they had bargained for.

The Shadows had abandoned any notion of taking him alive. It was either him or them. But in the narrow confines of the alley, their superior numbers gave them no advantage. Sorak did not remain still for so much as an instant, and the elves found themselves only getting into each other's way.

Fighting with a fury he had never felt before, Sorak parried, struck, slashed, kicked and slammed into his opponents, and they fell one after the other. In the midst of the melee, he caught a glimpse of a familiar face.

"*Edric!*"

The elf paled and took to his heels, but there was no chance to give pursuit.

Three elves remained, and they suddenly found themselves fighting for their lives. Sorak gave them no chance to retreat. He parried one blow, turning the blade aside, and stepped in, stabbing Galdra deep in the elf's stomach even as he blocked another stroke with his sword. He shoved the dying elf's body away, spun around, ducked under a slash, and drove his blade up into his attacker's throat.

The one remaining elf turned and ran in panic, but he never got farther than two steps. Sorak brought him down, tackling him from behind, and drove the broken blade into his back. He came up quickly, spinning around, but there were no more opponents. Edric had fled, but the others all lay dead or dying in the alley.

Then he heard a soft moan.

"*Sorak. . . .*"

Ryana lay facedown in the alley in a large and rapidly spreading pool of blood. Sorak ran to her and crouched by her side, gently turning her over.

"Ryana!"

When he saw her wound, he knew there was no hope. No hope at all. The spark of life was already fading from her eyes as she gazed up at him.

"Ryana, *no* . . ."

She tried to breathe in shallow gasps, but blood

bubbled up from between her lips. She coughed and made a terrible, grunting, choking sound, and managed to gasp out just three words before she died.

"I . . . loved . . . you. . . ."

Sorak stared with stunned disbelief at the limp and lifeless body he was holding in his arms, and his mind tried to reject the unacceptable reality. He shook her, and called her name over and over again, and finally, as the awful knowledge sank in, he threw his head back and screamed, one long, drawn out, inarticulate wail of agony and despair. And in that frenzied, tortured cry of unutterable pain, something new and terrible was born.

TWELVE

"*Nomad*!"

He spun around, his sword poised to strike. He did not know where he was. The street was unfamiliar. He had been wandering around for hours in a semi-fugue state, looking for the one Shadow who had escaped. *Edric.* The thought of finding him was foremost in his mind, driving out everything else.

But the man who faced him in the dark and empty street was not Edric. He was a human, slight in stature, dressed in a dark, hooded cloak. His face was wrinkled with age, as was his hand, which he held across the lower part of his face, miming a veil.

Sorak simply stood and stared at him. In one hand, he still held the sword of Valsavis. In the other, he held the broken blade. Both were bloodstained.

The old man lowered his hand and came forward, hesitantly. "We have been looking for you," he said, as he approached. "We know about what happened. By the time we got there, it was too late. Words cannot express our sorrow."

Sorak said nothing. He just stood there, motionless.

"You are hurt," the man said, reaching out toward him, then drawing his hand back. "You are losing blood. Please . . . come. Let me help you. You cannot wander the streets like this. There is danger. *Please* . . ."

The man reached forward once again, slowly and deliberately, and took his arm. "I am Andreas. I have some skill at healing, but I cannot do it here, out in the street. We may be seen. Please, come with me. In the name of the Path and the Way, please come. . . ."

Numbly, Sorak allowed himself to be led down a series of deserted back streets and dark alleys until they came to small tavern on a side street, near the merchants' plaza. It was late, and the tavern was closed for the night, but the old man knocked softly on the wooden door: twice, then a short pause, then three times, then a pause, then twice again. The door was unbolted from within, and they went inside.

It was dark within, and the benches had been turned upside-down and placed on the tabletops for sweeping of the floor. The man who had admitted them was human, middle-aged, and portly—balding on top and dressed in loose brown breeches, sandals, and a slightly soiled white tunic. He bolted the door again behind them and said nothing. He merely conducted them back to the bar, behind it and to a small storage room.

At the back of the room was a beaded curtain. He drew it aside and beckoned them through, but he did not follow them into the dimly lit chamber. Within stood a long table with several benches pulled up to it and three thick candles spread out along the tabletop. Seated at the table in the back room were three men in white robes, who immediately rose to their feet as they came in.

"You've found him, Andreas!"

"He's hurt!"

"Bring him here, quickly!"

They gathered around him and led him to a bench, easing him onto it. He felt them trying to take the weapons from his hands, but his fingers were tightly clamped around the hilts, as if of their own volition, and would not let go.

"Do not be afraid," one of the men said. "You are among friends. There is no need for these."

"Let it be," Andreas said. "He needs something to hold onto. He has suffered a terrible shock."

Andreas removed his cloak, revealing the white robe of the Alliance, and knelt in front of him, taking each of his hands gently by the wrists. He breathed deeply, closed his eyes, and concentrated while the others watched. Gradually, Sorak became aware that the old man's hands were growing warm. The warmth seeped into his wrists and started flowing up his arms. He felt the heat increase as Andreas breathed more deeply, drops of perspiration forming on his forehead. Sorak felt the warmth reach his shoulders and start spreading across his chest. The heat increased, flowing down his torso, into his legs, and rising into his neck, suffusing his face and head.

The cuts and slashes on his body slowly closed and began to fade away. He felt a warm, comforting, drifting sensation, as if he were floating on a summer desert breeze, and the pain slowly went away. He breathed more deeply, and his eyelids fluttered. His muscles relaxed, and he felt the blades drop from his fingers to the floor.

Abruptly, his body stiffened with a sharp, jerking spasm, and the jolt broke the contact with Andreas, who cried out and fell back on the floor, releasing him. Sorak heard the alarmed voices of the men around him, but they seemed to be fading away into the distance.

"What happened?"

"What's wrong?"

"I don't know. . . ."

Then everything was spinning as the room went away and Sorak found himself out in the street, striding down a dark alley, a cloaked and hooded figure walking just ahead of him. But it was not he walking through the alley. It was the *other,* the killer, and as the hooded figure turned into a side street and looked back briefly, Sorak recognized the templar he had seen before in his last vision.

The street they had turned into looked familiar. And an instant later, the realization struck him that it was the same street he had walked down with Andreas moments earlier. The door to the tavern they were in was just ahead. They were coming *here*.

Panic rose in him. He had to warn them, somehow, but he did not know how. He could not break free of the vision. It felt as if he were having a terrifying nightmare, one in which he knew he was dreaming, and he kept desperately trying to wake up, but just could not shake the dream.

He struggled to wrench free as the templar paused outside in the street, just by the door. In his shared perception with the *other*, Sorak saw the door in front of him, felt it as the killer kicked it in, and then saw the interior of the darkened tavern rushing past as the killer ran through it, heading toward the bar and the back room.

The tavernkeeper came rushing out, brandishing a blade, but the killer sidestepped his lunge smoothly and crushed his chest with one powerful blow.

From somewhere beyond the curtain, Sorak heard the front door of the tavern splinter, heard the alarmed reactions of the men, but it all seemed very far away. The effect of the shared consciousness increased as the killer drew closer, moving swiftly, vaulting the bar and running through the storage room, plunging through the beaded curtain. . . .

Then Sorak saw himself through the killer's

eyes. He saw the killer sweep one of the white-robed men aside as he raised his arms to cast a spell. One powerful blow sent him reeling back against the wall with stunning impact, and then the killer seized Andreas, grabbing him by the throat. . . .

With a desperate effort, Sorak's mind screamed, *STOP!*

Kah froze. Yes, that was her name—Kah. And, yes, the killer was a she.

She had heard the shouted command, but not aloud. It seemed to explode within her mind. For a moment, she simply stood there, confused and puzzled, using Andreas as a shield so that none of the others could throw a spell at her. Then her gaze focused on the elfling sitting on the bench before her, and she saw him gazing back at her, unafraid, eyes blazing.

Sorak slowly rose to his feet, his gaze locked with the deadly mul's. "Release him," he said aloud.

Kah heard the command echo in her mind. *Get out of my mind*, she thought, a chill clutching her.

No. Release him.

This time, he had not spoken aloud, yet she had heard him clearly. More significantly, *he* had heard *her*. The realization struck her with a shock. She spun Andreas around and held him in front of her, a powerful arm clamped across the throat. For the first time in her life, someone had *heard* her. She had communicated.

You can hear *me?*

I hear you. Release him. He has done you no harm.

The other members of the Alliance cell all stood perfectly still, staring with a mixture of fear and fascination. They could not hear the exchange but knew something was happening, something powerful and momentous, and those of them who were sensitive could feel the vibrant emanations of psionic energy in the small back room.

I must kill him, Kah communicated. *I must kill you all.*

Why?

The master wills it. He bought me. It is what I do.

And in that instant, as Kah thought of Ankhor, Sorak saw him in her mind and knew everything. A cold rage welled in him, a fury and hatred unlike anything he had ever known. He understood then what had been born in Ryana's death, and he embraced it.

I am the master now. Release the old man.

No . . .

Release him. . . .

Kah felt her right arm tremble. Slowly, involuntarily, she loosened her hold on Andreas. She fought to clamp her arm tighter against his throat, to squeeze the life out of him, but her own arm resisted her, fought her, pulled away. She redoubled her efforts, sweat forming as the powerful muscles of her arm and shoulder stood out with the strain.

GET OUT! she screamed inwardly.

Release . . . him . . . now!

Gritting her teeth, Kah fought the inexorable pull, but she was losing the battle. Slowly, her arm came away, and Andreas drew in a hungry, gasping breath as he broke free, falling to his knees, clutching at his throat, straining to draw air into his tortured lungs.

In that moment, a bright blue bolt of thaumaturgic energy lanced across the room and exploded with a blinding glare as it struck one of the Alliance men squarely in the chest. He screamed, hurled back against the wall, and the scream was cut off as his body flew apart into chunks of viscera and incinerated flesh.

The room became a blinding latticework of energy bolts as the remaining Alliance adepts responded to the templar's attack.

Livanna's assault broke Sorak's psionic link with Kah, and she charged in with a snarl, but Sorak ducked beneath her lunge and rolled, coming up with Galdra in his hand.

As energy bolts flew back and forth across the room, igniting everything around them, Kah spun and charged again. Instead of trying to avoid her lunge, as she expected, Sorak stepped right into it, slamming into her and driving the broken blade deep into her huge, powerful midsection.

The breath whistled out of the mul in a startled gasp, and she stared in shock at the blade buried in her stomach, then looked up at Sorak, their faces only inches apart. With an animal growl of fury, she grabbed him by the throat with both hands and started squeezing.

No!

She felt him boring into her mind like an auger

and fought the savage intrusion, but felt her hands resisting her, opening slowly despite all her efforts to close them around his throat.

NO!

The command was punctuated with a jerk as Sorak twisted Galdra in her stomach and pulled up, ripping her insides. Blood trickled from the corner of her mouth, and waves of pain washed over her. Her fingers slipped from around his neck as her eyes started to glaze over, and a moment later, it was finished. Her huge body went limp, and she collapsed to the floor, lifeless.

The spell battle, in the meantime, had progressed to the front room of the tavern as Livanna beat a hasty retreat. Though she had killed two of her antagonists, two more remained. Andreas had struggled to his feet after the initial assault, and despite already being weakened by the healing, had joined the one remaining Alliance adept in the counterattack.

As Kah slipped off his blade and fell lifeless to the floor, Sorak retrieved his other sword and left the room. He plunged through the beaded curtain to the taproom, which was already in flames.

He ducked down behind the bar as an energy bolt hurled by Livanna passed overhead, and then he heard a scream, cut off sharply as another Alliance adept met his end.

He came out from behind the bar, staying low and moving quickly, Livanna was facing off against Andreas. They both threw their spells at the same time. Andreas cried out and fell as his right arm was vaporized, but his bolt of energy struck Livanna in the legs as he fell.

She screamed and fell to the floor, a double amputee. The intense heat of the energy bolt had instantly cauterized her wounds, but she was legless from her thighs down and continued screaming, writhing on the floor in agony.

Sorak ran over to Andreas, but one glance told him there was nothing he could do. Already weakened by the healing spell he'd cast, the old man had thrown everything he had into his last spell. He had used up all of his remaining life force, sacrificing himself, leaving behind only a withered corpse.

As he straightened, Sorak saw Livanna struggling to drag herself toward the door. He crossed the burning room in several quick strides and pinned her to the floor, a foot in the middle of her back. The flames were spreading rapidly, and the tavern was filling up with smoke and the sounds of crackling fire. He bent and turned the templar over, pressing the broken blade against her throat.

Livanna stared at him with loathing, and as her lips moved to cast a spell, Sorak went in.

He focused his burning hatred upon her brow, and his mind tore into hers, psionically smashing its way past all resistance, driving to the core the way a termite bores through wood. He found everything he wanted in there—her plot with Ankhor and the mul; her bargain with the Shadow elves to betray Ankhor and clear the way for Nibenay; her spell link with the treacherous Edric.

He brushed everything else aside and seized on the spell link, focusing his energies on it . . . and he tore it out, appropriating it.

As he withdrew from the templar's mind, he left her ravaged, her consciousness psionically shredded. Her eyes stared up at him emptily, seeing nothing. He left her a crippled, mindless shell. She would survive, but not long. He glanced around at the conflagration. Not long at all.

As he stepped through the smoke pouring out the busted front door of the tavern, he saw a crowd gathered in the street. They stared at him and pointed, but he did not pause. He came toward them, and they hastily moved aside to let him pass. In the center of the street, he hesitated only a moment, cocking his head to one side slightly as if listening, then set off at a run for the gaming district.

* * * * *

The audience, composed almost exclusively of males, broke out into wild cheering and applause as Cricket shed her clinging, diaphanous gown and stood before them clad only in a tiny strip of cloth and a silver ankle chain. Seated among the male patrons were the other dancers, who had stopped hustling their customers long enough to watch the new girl and see what she could do. Cricket saw in their expressions a mixture of responses—admiration, envy, resentment, hunger—reactions she had seen often before.

The one response she had never seen, and wished she could, was someone who enjoyed her dancing merely for its own sake. Once, so long ago it seemed as if it were another lifetime, she had danced for the sake of dancing, for the simple joy it brought her. Now, it had become an exercise in manipulation.

Unlike other dancers, who wasted little time before disrobing, she had left her gown and scarves on through most her dance, only removing them slowly and provocatively at the end. The other dancers sold the fantasy of wantons, lustful, desirable, and easily available.

Among them, her presentation was unique. She was not a trollop, but a graceful half-elf girl, demure and feminine, conscious of her body and the joy it could bring. Instead of flaunting open sexuality, she showed flirtatious femininity. Instead of lewd gyrations, she presented charming sensuality. Instead of brassy provocation, she danced subtle invitation, with a shy surrender at the climax. It never failed to drive them wild.

Yes, she thought, that she could do. But in the end, it was merely illusion, a paltry substitute for a reality she had never even known.

She had thought it would be different in Altaruk. Yes, the house was larger and catered to a more well-heeled clientele. Yes, the pay was better, and the tips more generous. And yes, the working conditions were improved, with larger and more comfortable dressing rooms and attendants to assist with costuming and makeup. But in all other respects, it was the same: the pressure to be more "friendly" with customers, the blatant sexual overtures from patrons and management, the crude shouted comments from customers, the constant groping, feeling, pinching. . . . In the end, only the place had changed. Even the faces seemed the same.

Cricket retrieved her gown and headed offstage, toward the dressing room. In the corridor, as she slipped the gown back on, she felt hollow, a sensual facade over deep melancholy. She had found a new job and new quarters, but otherwise, nothing had changed. She was still just going through the motions of a life.

What was the point in holding out for an ideal that did not exist? What was the purpose in waiting for a hero when, in the end, heroic talk led only to base actions? Why bother to believe in virtue, love, and honor—mere masks for ambition, lust, and expedience? If men told lies, was she any better for selling them illusions? Why stop there? Why not simply sell it all?

She came to an abrupt halt as she entered the dressing room, eyes widening in surprise. The other dancers were outside, working the crowd, but she was not alone. Edric sat in a chair before her, legs casually crossed. His hands were toying with a dagger.

"What, no greeting for an old friend?"

Her lips turned down into a sneer. "You bastard," she said. "You never were my friend. You lied in everything you said."

"Well, in many things, perhaps, but not everything. I said you were beautiful, and so you are. I said you could drive them wild, and so you can. I said the same elven blood flows through our veins, and so it does. I also said I was tribal.

"I did lie about the boy, though. It was part of the role I chose to play. My true tastes do not happen to lie in that direction."

"I can't believe you had the nerve to come here after what you did," said Cricket. "What do you want?"

"You," said Edric.

"*Me?* You must be joking!"

"Actually, I had other plans when I arrived in Altaruk, but as luck would have it, things did not work out. My luck, it seems, has not been good of late. Now, I need to leave town with some alacrity, and it strikes me a hostage will improve my chances."

Cricket turned and bolted for the door, but Edric moved quickly, catching her just as she stepped into the hall. He seized her arm and twisting it behind her as he brought the dagger to her neck. "Don't be a fool," he said. "This is no life for you. You'll wind up like the other sluts. It doesn't have to be like that. You were tribal once. You can be tribal once again, a lady of the Shadows, free and proud, beholden to no man."

"Except to you?" she said. She snorted her derision. "How could I possibly resist such a charming invitation? A dagger at a lady's throat—truly the height of gallantry."

"I readily concede I am not much of a gallant," Edric said. "But then, of course, you are not much of a lady. Granted, we are starting off rather awkwardly, but though you may not appreciate it now, I am doing you a favor. You have far too much potential to waste yourself on a life of degradation in a pleasure house."

"Becoming your woman would be an even greater degradation," Cricket said.

One of the large, muscular bouncers appeared before them in the hall. "What's going on here?"

"Step aside, you thick-headed lout," demanded Edric, "else I will slash her throat from ear to ear."

The bouncer's eyes grew wide as he noticed the dagger against Cricket's neck. He backed away several steps, then moved aside to let them by. As Edric passed the bouncer, he suddenly shoved Cricket into him, trapping him against the wall. With a quick, deft stroke, he plunged the blade into the bouncer's side, then jerked Cricket back again as the man slid down against the wall.

"*Why?*" asked Cricket with despair.

"To insure he didn't do anything foolish, and as an object lesson to you, my dear," said Edric. "The same will happen to anyone who tries to interfere, so keep that in mind if you want to avoid any more bloodshed.

"Now we are going to go outside together and walk calmly toward the door. If anyone tries to stop or question us, get rid of him quickly, or I will."

He urged her out into the main room, where one

of the other girls was dancing on the stage. They kept close to the wall, moving around toward the front door, Edric walking close beside her, holding onto her and using his body to shield the dagger.

They were almost to the door when it opened, and Sorak came in.

Edric stopped, cursing under his breath. Cricket saw Sorak's gaze quickly sweep the room, and then focus on them. He drew his sword. In an instant, several bouncers moved toward him, but Cricket yelled out, "*No!*"

All eyes turned toward them. Edric jerked her arm up painfully behind her back and pressed the edge of the dagger under her chin. All conversation stopped. A moment later, so did the music. Everyone quickly moved back out of the way except the bouncers, who stood watching alertly, tensely, unsure what to do.

Sorak gave them a quick glance. "Stay out of it," he said. "He's mine."

"Move aside, Nomad," Edric said, urging Cricket forward. "Back off if you want the girl to live!"

"And if you kill her, then what?" Sorak asked, moving closer, staring at Edric intently.

"Then you will have another death on your conscience," Edric said. "The priestess died because of you. You want this girl to die on your account as well?"

"The only one who's going die here is you," said Sorak, still coming toward them.

"Stop right there!" said Edric. "One more step,

elfling, and I'll cut her throat!"

"Go ahead," said Sorak, advancing. "Try."

Edric tried to press the blade in closer, to draw blood and show that he meant business, but he suddenly discovered his hand would not respond. He tried again, but his entire arm began to tremble as he strained against a strong, invisible force. It was as if his own muscles resisted him.

Sorak simply stood there, staring at him, concentrating, and suddenly Edric understood what was happening. The Nomad was using psionic force against him.

Fear shot through him as he realized he was powerless to resist. He grunted, straining against the force, and Cricket held her breath as she saw the dagger trembling before her, just below her chin. But slowly, steadily, it moved away.

Edric's wrist cocked as he fought against the pull, and the dagger blade pointed back toward him. His arm shook, and slowly started to bring the point closer to his face.

With a cry, Edric released his grip on her arm, and as she lunged away, he grabbed his right wrist with his left hand in an attempt to keep the knife away. Then he stumbled, off balance, as the force abruptly went away. The bouncers started to move in, but Sorak turned his blade toward them.

"I said, stay back!" he cautioned. "I'll kill the first man who tries to interfere."

"We want no trouble here, friend," one of the bouncers said. "Take your quarrel outside."

"No," said Sorak. "He dies here and now."

Cricket cried out; Edric had snatched up a chair and hurled it at Sorak's head. Sorak ducked aside, and the chair missed him. Several of the bouncers cut off the elf's retreat. Edric glared about, panicked, but there was no escape.

Sorak glanced down at his sword. "No," he said. "This would be too easy. And too quick." He sheathed it.

Edric lunged.

Sorak drew the broken blade. It sparkled with a blue aura as he blocked the knife thrust, turning it aside and sidestepping in one smooth motion. He slashed Edric with a sharp, upward sweep of his arm. The elf cried out and brought a hand up to his ear, which was only a bleeding hole. It had been neatly severed, and blood poured down the side of his face.

He came in with a cry, slashing wildly.

Cricket watched with horrified fascination as Sorak danced aside, and the broken blade flicked in once more, opening a deep gash across Edric's face. The Shadow screamed and staggered as the crowd surged back, giving the combatants plenty of room, but shouting their encouragement, all the same. Rather than trying to stop the fight, the bouncers worked to keep bystanders out of the way.

Edric lunged in again, and Sorak's blade rang dully on his obsidian one as a piece of Edric's knife flew off. Once more, Sorak followed his parry with a lightning slash, opening a deep cut in Edric's shoulder. Edric backpedaled, staring with dismay at his obsidian dagger. The point had been knocked off.

Sorak reached down and pulled a steel dagger from his boot. "Here, try this," he said, tossing it to him.

Edric caught it and threw aside his own ruined blade. He was breathing heavily and bleeding profusely from his wounds. His eyes had a wild look. He was overmatched, and there would be no possibility of yielding. The elfling meant to kill him, slowly cutting him to ribbons. A look of determined resignation came into his eyes.

"Finish it," he said, gasping for breath. "Come on, finish it, you misbegotten half-breed bastard!" And he charged in.

Sorak attempted to sidestep the rush, but Edric anticipated the move and compensated, leaving himself wide open as he stabbed down hard with the dagger. With his free hand, Sorak grabbed Edric's wrist and simultaneously drove the broken blade into his midsection. Edric gave out a hissing gasp, and his eyes opened very wide. He coughed, and a bloody froth appeared on his lips.

"I salute the Crown of Elves," he said in a constricted voice, and spat blood into Sorak's face.

Sorak pulled out the broken blade and stabbed it in once more, directly into Edric's heart. The Shadow made a brief, gasping noise, then his eyes rolled up, and he died. Sorak shoved him back onto the floor, then wiped the bloody spittle from his face. As he turned and walked away, the crowd parted for him quickly.

Cricket watched him go, then ran up and bent over Edric's body, retrieving Sorak's knife from his dead fingers. She hesitated for a moment, then ran after him.

* * * * *

Ankhor stood on the veranda outside his private quarters, looking out over the town as the first faint light of dawn appeared on the horizon. In the distance, he could see flames rising near the market plaza as the fire brigade fought to extinguish the blaze.

The previous evening, Kieran had gone with the house guard to investigate a report of an armed brawl in the shopkeeper's district. He had been instructed to send a guard back with news of what occurred. Kieran had come back himself to tell him what they'd found.

"The fight took place in the alley by the shop of Lorian the Bootmaker," he had said. "Lorian himself saw nothing. He wisely stayed inside when he heard the commotion. The alleyway was littered with corpses. All elves, save one, and that one was the priestess, Ryana. Sorak's lady." The mercenary's gaze was hard. "It was an ambush by the Shadows, that much was obvious, but they got far more than they had bargained for."

"What of Sorak?" Ankhor asked.

"There was no sign of him."

"Dead, you think?"

Kieran shook his head. "He was seen wandering

the streets, wounded, clutching bloody weapons. His current whereabouts remain unknown."

"A tragedy," said Ankhor, silently cursing Edric for botching the job.

"Indeed," said Kieran, keeping his face carefully neutral. "I wonder how the Shadows knew where he would be."

Ankhor shook his head. "They must have followed him from the caravan plaza. The crowd was large; the raiders could have blended in easily. Sorak must be found. If he is hurt, he may have collapsed somewhere. . . ."

"I have already instructed the guard to comb the streets for him," said Kieran.

And it was then that they had noticed smoke rising from the rooftops near the merchant plaza. Kieran had departed quickly to investigate.

He sent back word that witnesses reported a mage battle in a tavern, that a number of charred bodies were pulled out of the blaze. One was a female mul. Another was also female, barely recognizable, and legless, but a blackened silver chaplet around her shaved head identified her as a templar of Nibenay, the Shadow King. Witnesses also reported seeing someone leaving the scene. From the descriptions, Kieran knew it was Sorak. His current whereabouts were unknown.

Ankhor could only guess at what must have happened. The Nomad must have gone straight to the Alliance, or else they had found him, and somehow Livanna and the mul had attacked that very cell. Ankhor knew the burning tavern had been a meeting place of the Alliance. It had taken months to place infiltrators in the support ranks of the Alliance to gather intelligence about the membership and gathering places.

It must have been purely a coincidence Sorak was there when the templar struck with Kah. Now both Livanna and the mul were dead. There was nothing to connect him with those two, but how had Sorak survived? The elfling had amazing luck. He had survived the ambush, and the murderous mul, and a senior templar of Nibenay. "There is a new viper loose in Altaruk."

"Trouble sleeping tonight, my lord?"

Ankhor stiffened as he recognized the voice. He turned around slowly. Sorak stood behind him on the veranda.

"Sorak!" Ankhor said. "Thank goodness you're all right. I've had the house guard combing the streets for you all night. I heard about what happened. I am so very sorry about Ryana."

"If you dare speak her name again, I'll cut out your tongue," said Sorak.

Ankhor's eyes widened. "What? Forgive me, but—"

"Aren't you going to ask me how I managed to get in?" asked Sorak.

Ankhor felt a chill go down his spine. He nervously moistened his lips.

"I imagine the question itself gives you the answer," Sorak said, "since I obviously did not come in by the front door." He looked out at the smoke rising from the rooftops in the distance, beyond the low walls of the veranda. "You have a lovely view up here," he said. "It appears the fire is almost under control. Some good people died there tonight. And two who very much deserved to die."

"I have no idea what you're talking about," said Ankhor.

"Oh, I think you do," said Sorak. "Livanna revealed much before she died. Against her will, of course, but she revealed it just the same. Shall I tell you all about it?"

"Who . . . who is Livanna?" Ankhor asked as a knot formed in his stomach.

"You mean who *was* Livanna," Sorak corrected him. "She was a senior templar of the Shadow King, with whom you had a bargain to sell out Altaruk to the defilers. Quite a complicated little plot you hatched. You hired the Shadows to attack your own caravan, to cause significant losses to the House of Jhamri and, ostensibly, to your own house, as well. Except your losses on that particular caravan would have been slight, and more than offset by your share of the plunder.

"Meanwhile," he continued, "the templar and your mul would systematically assassinate members of the Veiled Alliance in Altaruk, defying all efforts to apprehend them, because of course, you would give them shelter and keep them appraised of all the movements of the guard. Lord Jhamri would be made to appear incapable of keeping the peace, and at the proper time, your own house guard would have caught the mul, who would have been killed in the attempt to apprehend her.

"You would have received credit for generously hiring the famous Kieran of Draj to protect the citizenry. By then, however, the Alliance in Altaruk would have been broken, and the way left clear for defilers to move in. Once they were in power, Lord Jhamri would be brought to heel and the House of Ankhor would become the most powerful merchant guild in the western Tablelands."

"The templar told you that?" said Ankhor. "And you actually *believed* this nonsense?" He shook his head and chuckled. "I have never heard such a fantastic tale in all my life!"

"Then here's another tale," said Sorak. "One that is considerably shorter but should amuse you all the same. The templar was planning to betray you. She had made her own separate agreement with your friend, Edric. He was going to assassinate you."

"Edric? Who's Edric?" Ankhor said. "I have never heard that name."

"Oh, but you have, my lord," said Kieran, standing in the open doorway of the veranda, behind Sorak. Neither of them had noticed his arrival until he spoke. "I told you all about him when I gave you my report."

"Kieran!" Ankhor said. "Thank goodness you're here!" He pointed to Sorak. "He's got an insane notion I've been involved in some fantastic plot!"

"Yes, I know. I heard," said Kieran, leaning

casually against the doorframe. "The funny thing is, I believe him."

"You can't be serious!" said Ankhor.

"I am completely serious," Kieran replied. "And I fear I'll have to take you into custody."

"You must be mad," said Ankhor. "You work for me! I hired you!"

Kieran raised his eyebrows. "As I recall, I was hired to serve the House of Jhamri."

"But it was *I* who paid your salary! Besides, what grounds have you to arrest me? You have no proof of these ridiculous accusations!"

"Perhaps not," said Kieran, "but then the prosecution of them is not my responsibility. I will simply lay the case before Lord Jhamri, and it will be up to him to make the final disposition."

"The final disposition will be made right here, tonight," said Sorak grimly.

Kieran shook his head. "I think not," he said. "You have had a busy enough night, my friend. I just came from the pleasure house, where I saw what you did to Edric. Under the circumstances, I can hardly blame you. I know how you must feel, and I share your grief over your loss, but I cannot stand by and watch you commit murder, however justified it may be."

"*Justified!*" said Ankhor in outrage.

"Yes, justified, my lord," said Kieran. "You were the one who sent Sorak and Ryana to the place where they were ambushed. I was there, if you'll recall, and you were most insistent, even to the point of saying they should go there right away. You also took care to see to it that I was occupied with my report to you and reviewing the full complement of the guard. Now perhaps one or two raiders might have followed them to Lorian's from the caravan plaza, but nearly a dozen would have been conspicuous. I spoke to Lorian and learned that they were not in his shop more than a few moments, and so the ambush must have already been in place. The Shadows did not follow them. They knew they would be there. And you were the only one who could have told them. I suspect that will be all the proof Lord Jhamri will require."

Ankhor paled. He could think of no response.

"I already have all the proof *I* need," said Sorak.

"No doubt," said Kieran, "but you are not the law in Altaruk, and regardless of who hired me, I have a duty to that law. I must apprehend Lord Ankhor and deliver him to justice."

"Do not speak to me of justice," Sorak said. "Ryana died as much by his hand as by Edric's. Keep out of this, Kieran. I'll not let you take him."

"And I cannot let you kill him," Kieran said. "Stand aside. I am still your superior officer, if you will recall."

"We are at cross purposes," Sorak said coldly. "I hereby tender my resignation."

Kieran shook his head. "Don't do this, Nomad," he said. "Please, I have no wish to fight you."

"Then give way."

"I cannot," said Kieran. He drew his blade.

There was a sudden crash of shattering pottery.

Kieran grunted and collapsed, unconscious. As he fell, Cricket stood revealed behind him, the shattered remains of a heavy vase in one hand.

"I . . . I couldn't figure out how to get the secret panel open," she said. "It took me a long time to find the lever—"

Ankhor lunged past Sorak and snatched up Kieran's blade. But as he moved toward Cricket, Sorak pulled Galdra from his belt and threw it. The broken blade streaked across the distance between them and struck Ankhor in the right shoulder. He cried out, and Kieran's sword fell from his grasp.

As he bent to retrieve it, Cricket rushed him, shoving him hard with both outstretched arms. He staggered backward, struck the low wall of the veranda, and fell over. His scream was cut off as he struck the courtyard—the smooth expensive tiles of yellow and blue—four floors below.

Cricket gasped and brought her hands up to her face. "I . . . I didn't mean to push him! I . . . I was afraid he would . . ." Her voice trailed off.

Sorak looked down into the courtyard. Several guards had rushed over to the body. From its position, Sorak could tell Ankhor's neck and back were broken. Matullus looked up and, for a moment, their eyes met.

"*Get him!*" said Matullus. At once, the guards rushed for the front door, their weapons drawn.

Cricket was pulling at his arm. "We must get out of here!" she said. "Come, quickly!"

Sorak turned and started back inside, toward

the secret panel, pausing only briefly to examine Kieran. He was already starting to revive.

"*Hurry!*" Cricket said from the open panel.

"Good-bye, my friend," said Sorak softly, then he followed Cricket through the secret panel. It closed behind them just as running footsteps sounded on the stairs in the hall.

EPILOGUE

Sorak lay on a cot in the small, spartan room on the second floor of the hostelry where Cricket stayed, a short walk from the gaming district. His eyes were shut, and he held a damp cloth against his forehead. It was late afternoon, and the intense ache was only beginning to recede. His psionic exertions had belatedly taken their toll.

He recalled what Elder Al'Kali, the pyreen shapechanger who had found him in the desert all those years ago, had told him.

She had made her annual pilgrimage to the summit of the Dragon's Tooth, the tallest peak among the Ringing Mountains, and as she renewed her vows, she heard a powerful psionic cry for help. His cry. It had traveled all that distance to reach her on a mountaintop miles from where he lay. She responded, flying down to find him, and it was that cry that made her bring him to the villichi convent after she had nursed him back to health. The villichi sisters were masters of psionics, and his power was the strongest the pyreen had yet encountered in all her many years.

He had always believed power came from one of the others of his inner tribe, for he had never been able to perform any of the psionic training exercises at the convent unless the Guardian or one of the others came to the fore. But now they were gone, and the power remained. Perhaps, somehow, it had been transferred to him when the others left; perhaps it had been there all along. But he would just as soon have remained ignorant of it if only he could have Ryana back.

Cricket had brought him to her room, by which time the pain had grown so great that he could barely stand. Without knowing what was wrong, she had put him to bed and tried to nurse him, but he had only wanted to be left alone. She had gone out, a while ago, leaving him to lie there with a pressure in his head that seemed unbearable, but at the same time, he was grateful for the pain. It gave him something he could focus on, something to keep him from dwelling on his grief over Ryana's death.

The door opened, and Cricket entered, carrying a leather pouch. She set it down on the small, round, wooden table and came over to the bed, bending over him anxiously. "How do you feel?" she asked.

"Better," he replied.

"The guard is everywhere, asking about you," she said. She hesitated, biting her lower lip. "Everyone thinks you killed Lord Ankhor." She took a deep breath and exhaled heavily. "As soon as you are well, I'll tell them the truth, that it was I who pushed him."

"No," said Sorak, pulling the damp cloth away and sitting up. "There is no point to that. I would have killed him, anyway. What you did was an accident. You were only trying to protect yourself, and help me. There is no reason you should bear the blame. I will leave town as soon as it grows dark. I have done what I came here to do."

"Take me with you," she said.

Sorak shook his head.

"Please."

"No, I cannot."

"I know who you are now," Cricket said, kneeling before him and taking his hands in hers. "I know *what* you are. You are the Crown of Elves. You are the one thing I always wanted to believe in. The one thing I *can* believe in. Let me go with you. Please. I want to help."

"I do not mean to sound ungrateful, but you would be more a hindrance than a help," said Sorak. "You would only slow me down and get in my way. And however sincerely you may try, you can never replace the one I have lost."

"I know that," Cricket said, gently. "She came to see me one night when the caravan stopped to camp. The night Edric's treachery was revealed.

We talked. She was very kind. Most women are not kind to girls like me."

"Ryana was kind to everyone," said Sorak dully. "When she died, a part of me died with her."

"I know I could never take her place," said Cricket, "but I would hate to think of you being alone."

"I want to be alone now," Sorak said. "After all, that is the true meaning of my name. Sorak, the nomad who walks alone."

"I will only follow you if you refuse to take me with you," Cricket said.

"That would be foolish. I could lose you easily. And while I am grateful for your offer, I do not want you with me. Do you want to end up like Ryana? I do not want anybody with me. Not now. Not anymore."

Cricket sighed with resignation. "Very well. I have brought some food, some supplies to take with you on your journey."

"Thank you." He had no money. The packs containing all the silver from Bodach had been dropped in the attack in the alley. By now, someone had discovered a windfall.

"Where will you go?"

He shook his head. "I do not know. I will go wherever the Path leads me."

"Well, wherever you go, you will need this," said Kieran, standing in the doorway. He tossed the broken blade across the room, onto the bed.

Sorak looked up. "For a big man, you move as softly as a cat."

Cricket snatched up Galdra and held it out

before her in both hands, facing Kieran. "You will not take him!" she said vehemently.

Kieran raised his eyebrows and held up his hands in mock surrender. "That's quite a protector you've got there," he said with a smile.

"It's all right, Cricket," Sorak said. "He did not come to arrest me." He glanced at Kieran. "Or did you?"

"No," said Kieran, entering the room and taking a chair. "I did not. So put the blade down, girl. You have nothing to fear from me, though by rights, I should turn you across my knee for that knock on the head."

"I'm sorry," Cricket said. "But I thought you were going to—"

"Yes, I know what you thought, and you were right," said Kieran. "However, that is moot. You solved that problem neatly when you pushed Ankhor off the roof."

"It wasn't her," said Sorak, recalling that Kieran was unconscious at the time. "It was me. I did it."

Kieran shook his head. "No, you didn't. I saw what you did to Edric. If you'd killed Ankhor, you would have done a great deal more than throw him off a roof. But do not concern yourself. No one knew Cricket was there except the two of us. Matullus saw you, not her. He thinks you knocked me senseless, and frankly, I'd prefer he think that rather than know I was felled by a dancing girl."

"You would let him take the blame, merely to protect your reputation?" Cricket said, outraged. "I won't allow it. I am going to tell the truth."

"You are going to keep your pretty little mouth shut and not complicate things," Kieran told her. "I was merely joking. I will take care of everything, but it will take some time." He looked at Sorak. "Lord Jhamri has ordered your arrest, and Matullus is eager to prove himself by bringing you in, dead or alive. I will tell him the truth of what has happened, and I feel confident I can convince him. He's a good soldier, but he's young and brash and overeager.

"Right now, tempers are running high. Jhamri feels the need to demonstrate his authority. Personally, I'd just as soon tell him the truth after you are out of town. Whether he believes me or not, he might be tempted to use you as a scapegoat. Ankhor was his partner, after all, and it would not be very good for business for Jhamri to reveal that his junior partner was involved with murder and betrayal. The whole thing will have to be handled rather delicately."

Sorak nodded.

"I once told you I owed you a debt," said Kieran. "It is a poor repayment, but for what it's worth . . ." He handed Sorak a small scroll. "That is a formal introduction from me to anyone who knows me or my reputation. It speaks of my regard for you, and requests that any assistance you request be rendered for my sake. There is also a crodlu tied up outside, at the hitching post, with two full waterskins and saddlebags holding provisions. After the sun goes down, if you make your way to the west gate, you will find it strangely unattended for at least an hour. No doubt, a miscommunication of orders."

"I am grateful," Sorak said. "But I have one request."

"Name it."

"Ryana," Sorak said. For a moment, he found it difficult to speak.

"I will personally see to whatever arrangements you may wish," said Kieran.

Sorak swallowed hard. "I would like to take her home."

"Of course," said Kieran. "When you leave tonight, ride west through the pass that will take you to the route to Tyr. Wait near the west entrance to the pass, and I'll bring her to you after sundown tomorrow."

"I am deeply in your debt," said Sorak.

"You owe me nothing," Kieran replied. "It is the least I can do, and I am glad to do it. My contract with the Jhamris is for a year of service. Exactly one year from today, I am going home to my estate outside Salt View." He removed a silver signet ring from his left hand. "This was my father's," he said, handing it to Sorak. "If you ever need me, send this to me there, and I will come."

Kieran stood and held out his hand. They clasped forearms, mercenary style.

"Until tomorrow," Kieran said. "Good fortune to you."

* * * * *

Sorak sat astride his crodlu, watching as two mounts approached through the pass. One bore a rider, Kieran. The other had a large, limp parcel wrapped in oilcloth strapped across its saddle. Sorak felt his throat constrict as the two crodlu approached. He rode down the slope to meet them.

They exchanged no words. They had both already said all there was to say. Kieran simply handed him the reins and nodded. Sorak nodded back. Kieran gave him the mercenary salute, right fist thumped to the left breast, over the heart, then he simply turned and rode away without a backward glance.

Sorak sat there for a moment, watching him go. Then he looked down at the still form wrapped in oilcloth and felt a tight pressure building in his chest. He took a deep, ragged breath as a tear rolled down his cheek.

"Come, my love," he murmured. "We're going home."

He turned and slowly rode west into the night, toward the Ringing Mountains.

Be sure to read the other books about Sorak's adventures!

TRIBE OF ONE

Simon Hawke

The Outcast
The Seeker
The Nomad

TALES OF GOTHIC HORROR BEYOND YOUR WILDEST SCREAMS!

Tapestry of Dark Souls
Elaine Bergstrom
The monks' hold over the Gathering Cloth, containing some of the vilest evils in Ravenloft, is slipping. The only hope is a strange youth, who will become either the monks' champion . . . or their doom.
ISBN 1-56076-571-2

Heart of Midnight
J. Robert King
Even before he'd drawn his first breath, Casimir had inherited his father's lycanthropic curse. Now the young werewolf must embrace his powers to ward off his own murder and gain revenge.
ISBN 1-56076-355-8

MORE TALES OF TERROR

Vampire of the Mists
Christie Golden
ISBN 1-56076-155-5

Knight of the Black Rose
James Lowder
ISBN 1-56076-156-3

Dance of the Dead
Christie Golden
ISBN 1-56076-352-3

Carnival of Fear
J. Robert King
ISBN 1-56076-628-X

Sug. Retail Each $4.95; CAN $5.95; U.K. £4.99

Available now at book and hobby stores everywhere!

Ravenloft® Books

DARK • SUN
WORLD

The PRISM PENTAD

Troy Denning

Searing drama in an unforgiving world . .

The Obsidian Oracle
Book Four
Power-hungry Tithian emerges as the new ruler of Tyr. When he pursues his dream of becoming a sorcerer-king, only the noblema Agis stands between Tithian and his desire: possession of an ancient oracle that will leac to either the salvation of Athas – or its destruction. ISBN 1-56076-603-

The Cerulean Storm
Book Five
Rajaat: The First Sorcerer – the only one who can return Athas to its former splendor – is imprisoned beyond space and time. When Tithian enlists the aid of his former slaves, Rikus, Neeva, and Sadira, to free the sorcerer, does he want to restore the world – or claim it as his own? ISBN 1-56076-642-5

The Verdant Passage
Book One
ISBN 1-56076-121-0

The Crimson Legion
Book Two
ISBN 1-56076-260-8

The Amber Enchantress
Book Three
ISBN 1-56076-236-5

Sug. Retail Each $4.95; CAN $5.95; £4.99 U.K

On Sale Now!

Don't miss these exciting

TSR® B • O • O • K • S

Captains Outrageous, or, For Doom the Bell Tolls

Roy V. Young

A wild and wacky tale of fantasy adventure! Three captains of the king's guard are sent on a madcap mission to find a bumbling wizard intent on bringing the world to an end.

Available May 1994 ISBN 1-56076-855-X

City of the Sorcerers

Mary H. Herbert

A new epic adventure set in the world of the best-selling Dark Horse series! Peace reigns among the Dark Horse clans, until suddenly, an evil from the past rears its ugly face.

Available July 1994 ISBN 1-56076-876-2

Go Quest, Young Man

K. B. Bogen

Laugh along as sorcerer Erwyn the Inexperienced, who has just graduated from magic school at the bottom of his class, sets a hilarious sequence of events in motion.

Available September 1994 ISBN 1-56076-898-3

The Hidden War

Michael Armstrong

A science-fiction thriller packed with futuristic combat and epic dogfights that comes to a mind-blowing climax in the virtual reality of cyberspace and the no-man's-land of outer space!

Available November 1994 ISBN 1-56076-921-1

Sug. Retail Each $4.95; CAN $5.95; £4.99 U.K.